Oshun
PUBLISHING

Oshun
PUBLISHING

Oshun Publishing Company, Inc.
7715 Crittenden Street
Box 377
Philadelphia, PA 19118

Copyright © 2009 by Leyton Wint.

Printed in the United States of America

First Edition: January 2009

10 9 8 7 6 5 4 3 2 1

ISBN-13: 978-0-9676028-4-4
ISBN-10: 0-9676028-4-X

cover design by Keith Sanders of Marion Designs –
www.mariondesigns.com

visit Prey for Love on the web
www.myspace.com/preyforlove

Prey for Love

Leyton Wint

Oshun Publishing Company, Inc.
Philadelphia

Acknowledgments

Thank you, God, for your guidance, grace, and enduring mercy. Your plan for me was hard to see, but when I was weak you carried me. There is no way that I could possibly remember every person who has enriched my life during this process and during my struggle. To those people whose names should appear here, but didn't, please note it was a slip of the pen, not a slip of the heart. I love you, and thank you all. Takia Miguel, your love and support have been amazing. For everything, I thank you (for a peek at a phenomenally talented sister, check Takia out on www.myspace.com/takiamiguelmusic). She is my favorite rapper; probably will be yours, too. My beloved daughter Yadae and son Jaylen – I love you both with all my heart. You inspire me in all I do. With a determined mind, and love in your hearts, you can do anything. To Karen E. Quinones Miller, my publisher, my mentor, and most importantly my friend; thank you for believing in me and seeing past my circumstance. Your brilliance is my guiding light. My loving family . . . too many to name: Wayne "Bigga" Wint, my brother; and my sister, (Maj.) Deveril A.Wint -- I am so proud of you both!. Marsha, Bjour, D'Sullivan, Dominic, Sophia, Debbie, Annie, Judine, Lerone, Archie, all my aunts, uncles, cousins, and others who supported me – I know I'm difficult, but thanks!. Karon Johnson, I can't wait till Canada. My strength is your strength. Jah guide, lioness. Thanks to all my good friends: Jamila L. James; my BFF, Matthew Siniscalchi -- the meaning of a friend. Naima Cook. Leslie Wood. Junior "Bizzie" Johnson (YESSS! RUDE BWOY). Anthony "Big Tee" Tolliver. Chaine Dorsch (where ever you are). Sandrea Jones. Samonda Dunston. Angela Stewart. Travis Henry of soBeach@rentals.com of Miami; look them up for a great spot to chill! Love to all my comrades behind gates: Tommy Johnson, Jason Pendergrass, Larry Cave, Ronald Simms, Mark Forbes, Terrence McDaniel, Sadrach Santiago, Emory Jones, Robert David, Craig Sweat, Nate Goddard, Eric Holloway (thanks!), Delansie Rodgers, Cameron Walker, and all the soldiers I forgot, stay strong. Live your dreams.

And lastly, to everyone who ever did me wrong: you are a part of my struggle, but also part of my accomplishment. However, I will not immortalize any cowardly men or conniving heartless women by naming them between these pages. You looked here for your name? It's not here. Now get on with your life!

*This book is dedicated with abounding love
to my dear departed mother,*

Elaine Joy Wint.

Not a day goes by that I don't miss you.

I envy the angels your company.

Prey For Love

Prologue

Havana, Cuba 1977

There were a lot of things she hated about her work that she had to put up with, but being beaten was the one thing she just couldn't abide. He had already punched her in her right eye and she could feel it swelling shut. She couldn't see out of it, but it only took one good eye to see that he wasn't going to stop. This wasn't her first time dealing with him. She knew how he got when he drank. Usually he'd take her out for dinner and then to a nightclub before they went to a hotel where he'd pass out. Most times she didn't even have to sleep with him. It was easy money. Some of her clients wanted her to listen to all their problems before the three minutes of bad sex. That hardly seemed worth it, but all her clients were government officials, high ranking soldiers, and wealthy business men so they paid well. Plus, the things she learned and the connections she made were invaluable.

As he drunkenly staggered around the room knocking over everything in his path, she silently prayed that he would just pass out. She never even remembered picking up her purse, let alone drawing the small revolver she kept tucked inside for emergencies. He seemed oblivious to the gun in her trembling hand as he lunged toward her. That step he took would be his last.

She fired.

It was strange to her that the shot wasn't nearly as loud as she thought it would be. She kept on squeezing the trigger like she'd been told to do if she ever ran into trouble. She only stopped when the repeated clicks of the empty gun and the acrid smell of cordite smoke burning her nose snapped her out of her trance.

7

When the first bullet struck him the snarl on his face contorted into a horrific mask. He clutched at his chest and tore his shirt open exposing the bullet hole and the trail of blood that ran down his torso. The four bullets that followed served no purpose other than jerking him around violently before he collapsed. That first bullet had killed him. He lay on the ground bleeding with the horrific expression frozen on his face. Surely in those last moments he had to have been regretting ever putting his hands on her.

In 1977 I wasn't even born yet, but in Havana a series of events was in progress that would shape my entire existence. Till this day I can't figure out if what happened back then made me, saved me, or enslaved me, but I guess that ain't really important. At least not as important as that I know it all started out with Helena Vasquez.

She had grown up poor in a small city nestled on Cuba's south coast called Cienfuegos. Maybe it meant something that the woman who would have such a huge impact on my life came from a city whose name literally translated to "a hundred fires." From the time she was very young she knew that she wanted more out of life than Cienfuegos and her poor family had to offer.

She was an exceptionally beautiful young woman and strong willed. It wasn't long after she turned 16 that she fell out with her father. At that time, in a male dominated society, it was unheard of for a young woman to defy her father. Her family turned their backs on her. Choosing to live on her own rather than be the black sheep of the family, Helena left home. She fled north to Havana hoping that life in the city might treat her better. She met a cold reality. After a few days of being hungry in the streets, Helena realized that the only way she could survive was by accepting some of the offers from men who propositioned her. Some local women of the night befriended her and before long she adapted their craft. With her youth and good looks she became popular with the more well to do gentlemen callers. Eventually she found herself working as more of a high-end escort than a prostitute.

That was how she came to be standing over the body of Francisco Cepeda holding a smoking pistol and crying alone in a trashed hotel room. She knew she should have run, but she couldn't will her legs to take the first step much less run away. It probably would have been of very little use because she frequented the hotels in this affluent section of the city regularly. No less than a dozen people had seen them together that evening. She fell on her knees and prayed over the body. Then she sat in a dark corner of the room crying and waited for the soldiers to come for her.

In a democratic nation she would have had an iron clad case for self defense. The Cuban justice system, however, had more to do with who you knew and who your family was. One of Helena's clients was a higher up at the Ministry of Justice. Unfortunately for her, Francisco was a wealthy restaurateur from a wealthy family. His family's reach went just a bit higher, and they were adamant about someone being held responsible for the murder. Helena was tried and convicted. She received a "lenient" 20 year sentence since it was obvious that Francisco was doing her bodily harm. In 1978 she began serving her sentence at La Cabaña prison just outside Havana.

With no help from her family she found herself alone in a rough third world prison with no help from the outside. It was the worst situation she could have ever imagined for herself. She stared out the prison windows every day praying that somehow she would be delivered from her nightmare. In the interim she made some significant underworld connections. In that sink or swim situation she developed her skills at making things happen by manipulating people. She survived the best way she knew how. All alone she realized the value of love, and she missed her family even though they had abandoned her. She swore that if God ever gave her a family, she would never abandon them.

Helena had accepted her fate, but in 1980 after she'd served just two years of her sentence, something remarkable happened. Somehow Fidel Castro and the United States government negotiated a deal that granted asylum in the U.S. for thousands of Cuban nationals. The plan included regular Cuban citizens as well as convicted criminals. With help from "a friend of a friend," Helena was freed from prison. She came to the U.S. in the summer of 1980 as part of the Mariel Exodus. It was her stroke of astronomical good fortune that took Helena to Miami and later to New York where we would eventually meet.

Her story of a young woman with a broken dream, a second chance, and a prayer for love seems to have been destined to intersect with my life... if I could have known what was coming, I probably would have run the other way.

Chapter 1

My flight landed in Miami just after 6pm, but for some reason it was still hotter than the surface of the mid-day sun. I walked through the airport with purpose. My Momma always told me my walk was two parts glide and one part stride, said I got it from my Daddy...didn't get much else.

I hadn't had my feet on the ground a full ten minutes when I turned my phone on, and it immediately vibrated to life with an in-coming text message.

"Ready?" came the one word question. It was a stupid one really, because in the murder for hire game either you're born ready, or you're living to die. I was born ready. The game chose me, and at a young age.

Nobody advertises, 'cept maybe them contract clowns in the back of "Soldier of Fortune Magazine," but I'm pretty sure there wasn't another 26-yearold working the east coast with as much confirmed "wet-work" under their belt as me. I had removed a total of 1,134 years of life from this earth. I wasn't doing geriatric cases either. The majority of my marks were in their prime. The math certified me as a pro. I was good, most likely because I had a love for the game. You could say I was a natural predator.

As I hopped into my taxi I actually thought about making use of the pad provided by my employer. I thought better of it and opted for a "roach motel" on the outskirts of Liberty City. There was a posh spread waiting on me in Coconut Grove all laid out with food, liquor and most likely wall to wall pussy. Cats would kill to stay in some shit like that. I was, and I wouldn't. I was always leery of jobs that came with too many perks. For one, a whole lot of comfort invariably made the work sloppy; and for two, I try to never make myself an inviting target. After a job was done you really couldn't blame a client for trying you. It's a logical progression really: 'You kill him for me, and then I kill you, thus insulating myself from the hit.' That's the way I'd probably do it myself. That's why I always get out of Dodge after a job.

The cabbie and I rode across town in silence. I was thankful he didn't try to make small talk because I needed time to think. Had he, or anyone else for that matter, struck up a conversation I had a flawless repertoire of names and places, all fake, designed to get a person talking more about themselves than me.

There was something about this gig that bothered me. It had come through the normal channels, so it wasn't a trust issue. There was just something in my handler's demeanor that told me she had a little more interest in this job than usual. If that was the case, it meant I might be breaking my cardinal rule: 'Don't mix business with whatever.' Some people don't mix business and pleasure; I don't mix business with anything.

All my work came through a woman named Helena Vasquez. I affectionately referred to her as 'Nana Helen.' She was my upstairs neighbor where I grew up back in the Bronx. Most of the kids I grew up around were either raised or babysat by their grandmothers, whom they called "Nana," so I took to calling Helena my "Nana Helen," and it just stuck. At 48, she wasn't nearly old enough to be my grandmother, but she never seemed to mind. She was an Afro-Cuban beauty with long jet black hair and a café au lait complexion. In another life she could have been a beauty queen. You'd exception of Nana Helen and a few friends I wasn't particularly close to. Instead of letting it bother me, I figured it was for the best. Nana Helen and I couldn't get much closer, but that move solidified our bond.

After my mother left I made it my business to sit down for dinner with Nana Helen a couple nights a week. I called myself checking up on her, but in reality she was probably more looking out for me than I was for her. So, one day after dinner she sat down at the table behind me as I washed the dishes. "You ever think of making what you do into a real business?" she asked over my shoulder.

She knew what I did; there was no pretense, so there was none in my reply.

"I do real business. I do a job, the client pays." I responded with a mixture of insult and annoyed in my voice.

"No, I mean make it more organized," she giggled at my indignation.

"What, you think I should file taxes, have an infrastructure?" I asked sarcastically.

"Yeah!"

"Yeah?" I shot back, surprised as hell.

"Well, of course no taxes, but infrastructure. Yeah"

I mulled it over in my head and it wasn't adding up. I'd been doing collections for two years by then and she'd never brought it up. Nothing was new with me. Why the sudden interest? Nana Helen had taught me plenty about women, so I knew there was more to it. Something was going unsaid, unusual for a conversation between her and me. I called her on it.

"Look, this dance we dancin' don't suit me and you. Remember how when I was little and when I wanted candy I'd ask you about your day, and all types of other foolishness?" I didn't wait for her response,

"Well, that's how you sound right now. It's obviously something more to this, so why don't you save us both some time and tell me what you're getting at."

She laughed a knowing laugh that said she knew she'd been caught. "Okay. You got me. Maybe I taught you too well. Leave those dishes. Come sit down; let me run something by you."

As she came clean, I realized the whole thing had been a designed play, especially the part where she brought it up while my back was turned so that I couldn't read her facial expression. A person's face told you plenty if you let it. She had caught me unawares, but it was my fault. Years ago she told me that women were one of the last things I'd understand, and until then not to trust a single one. Petty or not, I received an early indication that the woman I trusted the most would deceive or manipulate me if it suited her. I wasn't mad at her, though. I'd learned to appreciate life letting me make a mistake here and there that didn't cost me much. Cheap lessons I called them.

As I sat down across from her, she took a bobby pin from her hair letting her voluminous silky black mane fall over her shoulders. She removed a cigarette from an open pack, lighting it and slowly exhaling. She smoked a Cuban brand called "Popular" that to this day I can't figure out how she gets here in the States. She thought, and then spoke, "You know Lex, you could be making more money. A lot of people want the 'malapaga' (bad payer in Spanish) to feel something. Why not get paid to teach lessons? Every person you go see you're ready to do it anyway. Why not make that your service?"

I thought for a moment before responding. She made a decent point, one I'd often considered, but I knew there was still more to it. I decided to push her buttons a little. "I thought about it, but nah, it's too much trouble."

There it was on her face. She was clearly dejected at hearing my response. Then I saw an almost imperceptible movement in her brow. She was strategizing, regrouping. I felt empowered. There I was turning one around on my sensei. But then came something unexpected. She took a long drag of her cigarette and her demeanor changed. Seemed like she gave up on the game and decided to come correct. She exhaled and leaned toward me taking on a more endearing posture. The conversation had taken a turn.

"All right, let's cut this game short. You win."

"You sure?" I rubbed it in.

"Here it is... I got this friend. Her daughter is caught up with this piece of shit dopehead living over in Edenwald Projects. The guy been beating on the daughter like she's a man. Her mother wants her to come home, but the girl is scared. The mother will pay you $2,500 to go pick up the daughter and give the boyfriend her regards."

It sounded easy enough, and $2,500 was good money for a one, two, step. I hated doing domestics, but I hated abusive men even more. A man who beat up on a woman definitely deserved a visit.

"Tell you what. I'm a little mad you ran the manip' game on me, but I'll do it 'cause seem like it means a little bit to you. I'll swing by here tomorrow and you can give me the particulars."

Before I finished talking she had fished a small manila envelope out of her purse that I only just then realized was sitting at her feet. Although I thought I'd exposed her ploy, it became apparent to me that I never stood a chance. She was a master manipulator and her student still had lots to learn. I took the fat envelope from her as I stood up to leave. She smiled and thanked me as I leaned down and kissed her on the forehead before leaving.

On my way out the door I ran back through the whole scene in my head making mental notes. Riding down in the elevator I thumbed through the envelope's contents. Inside were 25 crisp ones, a photo of the seemingly happy couple and a slip of paper with some info scrawled in Nana Helen's perfect cursive handwriting. I had everything I needed, so I figured I'd head over there on the weekend.

When that Saturday rolled around, I was anxious to head over there and get the contract squared away. I couldn't imagine a dopehead being much trouble, and judging from the picture it looked like dude would be a walk in the park. His face had that gaunt look that most long term users get. He looked like he was wearing one of those masks from the movie "Scream." Undernourished, and surely underweight. I made up my mind that this job was going to be a piece of cake

That morning I strolled over to the projects nonchalantly with not much idea as to how I was going to do things. As I walked along the street looking for the building, I didn't stand out at all. I fit in like just another one of the kids in the park. The address was already committed to my memory along with all the other info from the slip of paper. I knew everything about Julissa Diaz and Richie Vega that I needed. She worked nights over at Mercy Hospital, and he was an unemployed junkie, a night owl. They were both certain to be home on a weekend morning. The prospect of easy money had me amped, so I took the stairs two by two to their third floor apartment. I had no idea that I had not been privy to one small detail about this gig; one that made all the difference.

At the last moment before arriving at the door, I decided on the direct approach. I knocked hard on the

Chapter 2

I touched down safely at JFK, and in my brief absence, the city seemed no worse for the wear. I wasn't missed. Nevertheless, I was consumed by a desire to straighten out this double booking situation. My mind couldn't even focus on much else.

I by-passed baggage claim cruising on auto pilot. I was in a trance spurred on by curiosity and rage. It had slipped my mind that I'd be met until through the throngs of people, my eyes found a man holding a sign. There was Bubby, my driver, with a makeshift sign that read, "L-Dub." I cracked a brief smile walking up to him, and he grabbed my hand in a hearty shake, clapping me on the back.

Lester Hood was a fifty-something older cat that use to run a cab stand in my neighborhood. He had a habit of calling everyone he spoke to "Bub," so people just took to calling him Bubby and it stuck. He was a smooth talking free spirited kind of guy, and we'd gotten tight when he use to drive me on my collection runs back when I was just starting out.

I wasn't making much back then, and he wasn't charging me much. We'd just ride on my runs telling jokes and shooting the shit. He always had good advice to give me and even better stories to tell. Let him tell it, he had seen and done just about everything. He had stories ranging from having dated Diana Ross to once seeing a catfish the size of a Volkswagen in the Ohio River. Had a way of making you want to believe him too. He was always on time, and he stuck to his word, so he was my wheel-man come hell or high water.

It brought a smile to my face seeing him despite what I had going on. About 5'10", graying at the temples, and overweight, he was still dapper with a Polo shirt and his golf hat on. He had a Romeo y Julieta Cuban cigar tucked behind his right ear. Mainly, my mood was lightened at trying to figure out what kind of car he'd come to pick me up in. He had a small fleet of various whips. All his rides were 'hood legends, and it made me think cars were the only thing he spent the $1500 a week I paid him on.

"So, what we riding Bubby? The L-Dog?" I asked, referring to the money green Cadillac Eldorado he'd dropped me off in.

"Nah, nah, Bub. I got something else today. She the coldest, you gon' see." He shook his head, mumbling something about a "cold bitch" as we made our way out to the parking garage.

Entering the airport parking garage, I was reminded of my dilemma and the scowl crept back onto my face as I pondered it.

"Ay, Bub! You done got that fire and brimstone look on your face like you had getting' off the plane. You can't be around squares with your face screwed up like that… it make 'em nervous," he chided me.

"True dat, Bubby. I just got a little somethin' on my plate," I explained.

"Must be a hell of a bone you mashin' on that got you like that. You usually ice cold. But fix your face…can't have you givin' this lady no bad vibe." As he finished his sentence, he pulled keys from his pocket and deactivated a car alarm. I heard the chirp and my eyes went over to a tinted out black BMW 850i. It was clean, a classic, and indeed a "cold bitch." The smile coming to life as Jaheim's "Just in Case" came blaring from the speakers. I paused there letting the beat wash over me for a moment before heading towards the back room Big Tee had converted to an office.

As I turned into the hallway leading to the back, the door to the storeroom swung open and out stepped a smiling Mila. She ran down the hall to me with outstretched arms and I swept her up in a warm hug. Next to Nana Helen and Bubby, Mila was as close as I had to a friend. My profession and all the 'cloak and dagger' shit that came with it made it hard to get too close to people.

We had gone to high school together. Mila Carrelli was one of a handful of white kids who went to Evander Childs High. What made her special, though, was how she carried herself. She was five feet seven inches of Italian beauty with jet black hair. Her dad was doing life in state prison for a botched armed robbery that left two cops dead. He left a ten year old Mila and her mother behind to fend for themselves. We had grown up in the same neighborhood, which consisted of mostly Black and Hispanic people, so she had a lot more flavor than the average white chick. She was street smart and tough. She had gone from bartending at the Third Rail to running the place. That left Big Tee free to handle his other affairs.

"Hey Playboy, long time no see," she said, looking me over.

"M.C., what's good homie? I see you hardly working." I joked.

"Nah, you got it twisted, I'm working hard. That storeroom kicking my ass. We can't all be young, gifted, and Black. Some of us gotta grind." She felt I was gifted because I'd never had a legit job in my life. She didn't know exactly what I did; just that it was illegal and lucrative.

41

"Ma, you must don't know what's good. You got the best hand. Wit' Big Tee you got job security," I explained.

"Yeah, but working here I ain't gonna get long money. I want O.G. paper; money long like train smoke, like you got. A girl like nice things," she complained.

"Shit, I'm damn near dead broke, shorty!"

"C'mon Playboy, you can't be serious. You got ten g's in your front pocket right now. Save the stories for the kids." She looked me in the eye with her head cocked to one side.

I laughed at how on point she was, then said, "Yeah, you got that. But you know I'm here to render unto Caesar. Ain't no beating death, taxes, and Big Tee. I've had luck with the first two so far, but the last one's a motherfucker."

"Well, you my Big Homie...look out sometime. I ain't tryna work here forever. I'm tryna retire early. Work ages you," she reasoned, then added, "When we gonna hang out again?"

"Shit, last time we kicked it you made me watch 'Love Jones' twice and painted my toenails."

" 'Love Jones' was a good compromise. Nia Long for you, Larenz Tate for me."

We both threw our heads back laughing about the last time we'd hung out. "I'll probably have some time soon. In the meantime I'll keep you in mind for the 'come-up'. You never know." I glanced at the door at the far end of the hall.

"Anyway, I know you got pressing matters to attend to, so just gimme a holla. Home, the cell, whatever. You know I don't keep no man, or should I say don't let no man keep me!" She said the last part over her shoulder as she sauntered out into the barroom.

I took the remaining few steps down the hall. As soon as I raised my fist to knock on the door, I heard a 'click' and the door swung part way open before I could touch it. I still hadn't gotten use to that. The entire bar looked like it hadn't been renovated in years, but Big Tee actually had the whole place wired up. There were cameras everywhere he felt was "respectable," and all the doors had locking mechanisms that he could control from his desktop computer or his Blackberry.

Stepping through the partially open door, I saw Big Tee behind his desk reclined in an over-stuffed chair smoking what was most likely a Cuban cigar and reading the sports section of the Post. At six foot, three inches and 300-plus pounds, Big Tee was a hulk of a man. He kept his hair cut low with waves spinning. He favored well cut Italian suits, and I never saw him with anything on his feet that wasn't made from some exotic creature, whether it be a snake, lizard, alligator. His demeanor was quiet, always allowed the next guy to finish talking before he spoke. When he did speak, he had a deep authoritative growl reminiscent of your dad telling you what you were gonna do. To most cats he was intimidating. If you knew him, he was cool as a fan; especially when he got to talking sports.

When I closed the door behind me, he spoke from behind his paper, "Hey young Lex, when you gonna make an honest woman outta Mila; meet her at the altar in her white dress? I can spare her for a few weeks for ya'll honeymoon and all that," he chuckled. He'd obviously seen us in the hall talking via his eyes in the sky.

"Ah, c'mon Big Homie! That's how rumors get started. Me and her is just cool peoples. Besides, I'm too big a proponent of the Black family, it's a lot of sistahs out there single and only a few good men," I said.

"I meant no disrespect to your status as a young Black nationalist my brother. I just know ya'll both young, get along well, and single," he said, soothing my ego.

"I'm equal opportunity and all that, but as far as my status goes, I got this fish on the line I just met coming back from Miami. She like that homie. Baby girl look like a young Jasmine Guy…things play out right, she might be a keeper," I said enthusiastically.

He set his paper aside at hearing my enthusiasm. Appraising my expression, he paused before speaking. "Is that right? She must be helluva 'cause you got that same twinkle in your eye you get about good hardware. Speaking of which, heard you had a little turbulence down the way?"

I didn't have to ask if he knew about the job being double booked. Big Tee knew things sometimes before the parties involved. Although we never spoke specifically about what I did for whom or to whom, I'd have been foolish to think he didn't know what I was. Still, we left a lot of things unsaid. The wall of gangsta silence between us spoke volumes. I was, nevertheless, slightly surprised to hear him make mention of an actual gig. I didn't know much, so I couldn't say much. "Yeah, it got crowded down there. They say too many cooks fucks up the soup, or whatever. It was more than likely just a mix up. I should have it straightened out soon, though," I explained.

"Ain't too much happen in this world by accident, and coincidences is a concept created by squares for squares. I fucks wit' you. Get that shit straight. Lemme know if you need any help." He sounded genuinely concerned.

I knew his offer was a real one, but I wanted to keep it in-house for the time being. I changed the subject, "The food at Alphonso's was excellent. Good lookin' out. Whay my account lookin' like?" I asked, inquiring about my bill. He supplied me on a couple jobs at a time. I paid when my number got up around ten grand. Working it that way was good for both of us. I didn't have to make a bunch of trips, and he didn't have to get his money piece by piece. Needless to say, he trusted me.

He held up one finger and began punching keys on an imaginary calculator. He paused and said, "Right now you at $9400...Cash or charge homeboy?"

I took the stack of bills from my pocket, removing six ones and laying the remainder on the desk in front of him. Standing and turning to leave I said, "I may need that 'big boy' I told you about for a piece of work I got coming up. I'll be in touch Big Homie...Oh, by the way, 'Phonso said..." I began but he cut me off.

"Man don't even tell me! 'Phonso been hating on my 49ers since back in the day when we played college ball out west. That fool's a fan of whoever go to the Super Bowl! Just holla at me when you ready."

I gave him a pound and let myself out. Stepping into the barroom I shot Bubby a slight nod, letting him know it was time to leave. On my way out, I stopped at the bar and handed Mila the $600 I had left over. I told her to buy everyone a drink on Bubby, and keep the change. Before she could protest, I was out the door and back in the coupe.

My last destination was obvious. We jumped on the highway and headed south to my lower Manhattan hideout. While stuck in typical evening traffic on the FDR Drive, I relaxed in the V and allowed my thoughts to drift back to Chaine. She was the most fascinating woman I'd ever met. Long legs, an ample-bottom, and a pretty face. The total package. Despite all my work related drama, I found myself undressing her in my mind. I would definitely be giving her a call. I didn't have much lined up for the next few days. In between jobs, I was free to do whatever. I hoped it'd be her. My happy contemplation was cut short by our arrival in front of my place. I grabbed my bags and thanked Bubby for the lift. I hopped out and glanced back at the 850's sleek lines. The car was a definite keeper, and perhaps Bubby's coldest yet.

The block he let me out on was a busy street in SoHo, right on the edge of Chinatown. It was lined with Chinese take-out restaurants, small stores, and warehouses. The area didn't appear to be much of a place to live. The tiny apartments over the stores were mostly inhabited by the immigrant families that owned and operated the neighborhood's many businesses. Mostly honest folks, they kept to themselves.

The place I rented wasn't exactly residential living space. In between two large buildings, one a warehouse and one a factory, was an alley that led to discreet rear entrances to both buildings. It was the 2000 square foot space above the factory that I called home. I'd taken a lease on the place from an elderly Jewish couple under the guise of using the place as an art studio and showroom. That was what the previous tenant had used the place for. The owners weren't altogether concerned with that. I took a 24-month lease, and paid the rent for six months at a time, in cash. They were happier than hogs in slop, and I was happy to never see them. The factory downstairs was rented by a Chinese outfit that manufactured "I Love N.Y." fanny packs. I'd seen them from time to time. I checked them out and they were 100% legit.

I crept through the alley making my way around to the massive steel door at the rear. Through that door was a freight elevator that I'd had modified to work by a key Nan Helen and I had the only copies of. The elevator brought you up in front of another heavy steel door. On the other side of this door was my lair. Once inside the door, I raced across the floor to the keypad mounted on the wall and deactivated the security system. I surveyed the cavernous apartment keenly, and saw that everything was exactly how I'd left it. Home sweet home.

My apartment, or my loft as I often referred to it, was a young bachelor's dream. First off, it had no interior walls, just some pillars here and there, but other than that it was all one big airy room with 30 foot ceilings and hardwood floors. Even the bathroom was just a big lion-footed antique tub with a shower with a sink and a toilet off in a corner. The toilet and sink were partitioned off with a Chinese screen, but I don't know why I got it because I never had company. Adjacent to the bathroom was my kitchen space which was small because of the two motorcycles I kept parked there.

There were no windows in the entire space, just brick walls. The place came with tons of track lights run all over. I guess for the art studio effect or whatever. At any time of day, it could be light or as dark as I wanted it. In the center of the floor was a plush black leather couch, and mounted on the wall in front of it was a sixty-inch plasma screen television. Against the wall behind the couch was an entertainment center with a stereo system I spent entirely too much money on, and no less than 1,000 CD's. On a chain from the ceiling in the far corner swung an Everlast punching bag. That corner had all my work-out equipment. There was a treadmill, pull-up bar, and a rack of dumbbells. Across the floor from my gym was my king sized four post bed. First thing I saw most mornings was the gym because it seemed I often needed to be reminded to work out.

In the corner by my bed was a metal spiral staircase that led up to the part of the place that actually was a loft. This was my sanctuary. Atop the stairs was a 20 foot by 18 foot room. At first glance it appeared to be just an office. There was a recliner on a throw rug and a desk for my laptop. Beside the desk was a small file cabinet. A potted plant and a bookcase completed the look. Truth told, I actually spent more time up there reading than anything. Reading however, wasn't what made the room important. When I was first moving in, I'd asked Nana Helen to find out the best type of safe for me to buy. She laughed at me ...Real hard. She told me, "A safe? Are you crazy? There's nothing safe about a safe. That just tells people you got something to hide, and where you're hiding it. Best thing you find a safe place in plain sight." That was when I'd had the bookcase installed.

I dropped the bag with my clothes and headed straight up the stairs with the bag containing the eighty million from the Miami job. The bookcase was filled with all types of various titles from classics to contemporary. I walked over and removed two American classics, Ernest Hemmingway's "A Farewell to Arms" from the top right, and Arthur Miller's "Death of a Salesman" from the bottom left. These seemingly unrelated and insignificant selections deactivated a pressure switch with a faint 'click.' The click was the disengaging locking mechanism that freed the entire bookcase to swing open. And there behind it was my candy store.

In a three foot by two foot hollow behind the bookcase, I kept the things I needed to keep safe. Neatly placed along the left side of the hollow was my contingency plan, should things ever go awry. Mounted on the interior wall were twin H&K MP-10 sub-machine guns, and beneath them were twin Ruger P-89 9 mm handguns. I like 'em in two's 'cause I figure I got two hands for a reason; no sense letting one hand sit idle while the other has all the fun. On the bottom below the guns was a wooden crate containing 24 Army issue fragmentation grenades. It was all courtesy of Big Tee's one stop shop. If I couldn't get myself out of any situation with all that; well, that meant I was in the wrong business.

On the right side lay a caramel colored Coach bag. That bag pretty much held my life savings, with the exception of a $250K I kept in a bank safety deposit box in case of emergencies. I was slightly dejected as I opened the bag and eyed the contents. There was $1.4 million and some change in there. The addition of the Miami money took the total to $1.5m. I sat there at my stash for a moment and regretfully pondered not having more to show for my work. I could have saved a lot more along the way. All the clothes I bought could be seen as a necessary business expense, but I also spent a lot on things I barely used. The plasma I almost never watched, and while I did ride one motorcycle regularly, the other one was a race bike that I'd only taken on a track twice. These were prime examples of poor fiscal policy.

The situation on the last job and Nana Helen's constant pressure had me seriously considering retirement, but financially I wasn't even close to ready. Things had a habit of going wrong when you least expected and were least prepared. Miami had been a smack in the face of a reality check. It was time to tighten up and begin formulating an exit strategy.

I closed up shop and headed downstairs with my mind's wheels turning. I decided to have a bath and relax a bit. I thumbed the remote control and cued up some music. Instinctively going through my pockets as I stripped off my clothes, I came across Chaine's business card. While the tub filled with water, I sat on its edge with two things on my mind. My future, and this incredible woman I barely even knew, yet couldn't stop thinking about. Were the two things related? Maybe somehow life was sending me signals.

I slid into the steaming hot water and soulful music filled every inch of my loft from speakers unseen. I soaked in the water to the sounds of Anita, Luther, Patti, and Sade. As Anita "Apologized," Luther told me the "Power of Love," Patti reminded me I was "On My Own," and Sade gave me the "Kiss of Life" I couldn't escape the feeling that something totally different from everything I'd ever known was coming my way.

Chapter 3

A few days later when the weekend rolled around, I found myself sitting on the edge of my bed staring at Chaine's phone number. I sat thinking of what to say, worried that the chemistry we'd shared in Miami may have been just a fluke. Thus far, I'd never had a problem approaching or calling a woman, but this was different. I actually wanted her to like me. I'd even told her my real name. Usually the women I dealt with were all superficial, and thoughts of a relationship never even crossed my mind. By the time they realized that everything they thought they knew about me had been a lie, it was too late. They looked up and I'd disappeared like a flame on a candle in the wind. I had never even brought a single one to my place. In my profession, keeping a woman was bad for business. Still, there was something about Chaine that made me want to know her, and in turn, I found myself willing to let her know me.

A little before noon, after quite a bit of hesitation, I dialed the number on the card. A few rings later, there was her voice on the line, "Hello, you've reached Chaine..." It was one of those voice mail answering services. I had a mailbox on a similar service. It was "stalker-proof." I laughed at the irony and hung up just before the beep. The service made it so a caller had to identify themselves and leave a number if they wanted to hear back from you. Basically, if I did that, she'd have my cell number and the option to call back. I considered it, but decided to go another route.

I picked up the phone and hit the redial button. "Hey Chaine, it's Lex from Miami International... The $20 Sprite drinking 'Floetry' fan...It's a lovely afternoon, I'm wondering if you'd join me for coffee. I'll be at the Starbuck's next to Washington Square Park at around 2 o'clock if you can make it." I hung up feeling a little better about the situation. This way Chaine would have to meet me on neutral territory.

I showered and got dressed. Opting for a casual look, I threw on some Rocawear denim jeans, an Iceberg t-shirt, retro Jordans, and a Yankee fitted. I didn't want to look like I was trying to impress her. Before heading out the door, I grabbed the "baby" Beretta .380 that I kept under my pillow and tucked it in my waist. I scooped up some cash and set the alarm on my way out.

Walking along the busy streets, I wondered if she would actually come. I had no way to know but had decided to take a gamble figuring, 'what's the worst that could happen?'

I cut across the park and made it to Starbuck's at about ten minutes after two. I anxiously scanned the crowded bar as I walked in, but she was nowhere to be found amongst the afternoon's diverse patrons. It was still early. I went to the counter and ordered a double latte. A couple vacating a good table in the back by the window caught my eye, and I grabbed my latte and headed over to secure the prime real estate.

I sipped and worked on a half-done N.Y. Time crossword someone had left behind. Periodically, I picked my head up and looked around the room and at the sidewalk outside the picture window. An hour passed and still no Chaine. I began to rationalize that maybe she lived way uptown and it could take her a while to get there. As it got even later and I began to accept that she might not be coming, I started kicking myself for assuming that this beautiful woman would somehow just not be busy on a Saturday afternoon. Or that she would just extricate herself from whatever she was doing because I had called. I had been reaching. I finished the crossword and saw that the theme of it had been "tragedies." Ironic. A glance at the clock said it was 3:45. It was time to give up. An hour and a half was all I could give up and still have my dignity intact.

In the interest of making the most I could of the remainder of the afternoon, I decided to head over to the park and do battle with the local chess hustlers. Not five minutes in the park, amongst the groups of onlookers and technicians at work, I found a graying older rasta-man looking for a game.

"You wan' spar Natty Dread?" I asked him with a Jamaican accent.

"How much a game you can afford to lose rude bwoy?" he asked.

"Sky's the limit, if you can fly," I replied, quoting an old reggae tune.

"Mek it ten a game, double afta' stalemate," he said, producing a pouch of well carved heavy wooden pieces.

We sat down at one of the park's many cement chess tables and went to work. He beat me two games back to back. My game was rusty the first game, and in the second I walked into a well laid trap. He was good. I settled down and managed to win two intense very close games. A crowd had gathered around us when I rallied in the third and fourth games, but as we got on to the fifth game, I noticed that they had all moved on. All the spectators were gradually drawn to a match being played a few tables down from ours. I couldn't quite make out the players through the crowd. Even some of the other matches had broken up to watch. I thought nothing of it because sometimes pro chess players or the occasional celebrity would stop through and play a few. In that fifth game, the dread got me. I'd over-extended my pawns, and left my king poorly defended. I decided to call it quits, figuring I'd watch the interesting match at the other table for a few before heading home. I paid the dread his $10 and gave him a pound.

Squeezing in amongst the gaggle of onlookers it was so packed I could barely see. I maneuvered to a position where I could see only one of the players and the board. I recognized him from my previous trips to the park. He was an NYU professor. Word was, he was one of the designers of the "Deep Blue" computer chess program that beat Bobby Fisher. I'd never played him, but despite his disheveled Albert Einstein look, I knew he was one of the best players in the city. From the look of the board, he was a couple of moves away from a win. After one or two evasive moves, his opponent accepted defeat and tipped over his king in submission. They shook hands and a small wad of bills was exchanged.

From the look of the board, he was a couple of moves away from a win. After one or two evasive moves, his opponent accepted defeat and tipped over his king in submission. They shook hands and a small wad of bills was exchanged. A small wager was the status quo in the park, but I zeroed in on something else. Delicate fingers? Manicure? Smooth skin? The crowd began to dissipate as the loser turned to leave. I craned my neck to see what I already knew, but I was no less astonished to find that the competitor had been a woman! On closer inspection I realized I recognized her. I stood there gawking dumbfounded for a moment before it clicked that it was Chaine.

Her look was different. In Miami it had been toned down, more reserved. This was more haute couture. But it wasn't just what she was wearing; it was like her whole persona was different. She was still very beautiful, but it seemed she was a different person from the one I'd me in the airport.

I was so surprised at seeing her I didn't have time to be pissed off that she'd blown me off to play chess. I stepped through the dispersing crowd trying to catch up with her as she walked away. I pulled up beside her a little ways down the path. She was impeccably dressed. 'Even fly for chess in the park,' I thought. She had on black high heeled Gucci alligator boots that came up to her knees with a short Marc Jacobs trench coat that came down to her thighs. Her hair was wrapped up in a Fendi scarf that matched her sunglasses and earrings.

"Remember love, it's not whether you win or lose..." I said as my stride brought me abreast of her.

A small smile crept onto her face, replacing what I thought may have been pouting. "I don't like to lose, but I figured I'd never get another game if I didn't let him win his money back." She said it playfully, but it was hard for me to judge how serious she was. No matter how serious she really was, I made a mental note that she had to be one hell of a chess player.

"So, you're saying you let the professor win?" I asked, stating the obvious.

She looked at me as though I had sprouted a second head. Her left eyebrow arched to an impossible height as she sized me up. She "tsked" as though I'd made the classic mistake of underestimating a woman. "Basically you're implying that it's hard for you to believe a 'girl' could beat him."

We stopped walking and she turned to face me with a hand on one hip waiting for me to play myself. I could tell from her posture she felt she had me in a "catch-22." She clearly didn't know who she was dealing with. "Actually Chaine, what I'm implying is that it seems pointless to me that you'd blow me off to play a game of chess that you couldn't even be bothered to win," I said, watching as the smug expression left her.

"You assumed a lot making a date with my answering service. Could be that I'm just out for an afternoon in the park and this meeting is simply a chance occurrence," she said with a sly grin.

"Could also be you couldn't make up your mind about seeing me," I said, calling her bluff. "Anyway, this makes the first time a woman ever stood me up in person." I looked into her eyes and I could see she was enjoying this. It was a game to her.

All of a sudden it dawned on me that the whole thing was a plot. She'd probably watched me from a distance and maybe even saw the dejected look on my face when I thought she didn't show. The situation I'd tried to make neutral had been manipulated. We stood there in a silent stand-off as the afternoon in the crowded park went on around us. There was an unmistakable attraction between us. I wondered how long she planned on being aloof and evasive.

"So, what now, Lex?" she asked coyly. "Would it soothe your ego a bit if I offered to buy you a cup of coffee?"

It seemed funny to me that she knew my ego was somewhat bruised. My eyes roamed down to her honey-dipped thighs and I was tempted to just let her have an easy win. There I was, being manipulated and liking it. The air of control, composure, and panache that normally surrounded me was somehow nullified by this woman. I couldn't ever remember feeling like this.

The competitive side of me took over and just wouldn't allow me to five in so easily. "I've had enough coffee for one day," I said. I saw a look of defeat sweep across her face. She hadn't expected to be turned down. I continued, "Maybe we'll get together and play chess sometime." I turned and began to walk away, leaving her frozen there.

I had gotten about five steps away when I heard music to my ears, "So, it's like that?" she asked.

I stood there a moment like I was in deep contemplation. In actuality I'd already had my mind made up. Standing there stalling was just payback for the whole Starbuck's thing. When I felt she'd had enough I let two parts glide and two parts stride gracefully put me back in front of her. Her eyes had become less confident at seeing the twist her little game had taken.

"What you want it to be like?" I asked, slowly closing the distance between us until we were face to face.

"I came, didn't I? I wanted to see you but..."

"Is this the part where you stop playing games?" I asked as I took her hand in mine.

She didn't answer; just put her arms around me. We stood there for a minute in a warm embrace. Although we were standing in the middle of Washington Sq. Park, it felt intimate. In those few moments that I held her close to me everything seemed to fall into place. I'd never been out to find romance, and I surely never sat around praying for love to find me, but somehow I knew Chaine and I had a future. When we finally separated, I could feel that vibe we shared in Miami returning.

We started to walk and talk. We people watched and made fun of the city's many different flavors of freaks and geeks. Strolling down Broadway holding hands an hour flew by before we knew it. One, or maybe it was both of us, had gotten hungry. We had already gotten as far south as Houston Street. I suggested we grab a bite to eat at Mekka, a trendy soul food restaurant.

The spot had a lot of ambience. In the restaurant's crowd of twenty and thirty-somethings, she wasn't overdressed, and I wasn't underdressed. At my suggestion, the hostess seated us in a cozy little corner, and before leaving, she told us what a cute couple we made. I agreed. Chaine blushed - beet red. She was even sexy when she did that.

Since I'd chosen the spot we decided she would order for the both of us. She had the crab cakes and ordered me a delicious honey mustard grilled salmon. When the waitress brought the food, Chaine ordered us a bottle of some wine I couldn't pronounce. I protested. Drinking wasn't my thing. It was a date, but I was still a professional and obligated to remain aware of my surroundings. The pistol on my waist might need to be drawn at a moment's notice. Anything outside of cautious could get you dead. I realized that my interest in her was making me say and do things I didn't normally do. The wine was no different. She twisted my arm for about 45 seconds and before I knew it, we had nearly finished the bottle.

There, in the back of the dimly lit restaurant, we sat and built the foundation of something that felt right. We sat closely at the table long after the food was gone. I ran my fingertips back and forth on the silky smooth skin of her thighs as she whispered in my ear about wanting to find that right someone. I let my hand wander towards the warmth between her legs. She playfully squeezed her thighs together on my hand. I told her I'd never met anyone like her and asked her about her dreams. She confided in me. She told me about her formative years. Growing up an army brat, she'd never spent enough time in one place to make real friends. Young and dumb at sixteen she left home and everything she knew behind in pursuit of love. It was a disaster that ended with her heartbroken, homeless and alone. Too ashamed to return home, she faced the cruel world alone. She was proud of the person she had become, but she regretted her decision. I sensed an intense wave of relief in her. As she revealed those parts of herself, I knew they were things she'd never told a soul.

Finally, she said something that I'd dreaded was coming. "Lex, I'm starting to feel so close to you. This is the most intimate first date I've ever been on ...but I hardly know anything about you. Tell me about you."

In that moment, I felt completely and totally conflicted. Thus far, I'd managed to keep the focus on her. I knew I was in uncharted waters. There I sat with a decision to make. Besides Nana Helen, nobody really knew me. We'd only just met, but the pounding in my chest told me she was the one. Maybe not on that first night, but I made a decision that I would let her in.

I told her the basics with the exception of what I did for a living. I started out with my emotionally unavailable mother, my delinquent father, and the bond I shared with my surrogate mother. It passed for family ties. My early years were a blur, but I managed a fair account of coming up in the Bronx. Some of my later years were trickier to talk about. I rode it out with some clever editing. By the time I was done, I realized that all I'd told her wasn't really that far from the truth. She didn't ask many questions, just listened really well and soaked up all I had to say. By the time I was finished talking, she was holding my face gently in her hands. Over the din of the patrons in the background, I could hear Kem singing "Love Calls." Truer words were never spoken or sung; there really was nowhere to run when love was calling your name.

When I was done talking, she looked deeper into my eyes than anyone ever had then leaned in and kissed me with soft lips that warmed me from the inside out. Her kiss quenched a thirst in me that until then I hadn't known existed. Every second our lips stayed locked it got more and more intense. We started groping and rubbing each other. I wanted to rip her clothes off then and there. Felt like it was ten degrees hotter in that little corner. We were at each other like teenagers in the back seat at a drive-in movie. We crossed the line from P.G. to R and X was fast approaching, but somehow she found some restraint.

She excused herself to the ladies room. I was tempted to follow her, but instead, I paid the check, hoping we were about to adjourn to someplace more appropriate. I gathered up her coat and her little black Gucci alligator bag, and went over to meet her by the door. The patrons who'd seen us all over each other gave me funny looks. I couldn't have cared less.

As I stood waiting for her to emerge from the ladies room, I offhandedly noticed that her purse was slightly heavy to be so little. I started to undo the clasp and peek inside when she came up behind me, slipping her arms around my waist. I was startled back to my senses. I figured it was probably just a phone and some personals that she had in there. I had a tendency to think like a technician and it was obviously carrying over into my personal life.

As we made our way out in front of the restaurant, I was already fantasizing about how the night would play out. I decided to be direct. "We having breakfast at your place or mine?"

"Lex..." I could hear apprehension in her voice, "I don't want this date to end. I really don't...but I got something to take care of first thing in the morning," she explained.

"How about we go to my place, and I promise to have you home before either of us turns into a pumpkin?" As the words left my mouth, I immediately thought about the impact of letting her see where I lived. I didn't care. In that moment, wanting to be with her became my priority.

60

"Don't think I don't want to. I really do. I have this early appointment, and I can't get out of it. We can get together again real soon, though." As she spoke, she took out her cell phone and began typing a text message. I tried to peer at her phone's screen and inside her bag, but she held both on an angle toward herself. My curiosity was renewed at wondering if maybe she had someone to go home to.

"Chaine, keep it real wit' me. If you got somebody else you gotta be with..." I said indignantly. I watched her face closely for tells, but all that came was that same coy smile from the park.

"It's cute you're jealous. I'm really feeling you...I got a pair of wet panties in my pocket to prove it. I just have this business thing in the morning," she explained.

"What business is that? And on a Sunday morning?"

"I'm a marketing consultant..." she said, but before she could elaborate, a black Lincoln Town Car pulled up beside us. I instinctively reached for my pistol but realized it was her ride when she motioned to the driver. It must have been a car service she'd been texting, but I didn't have a clue how they responded that fast.

"Here's my ride. I'm really sorry we had to end this. Why don't you leave a number I can reach you at on my service so we can finish what we started?"

"You don't leave me much choice." I replied.

"Don't be like that," she said, putting her arms around my neck, "I promise I'll make it up to you." She kissed me long, deep, and hard. I felt her hips grinding against mine. We both wanted more. Our lips parted slowly and she traced the outline of my lips with her tongue. I saw stars. I stood there clinging to her and not wanting the moment to end. She tore herself away from me, and gracefully seated herself inside the sedan pulling in one sexy leg at a time. As the sedan pulled away from the curb, she lowered the window and blew me a kiss.

I stood there on the sidewalk for a minute or two after she'd gone. I was stuck on stupid. A lot of the mistakes I was making were obvious, but the only thing that really mattered to me was being with her. While I walked the few blocks back to my loft, I called her service and left my number. The cityscape seemed to move around me. I floated as if I was riding along on an invisible cloud.

When I got home, I sat on the couch wondering if she would call me sooner, or later. There wasn't much on television, but I let it watch me hoping to get distracted or fall asleep. Around midnight I drifted off. My dreams were of her.

The following morning, I woke up around nine and saw that I'd slept on the couch. I shook my head at how the previous day's escapade was altering my life. In an attempt to normalize, I decided I needed a good work-out to help me snap out of it. After hitting the heavy bag, I did so many pull-ups and push-ups I lost count. To finish it off, I got on the treadmill and ran until my sweats were soaked to the bone. I was just grabbing a towel when I heard a noise I momentarily mistook for an intruder. I quickly realized it was my phone vibrating on the kitchen counter. Rushing over, I switched it on expecting Nan Helen with something work related.

"Talk to me," I answered.

"Hey sexy! I'm downtown. I got bagels. Where should I bring 'em?"

It was Chaine. Here voice just about floored me. I steadied myself on the counter. Hearing my silence, she continued, "Lex...we are still on for breakfast, right?"

"Oh, uhh…yeah. Yeah. You just caught me working out," I replied, trying not to sound stupefied.

"Well, this food ain't gonna eat itself. Where are you?"

I gave her directions to my street. She said she'd be there in five minutes. That didn't even leave me time to shower. I grabbed my keys and headed out front to meet her. Not a full two minutes had passed when she came strolling down the block.

The first thing I noticed was that her look was different again. Her skin had more of a bronze tone like she'd been tanning. She was dressed down in tight Baby Phat jeans and a baby tee that read "Spoiled Brat." She had custom Air Force One's on and her hair was in a bun. Her look was 'hood, but she looked so damn good! In one hand, she held her phone, and in the other she had a brown paper bag. When she saw me, she smiled and ran up to me, planting a quick kiss on my lips.

"You live around here? I didn't even know you were Chinese," she joked.

"Why the Black man and the Asian man can't live as one?" I replied.

"Okay Mr. Ambassador, I'm hungry so lead the way."

I walked down the alley in silence and she followed. She was quiet but her face told me she thought it was odd. In the elevator, she looked my sweaty clothes up and down and jokingly held her nose. I opened the door and stepped aside for her to enter first. She walked in and she seemed taken aback by either all the space or all the toys. She walked into the middle of the room by the couch and spun around taking it all in. I could tell she was impressed. I spoke to her from the kitchen, "Can I get you something?"

She paused and looked around the room like a kid in a candy store before speaking. Putting a finger to her lips, she said, "Yeah, I'd really like to ride that Honda Fireblade sitting in your kitchen," she said, referring to the race bike.

Her ability to identify it surprised me. She knew motorcycles. This chick was a keeper! "That one's not street lega. I'd be happy to take you for a ride on the R-1, though…that is, if you think you can handle it?"

"I don't do Yamaha. And who said anything about you coming with me," she replied, in a feisty tone.

"So, what you bring us to eat? That work-out got me hungry as a hostage," I said changing the subject.

"I told you, bagels. But don't you think you should wash up first?"

"Well, it crossed my mind, but my bathroom isn't exactly private. I didn't want to be rude."

"It's only a body…ain't even like it's a dead body! I can stand it if you can. Better yet, I'll promise not to peek," she said laughing.

Before she finished speaking I had already started undressing. Unfazed, she went to the kitchen and started fixing us something to eat. I didn't tell her where anything was, but she just made herself at home and found what she needed. I grabbed a towel and walked across to the tub naked. She watched me out from the corner of her eye. As she checked out my body, she gave an approving nod and smile. I was ripped up from the work-out and apparently, she liked what she saw. I took a quick shower while she fixed us coffee and toasted bagels with cream cheese.

While I showered, I couldn't help but revisit the time we'd spent together the previous day. After my shower, I dried off and threw on some sweat pants. Standing alone, half naked in a room with her had me slightly turned on. I approached her with a significant bulge forming in the front of my sweats. Rivulets of water glistened on my skin. She bit her bottom lip as I came toward her, and she fixed me in a gaze that told me we had the same thing in mind. I wrapped her in a strong embrace, and I began to kiss her softly. The room seemed to spin. She moaned as our tongues intertwined, but she stopped abruptly and pulled away.

"What about breakfast?" she asked.

"This is exactly what I had in mind. I'm real hungry...think you can satisfy me?" I whispered in her ear, while grabbing two handfuls of her ass.

She giggled and looked me in the eyes. There was electricity in that stare. She playfully pushed me away from her and began to undress. I watched her slowly reveal the same flesh I'd fantasized about as she pulled her t-shirt over her head. She wore no bra. Her perky breasts defied gravity like two juicy mangoes suspended in mid air. The bulge in my pants became a full erection and seemed to be reaching out for her. She kicked off her sneakers and peeled off her tight jeans. Standing there in front of me in a pink LaPerla thong, she undid her bun and shook loose her silky brown hair. It was like being awake, but still in a dream. Her face was beautiful and her body was the picture of perfection. She undid the drawstring of my sweats and pulled them off. Her eyes drifted down to my throbbing rock hardness. We both just stood there for a minute drinking each other with our eyes and savoring the moment.

Like a savage beast, I swept her up in my arms and drew her to me. I vigorously kissed all over her neck. She threw her head back, inviting me to explore her. Slowly taking my time, I gently suckled her tender breasts. Her skin was smooth as satin, its texture was like whipped butter. As I softly bit her erect nipples, her unabashed moans filled my spacious apartment like the crescendo of a sweet symphony. With tremendous attention to detail, I licked, kissed, and sucked every part of her upper body, working her into a near orgasmic frenzy. I grabbed her supple thighs and lifted her onto the kitchen counter. She took hold of my pulsating member and deftly began to stroke it.

I couldn't wait another second.

I pulled her to the edge of the counter. The moment seemed timeless. She moved the fabric of her panties aside and guided the head of my long, thick manhood inside her. The instant I entered her, I let out a long deep moan. Her flowing juices coated me inch by inch until I found myself submerged within her. She felt like cotton dipped in warm honey as her walls stretched to accommodate me. I stroked her long and slow. As I explored her, I discovered a comfort and satisfaction that was like nothing I'd ever imagined, much less experienced.

As it turns out, Chaine was a screamer. Neither of us gave a damn. She kissed me, probing my mouth deeply with her tongue. Suddenly, her rhythm changed. She wrapped her long legs around my back and began grinding and rocking her hips against me. I lifted her off the counter top, and increased my paced. I wanted to be more inside her. Not just deeper, but it was like I wanted to "be" in her, to exist within her. She clung to my neck and sung my praises at the top of her lungs in a language I could barely understand. I continued to stroke her as she bucked and thrashed violently. Her juices ran down my legs. Beads of sweat poured from my body as if I'd worked out all over again. I felt the brink of orgasm, and I pushed myself still deeper inside her. Her body trembled intensely for a few moments, and then she went limp. I followed her over the edge, exploding in a climax that surpassed anything I'd ever felt in my life. I gently set her back down on the counter top. My knees had come weak.

I thought it was over, but that was just the beginning. Chaine recovered with remarkable quickness.

After I'd held her for a minute, she hopped down off the counter and led me by the hand over to the couch. Following behind her, I watched her ass in that thong. I felt almost fully rejuvenated at the sight. She had a body that could motivate any man.

Standing in front of me, she aggressively pushed me down onto the couch. I grabbed the remote and hit a few buttons. "Floetry" filled the air reminding us all we had to do was "Say Yes." She smiled. That smile could melt a man. She got on her knees in front of me and breathed new life into my semi-hard erection. She took her time and I gripped the couch so tightly that I nearly ripped the soft leather. The sound of the stereo's sensual sweet serenade surrounded us while she made love to me with her mouth. When I couldn't stand another moment of the ecstasy, she took off her thong and climbed on top of me. She rode me front, back and sideways. I laid back and let her have her way with me.

Chaine and I went at it for most of the day, only pausing for a cat-nap intermission here and there. She slept over that night but we didn't sleep much. We had passionate sex in every position known to man on just about every surface in my loft. It was crazy how sexually compatible we were. We fit together like a hand and glove. Sometimes after going at it, we'd just lay back and laugh out loud at how good it was. We slept a little, and played love games for most of the night.

I'd be hard pressed to say which one of us had the most fun. When morning came, we held each other tightly. Neither of us wanted it to end, but I had a job to prepare for and she had work. showered and got dressed. I walked her downstairs where she kissed me goodbye before jumping in a cab. It was the first time in my life I was ever sad when someone left me.

Chapter 4

That afternoon I began making preparations for my next job. It was a nice day, so I decided to ride my motorcycle uptown to see Nana Helen and Big Tee. I figured that maybe the adrenaline rush might be comparable to what I'd felt with Chaine. Maybe it would satisfy my soul, and the ache of longing I'd felt since the moment she'd gone. I sported some old jeans, a wife beater, Tims, and a Vanson leather jacket. I strapped on my "baby" Beretta in an ankle holster, grabbed my helmet, and headed out. The afternoon congestion of the downtown streets didn't afford me much opportunity to indulge the powerful 1000cc motorcycle. Bumper to bumper on the West Side Highway only further defeated my purpose, and by the time I made it to Nana Helen's, I was feeling more frustrated than when I started out.

I let myself in her place and was greeted by the pleasant aroma of Cuban cuisine. Yellow rice, black beans heavy on the garlic, and roasted chicken that seduced my senses before the first taste. In the kitchen, I found Nana Helen throwing down. Usually just the smell would have had my mouth watering, but today I was strictly business. I came in, gave her a kiss on the cheek, and plopped down in a chair at the kitchen table.

Noticing I had my helmet with me, she said, "I see you flying around on that 'death rocket.'"

"Ah, c'mon. Not this again. I…"

She cut me off, "I don't care how good you ride. It's not you I'm worried about. This city has six million maniacs and, most of them have a license. They're what scare me."

"Lemme guess, I'd be safer in a car," I said sarcastically.

"Well, you do have a driver on your payroll."

She had a point. Even if she didn't, arguing with her was usually a losing battle. She had a way of verbally trapping you. I took the smart way out and changed the subject. "I met this girl. I'm kinda feeling her."

Her focus changed. I was no longer secondary. She put a lid on the pot she was stirring and turned down the fires on the others. She dried her hands on a towel as she sat down across from me. I had obviously said something that caught her attention. She looked at me sideways before speaking, "Tell me about her, and leave out the part about her being beautiful…I know how you do."

I excitedly took off describing Chaine at length. She listened attentively nodding and smiling here and there. The part about the earth shattering sex I kept discreet, but I knew I was gushing. The only part I wasn't totally honest about was bringing her to the loft. Nana Helen would never approve. When I was just about through, I added on that I was seriously considering getting out of the murder for hire game.

She stared at me for a minute studying me closely like she was trying to identify a speck of lint on my eyebrow. I fidgeted under her examination. When she finally spoke she said, "What's she do?"

"What 'chu mean 'what she do?'" I shot back defensively.

"Where she work? McDonald's,? She a doctor? She a trust fund baby?"

"Oh…" I stalled, "She's a ummmm…a travel agent."

"Must be one hell of a trip she took you on! I've never seen you like this. You glowing like 'Bruce

Leroy!'" We both burst out into laughter at her joke. "I've been telling you for the longest that this game is getting old...So, if this girl is helping you see straight, I think I like her already."

"Yeah, just a couple more gigs and I'm out," I said.

"Why a few more, why not quit?" she stopped smiling. "Maybe Miami was a sign. You could do the 47th street job and be done with all this shit."

"You keep bringing that up. Robbery ain't my game. I told you I'd think about it. In the meantime lemme get the info on that corporate gig," I said, growing impatient.

"I just want you to quit while you're ahead. That one job would guarantee you retire comfortably. Is that such a bad thing?"

"That's what you want me to do. I'll think about it, but it ain't that simple to change gears. In the meantime..."

I didn't get to finish. She got up and walked to her bedroom. When she came back she dropped a manila folder in my lap and said two words: "Do you." All the sound was sucked from the room as if by some giant unseen vacuum. I rose, snatching my helmet from the floor, and left.

As I let myself out, I felt confused. Why was Nana Helen pressing me so hard to do that heist? She'd never been one to press me about doing something till now. The other day she'd said the Miami situation was probably just a mix up, now it was my cue to quit. It didn't add up. Helena Vasquez was a psychological technician. Everything she said and did was for a purpose. As far as her question about Chaine, I should have seen that coming. What she did for a living was the only thing I'd left out. That was an amateur mistake. For the moment, all I could assume was that Nana Helen really wanted me out of the game. Maybe that was in my best interest, but first I needed to get my paper right.

Almost everyone who lived in Nana Helen's building came and went via the elevator. I went into the stairway and sat on the stairs. I spent the next hour there studying the dossier she'd given me. By the time I finished, every detail was etched in my memory up to and including my next mark's shoe size. The file told me so much about him that it was now as though we were closely acquainted. From his photos, I could easily pick him out in a crowd...or pick him off in one. The file also gave me a few possible locations to intercept him. I saw they were all in Norfolk, Virginia. I hoped Big Tee wouldn't have a problem with that. After destroying the file and throwing the remnants down the incinerator, I headed over to the Third Rail to find out.

The afternoon crowd at big Tee's spot was thin. Just a few old heads sat at the bar with what were probably the day's first beers. Nobody so much as even noticed me coming in, with the exception of maybe Big Tee and his eye in the sky.

Mila was behind the bar with her back to the customers, reading a gossip rag. I quietly climbed on the stool directly behind her, and waited for her to notice me. After a quiet minute, she towered the magazine and spoke without turning around. "You know Lex, some people would be annoyed bein' crept up on like that."

"Yeah, that's them. What about you?" I replied.

"Me? I gave you a pass because I knew it was you."

"You psychic now?" I asked.

"No, fool, you pulled up on your loud bike. People come in here to get drunk. They can barely drive much less handle a motorcycle," she broke out laughing and turned around giving me a hug across the bar. She smelled good.

"How was your weekend?" I asked.

"Boring as hell. I used the money you gave me and signed up for a real estate seminar. I learned some shit, but real estate is slow money."

"Shit Mila, you don't know what's good. Slow money is hard to blow money."

"You just got all the sense. What did your smart ass do this weekend?" she asked.

"The 'grown up' with a fine red bone."

"What's with dark brothers always chasing light women?" She leaned back waiting for an answer.

"Homie, that a black thing you wouldn't understand," I smoothly replied, before breaking into laughter.

"Oh, puleeze. Spare me playa, believe me, I heard it all before."

"I bet you have. Remember? I was there in high school. Chicks called you 'Queen of the Jungle' 'cause of all the brothers that came down with jungle fever."

"Lemme find out you a closet racist. You got a problem with interracial dating?" She asked, crossing her arms in front of her.

"Hell nah! I'm an equal opportunity employer...Speaking of which, I'm thinking about taking this job; I could use your help if I do."

"Oh yeah?" she leaned back trying to gauge how serious I was. "What kinda job, what kinda dough?"

"Diamond district, train smoke money."

"What you need me to do?" she asked.

"I ain't even sure about it yet, but I'm thinking I'ma need you to play 'Decoy Joy.'"

"Sounds like you still need to connect the dots. If you decide to make it happen, I'll ride with you, though."

"Consider yourself on stand-by," I said as we shook hands. "Right now, I need to go holla at Big Tee."

I wasn't altogether sure about taking down that score because Nana Helen's pressure game was giving me doubts, but it wouldn't hurt to have a back-up plan. Supposedly, that heist would be good for upward of $5m; my end would probably come out to about $3m, $3.5m tops after I broke off Mila and Nana Helen. On the other hand, if I put my nose to the grindstone and the right people needed to get dead, I could probably build my stash to $5m in the next 6 months. From there it would be game over. I was off to a good start because this week's gig was paying $300k. For some reason, corporate work always paid more. I guess people in business just wanted their marks dead more, or it was probably that they just had the cash to get it done. Either way, irreconcilable differences were what kept me in business.

As usual, Big Tee's door popped open without so much as a touch. I walked in and I was surprised to see he had company. In the chair opposite big Tee sat Fast Black, a local pimp/hustler. He looked up briefly and recognized me with a slight head nod. I had done some work for him when I was doing collections way back when. I noticed something was off about Black's usual confident talkative swagger. When I stepped all the way into the room, I saw that Fast Black's demeanor was off because Big Tee had the business end of a shiny nickel plated .50 caliber Desert Eagle pointed at him. There was thick tension in the room. I spoke apologetically for interrupting. "Oh, my fault. I didn't know you had company Big Homie." I addressed Big Tee, locking eyes, trying to get a sense of what type of time he was on. He'd let me in his office for a reason.

"Nah, young Lex, you straight." He put an ice cold killer scowl on his face and looked at Black, "Fast Black here was just about to leave us."

As if on cue, I turned and shut the door. If Big Tee was about to move, I would back his play. I stepped a few feet to Black's left. No sense in getting blood on my clothes. With that cannon pointed at him, I surely wasn't gonna stand anywhere behind him. Between Big Tee's mean mug and my 'anything goes' posture, Fast Black became visibly shaken. I smirked at the thought that his brightly colored suit suddenly made him look like a clown. No one spoke for a few moments, just one icy stare. Big Tee instilled the fear of a higher power in Fast Black in those moments.

Finally, Big Tee spoke, "I got other shit to do than hefty bag yo' bitch ass right now. Maybe we done come to an understanding?"

Fast Black's mouth hung open. He was terrified and couldn't speak. I whipped my head around looking at him like he was crazy. I knew he had to speak now or forever hold his peace. Maybe I sent him a telepathic signal because he began to vigorously shake his head yes. That nod saved his life. Big Tee uncocked his pistol and lowered it slightly. The door 'clicked' open. Fast Black quickly rose and turned to leave. The sound of Big Tee's voice froze him in his tracks. "Be clear on one thing...Fourth St., Park and The Hilltop are now officially off limits."

We both studied him for a response. "Nnnnnn, nnno problem, Big Tee," he stammered.

Big Tee nodded, dismissing him. He fled the room with an awkward version of a pimp strut. The vapor trail he left behind told us he'd shit himself. I looked at Big Tee and smiled. "I'ma stand if you don't mind. 'Cause I don't think that brown stripe came with the pimp suit!" We both laughed.

"That fool been tryna' gorilla pimp some lady friends of mine that wanna be independent contractors. If you hadn't come through, I was finna' send his ass to the crossroads," he said.

"Shit, you nearly scared him to death with that shiny ass burner. I don't know why people mess with them chrome and nickel plate joints. 'Bling Bling' is for jewelry, playa," I joked.

"We can't all be ghetto commandos. The 'hood ain't for tactical, it's for practical."

"I'll keep that in mind next time I'm in a project staircase. As of right now, though, homie, I need some exotic hardware and the location ain't exactly a popular spot," I said, shifting to business.

"This s'pose to be a test? Anything. Anywhere Lex. How you gon' doubt me? If I tell you a roach ca' pull a coach, get a rope," he replied.

I smiled at his colorful metaphor. He was right. Anything, anywhere had never been a problem. I picked up a pen from the desk and scrawled my order and the destination on a post-it note. After I handed him the slip of paper, he smiled and said, "That's nice...that's real nice. It'll be ready for you in 48 hours."

"I appreciate it, I'll see you when I get back," I said, giving him a pound.

"Yeah, and Lex?" he said as I headed out the door. I turned around as he continued, "I like how you held me down. You saved me from havin' to body ole' Fast Black. You a real rider, let me know if you ever need me."

"Fo sho'," I replied, and left. In the back of my head for some reason, I got the funny feeling that I would actually need Big Tee's help at some point.

I spent the next two days at home doing research on the lay of the land down in Norfolk, VA. I'd been through there but never on "business," so I was vaguely familiar with the terrain. Via the internet, I downloaded detailed local maps that helped me pinpoint distances around the places my mark would be the following day. My plan was to take him down from a distance. He had business meetings throughout the day, and I couldn't chance any collateral damage on this hit. Businessmen were usually somebodies, and to clip one of them in the process would draw extra heat. If someone wanted one of the mark's colleagues dead, I damn sure wasn't gonna do it for free. So, I was figuring on playing sniper. One shot, one kill.

Chaine and I played a little "text tag" here and there. She even sent me some very "interesting" flics off her camera phone. Late night we talked on the phone till the wee hours of the morning. Neither of us could find the time to hook up, but we made plans to get together on the weekend. I had a serious jones in my bones for her. From the erotically ambitious flics she sent to my phone, it was apparent that she had one for me too. The weekend couldn't come soon enough, but in the meantime, I put on my game face. It was time to work.

Early Thursday morning, I stood at the curb in front of my place waiting for Bubby to come scoop me up. In this particular instance, I looked out of place. Amidst the local workers of various nationalities shuffling off to their menial jobs, I stood out. For this job, I took on the look of my prey. I could have been on my way to Wall Street in the $3,000 made to order black Roberto Cavalli suit I was rocking. The suit and tie look went well with my six foot frame, but I couldn't see it for every day. The silver Hugo Boss aviator frames I wore glinted in the sunlight and perfectly complimented the white gold Rolex Submarine timepiece on my wrist. I completed the look with some mean Salvatore Ferragamo loafers I'd had re-soled with rubber. In my profession, rubber shoe soles were a must. You never knew when you would need to get gone in a hurry, and I was certain leather soles wouldn't help your odds in a fight very much.

I heard tires screech and a heavy motor bend the corner of my block. Before I looked up, I knew it was Bubby. He came to a tire squealing halt right in front of me. Today, Bubby had outdone himself. He had come to pick me up in a cherry red 1965 Corvette. This car was the quintessential classic. From the looks of the immaculate paint job, the shiny chrome, and the smooth growl of the power motor, I could tell it was in pristine condition. I stood there for a few moments looking the beauty up and down. Bubby gave me an approving nod as I took my time admiring the ride's sleek perfection. I hopped in, and he said four words to me, "This bitch the coldest!" I nodded in agreement as we rode out in total silence to LaGuardia airport. We were two connoisseurs enjoying the ride in a feat of automotive genius. Words were insufficient.

We pulled up in front of the terminal with Bubby downshifting and bringing us to a dramatic stop. Maybe he'd wanted the extra attention, but in that car, it came guaranteed. I politicked with him for a minute and made sure he had my return info for the following day. The travelers, cab drivers, and airport porters milling around had all taken notice of our arrival, but had since gone back about their business. As I stepped out of the ride, they craned their necks trying to figure out who I was. They lost interest only once they were certain I wasn't 'Diddy' or some other glitterati. Actually, I was glad to be free of the few brief moments of attention. I walked through the automated doors and checked in. With just a small carry on bag, I cleared security in what seemed like record time. My flight departed on time and with little or no fanfare. The small commuter flight touched down in Norfolk 45 minutes later. As we got off the plane, I took note that there had only been 20 or so passengers. I wondered how it was that an airline could even stay in business. Maybe that's why they were all hollering broke nowadays.

The airport was small and had so little going on inside that although it was 9 a.m., it didn't even seem as though it was open. I breezed right through and caught one of the taxis idling out in front of the entrance.

My first stop was Jillian's, a large multi-level upscale restaurant located on the waterfront. My mark would have been having a business lunch there with three of his associates later on in the afternoon so I went there and ordered breakfast, just to get a good look at the place and see if it would give me an opportunity to take him down. If not, I had a few other spots he was supposed to be at during the day. Someone had done their homework on the guy and wanted him dead for certain.

The moment I was seated inside Jillian's I knew it would be the perfect spot for the hit. The entire south wall of the restaurant consisted of large panes of glass. Diners could enjoy their meals with a nice view of the water. I purposely asked the waitress to seat me by a window. I could already tell I would have a clean shot at him almost anywhere he would be sitting in the room. I had just two things left to figure out: for one, there was the thickness of the glass panes, and second, I had yet to choose where I would take the shot from. Happily, I found out that the owners had spared some expense in construction. The plate glass windows were no more than a half inch thick, nothing that would affect the trajectory of my shot. At least not what I'd be shooting!

It appeared I was just another customer staring out of the windows onto the world, as I picked over scrambled eggs and turkey bacon. I was actually trying to make up my mind on my second problem. That was choosing one of three places to shoot from. To the right was a Naval ship yard, and I surely wouldn't be taking my shot from on federal property. On the far left, out across the water, were some nice private homes, and I could make out a tire swing and a tree house in one of the yards. Bad idea. About 500 yards on the other side of the water was an office building. That was my best bet. Even though I didn't know how easy it would be to get into it, it beat the shit out of shooting from a ship or atop a grassy knoll.

I left the waitress a decent tip and cut out. Walking through downtown Norfolk, I seemed to be just another business type. As I walked along, I nonchalantly thumbed the keys of my cell phone. The message I sent was perhaps the most common one in America, "Where U at?" In just moments, the phone vibrated signaling a response. It read: "Kinko's can copy blueprints! Good Luck." Reading the message, I chuckled to myself thinking that Big Tee would never cease to amaze me. When I received the text, I was just a few blocks away. I lengthened my stride, eager to see if Big Tee had been able to get exactly what I wanted.

The small Kinko's store was completely empty when I walked in. I went up to the counter and rang the bell. Seconds later, a disheveled Biggie Smalls look alike in a Kinko's smock and visor cap emerged form the back. He stood there quiet for a moment giving me the once over. It was probably the suit. I spoke, breaking him out of his trance, "Good morning, are you open for business?" I asked.

"Oh uhh yeah. Yeah. How can I help you?" he replied, but the look in his eyes told me he knew why I was there.

"I need some blueprints copied."

His demeanor became more laid back as he responded, "Yeah, playa, I ca' do that for you. Hold tight a minute, I'll be right back." He disappeared to the rear of the store for a few minutes. I heard some shuffling and boxes moving around. When he came out, he laid one of those tubes that architects carry blueprints in on the counter. I smiled ear to ear at the ingenuity of it.

"That's you right there, playa. The Big Homie said to tell you, 'if he say a duck ca' pull a truck, just hook him up'," he said smiling.

I nodded in agreement as I picked up the tube, which was heavier than it looked. Giving him a closed fist pound, I said, "True story," and turned and left.

Twenty minutes later, I was stepping out of a taxi in the parking lot adjacent to the office building I'd scoped out from Jillian's. When I saw the company logo and read the sign out front, I breathed a sigh of relief. It would be no problem getting into Jones and Simpkins property management firm. I strolled through the double glass doors, casually glancing around the lobby with my "blueprints" in hand. There was one rent-a-cop armed with a flashlight seated at a desk by the elevator reading a paper. I walked right past him and pressed the button on the elevator like I owned the place. He started to speak but looked me up and down and changed his mind. His eyes told me he assumed I had business there. The elevator doors sprang open, and I hopped on.

I rode to the top floor of the 15 story building. On the floor, various workers went about their business. No one even glanced my way. Perfect. I made my way into the stairway. One flight up, it took me no more than 30 seconds to disable the alarm on the roof access door. Stepping out into the midday sun, my Rolex told me it was 11 a.m. I had one hour until show time. From the northeast corner of the building, I had a direct line of sight to Jillian's. The air was calm, but the downward angle and the window pane might require me to adjust my shot slightly. Other than that, it wouldn't be difficult, at least not for me.

It was time to get the "Big Boy" ready. Inside the tube I picked up from Kinko's was my weapon of choice for the day's job, a Dragonov .50 caliber sniper rifle. I carefully removed the parts of the gun from the tube. Even in its partially disassembled state it was a thing of beauty. This Russian-made killing machine was in a class by itself. It was the epitome of long range weapons, and favored by upper echelon assassins all over the world, including the U.S. government. The Dragonov was effective even from over 1000 yards out. My 500 yard shot was well within range. I screwed in the barrel and attached the walnut stock. Then I connected the powerful Nikon scope. With that scope I could split a hair on the guy's head. The right hardware made all the difference in this business, but besides that, I suppose one had to have some measure of talent. I had talent. I was a natural. With everything ready to go, I sat there on the roof waiting.

Soon it was "that" time and I took my position at the edge on the building's northeast corner. Looking through the scope I scanned the dining area. The man I'd come to see wasn't there yet, but I was pleased and amused that I could read the day's special off a menu that sat on a table. Fifteen minutes had passed when I saw a group of four men in suits walk into the dining room. One of them gestured towards the far corner of the restaurant, and the hostess led them to a booth in the back. As they crossed the room, I studied their faced, and there was my mark among them. I knew his face the moment I saw him.

When they'd been given menus and seated, I realized I had hit the first snag of the day. The men sat in the booth with two on each side, but all I could see of my mark was the top of his head. He sat on the inside, and the high back of the booth obscured my view of him. Of the entire restaurant, this lucky fool had sat in the one place I couldn't see. I had a view of about an inch of the top of his head, but with so little target I risked missing him or only grazing him. I'd probably only have just the one shot, so I had to wait it out. The men ordered steaks and beers. They joked with the young waiter and periodically answered a cell phone or checked a Blackberry. It was the typical business lunch. It ran long.

They had finished eating, and I suppose were discussing business matters when a waitress came over. She was tall with blonde hair. Although she wasn't the same woman who'd served me earlier, there was something vaguely familiar about her. I didn't get a long look at her face. She turned her back to me, and I saw she had a real nice ass. My guess was she had talked the waiter into letting her serve the men dessert so she could get a bigger tip, then they'd probably just split it. Smart. It seemed to work too because the men at the table stared hard as she walked away after taking their order. Seemed I knew that walk, but I wrote it off. I had to focus. I was becoming frustrated after standing in the same position for over an hour.

The waitress returned carrying a tray of coffee and cakes. She leaned over the table giving the men their orders and for a few seconds I had a very enticing view. My mark must have had the same thing on his mind because he popped his head up out of the booth craning his neck to watch her walk away. I would have had a clean shot just then if I hadn't been watching her too. Her walk was so seductive, but I chastised myself for being sloppy.

The men sipped their coffee and laughed at some joke I couldn't hear. Suddenly, the man that sat beside my mark stood up. He moved aside to let the mark out to go to the bathroom or something. My muscles tensed as I prepared to take the shot. I trained the crosshairs of the scope directly on his face as he slid out. Looking at his face as I waited for him to stand upright I noticed he did not look well. Maybe the combination of beer and coffee didn't agree with him. His complexion was pale. As he rose, I readied my finger to squeeze the trigger. Just as he came to his full height, he began frantically clutching at his chest. He moved erratically and I hesitated to fire waiting to see if he'd be still for a moment. He lurched forward and collapsed. On the floor he went into convulsions flopping around like a goldfish out of its tank. His associate bent down to help him as the violent spasms took control of his body. The other two men at the table rushed to his side as well. Other patrons looked on, horrified at the scene unfolding in front of them. There was now a crowd gathered round him, and I couldn't take a shot if I'd wanted to, unless I wanted to shoot his feet. That was all I could see. Then his feet became perfectly still.

My mark was down for a few minutes when I heard the wail of an ambulance siren in the distance. If he'd been choking someone would have tried to help. The best guess I could make was that maybe he had a heart attack, but what were the odds of that? I looked down through the scope and saw paramedics feverishly working on him. Strangely enough, I was hoping they'd save him so I could kill him. They worked on him for ten minutes, desperately trying to resuscitate him. After that they exchanged grave looks. The paramedics gave the mark's associates an apologetic nod. He didn't make it. The man I was there to kill had died right before my eyes.

Although I was tempted to sit there on the roof contemplating what I'd just seen, I couldn't. My instincts took over. In moments I had my weapon disassembled, and I popped the top back on the plastic tube as I entered the stairway. I took the stairs all the way down to the second floor. On two I emerged from the stairwell. It was lunchtime and the floor was deserted, save for a couple people working at their desks. They paid me no mind. I dropped the tube in a garbage can and kept on moving right to the elevator. The lobby was empty. Flashlight cop must've been at lunch too, which suited me just fine. I put my shades on as I walked out of the building.

As I walked quickly up the street I realized something…I hadn't done anything, so I had no reason to rush. For the rest of the couple of blocks I walked slowly. There was only one thing on my mind: the odds of a man dying of natural causes when you were about to kill him were astronomical. There was only one theory that made sense. My mark was assassinated by another contractor. The job had also been double booked. Twice in two weeks was no coincidence. This was a serious problem. I caught a taxi back to the airport. Needless to say I was anxious to get back to New York, and I didn't stay in Norfolk a minute more than was necessary.

Chapter 5

It was early evening when I landed back at LaGuardia. I must have been the first one off of the plane, and I walked briskly through the busy terminal. Had I moved any faster there would have been a lot of attention on a Black man in an expensive suit running through the airport. If not for almost running Bubby over near the baggage claim carousel, I would have shot right past him. He was trying to talk but my demeanor, fast walk, and stern expression told him I was in a hurry. Bubby was far from slow; he knew when it was time to get gone. He fell in a step behind me, and we briskly made our way out of the airport.

When we got to the parking lot I slowed slightly so he could lead us to where he had parked. The 'vette was nowhere in sight, but I looked around for it expecting that he'd be driving the same car since it was the same day. Not Bubby. An alarm chirped and headlights flashed. This evening he was pushing a '94 Impala. Even in the garage's low light I cold see it had a mother of pearl flip-flop paint job. It was real clean, but in my present state all I could think of was getting uptown. He must have read my mind because as soon as we shut the doors he peeled out of the parking area with tires smoking.

Bubby got us up to the Bronx in record time. He never slowed down a bit until we were pulling off the Bronx River Parkway at the Gun Hill Road exit. In that moment I was thankful that Bubby stayed in a ride with some power.

Pulling up in front of Nana Helen's building, I barely let the car come to a complete stop before I hopped out. As I dashed into the building, Bubby revved the motor indicating that he was staying put with the car running. He was a rider. I was glad I didn't have to tell him it was prime time.

I pounded on Nana Helen's door without rhyme or reason. In that moment I couldn't have remembered our little code knock if I'd tried. As I fished my keys out of my pocket, I heard the sound of bare footsteps on hardwood and then the peephole. The locks tumbled, and she opened the door cursing at me in rapid Spanish for knocking on the door like I was crazy. I paid her no mind and stormed past her into the apartment. She was wearing a silk robe, and a lit cigarette burned in the ashtray. As soon as she closed the door I spun on my heels and started yelling, "This shit an't gon' work! Twice in two weeks is not a misunderstanding. I let you tell me Miami was a coincidence, then this bullshit gon' happen again? I don't know why I ain't see this shit coming."

She crossed her arms and waited a few moments after I stopped yelling to make sure my tirade was over. Silent seconds passed and then she spoke, "Look, Lex, I told you this game was getting old. Now you wanna come in here yelling like..."

"I don't need no 'I told you so's' right now. You the one that books the contracts. Don't try to act like I'm just putting all the blame on you," I said cutting her off.

"All the clients know the rules, one contract, one hitter. How you expect me to make them stick to it? I do my job."

Nana Helen had a point. I realized that in my frustration I was standing there yelling at the wrong person. That thought calmed me down somewhat. Now was not the time for me to be yelling at the one person I could trust. I changed my tone. "You know what? You right. I was foolish expecting to be the only game in town." My voice gradually lowered.

"Being the best doesn't make you the only one getting work," she added.

"Alright. So, what do you suggest I do? I'm not really in a position to up and quit. Can't we step the game up? Maybe take more exclusive contracts?"

"High end contracts don't guarantee anything either. You'd still have to worry about crossing paths with other contractors," she replied.

"What about work overseas?" I asked. I always shied away from international contracts, preferring to stay in my east coast comfort zone. International work paid two and sometimes three times as much as state-side work, but getting hardware overseas might prove difficult. Still, at this point, I was willing to chance it. Double the pay meant I could retire in half the time.

"For all you willing to go through with overseas work, you could just do that job on 47th street. It's a lot less trouble for a lot more money."

"Right now I ain't tryna' do that. I've had it on the back burner, but I just can't see myself running up in a spot 'cause I have to. I'm a professional hitter. You can't be 'bout to tell me it's nobody left out there who need to get dead."

"There'll always be contracts Lex," she said. Becoming frustrated, she raised her voice, "When is enough gonna be enough? You willing to go to the ends of the earth to avoid doing what I want you to do."

"So now that's what it's about? You see a little boy standing in front of you?" I looked to my left and to my right for dramatic effect. "Don't nobody tell me what to do! Now you can either book me something outside the country and collect your percentage, or I can handle the shit myself."

As I turned to leave, her mouth was open but she didn't utter a word. It looked like tears began to well up in her eyes, but she held it together. I couldn't ever remember talking to Nana Helen that way, but I was getting fed up of her trying to run that heist down my throat. The crazy part of it was that I had been considering it. Maybe left to my own devices I'd have convinced myself. The hardware wasn't a problem, and Mila was down for it. I had the means to do it, but I just couldn't bring myself to do it under pressure. In a pressure situation I had to stick with what I knew. I knew hits for hire. When I reached for the doorknob she finally spoke, "Okay, Lex, have your way. I'll have something lined up for you for next week. I see it's gonna take more than I can say or do to change your mind. Once upon a time you use to listen to me."

I never had a chance to respond. She turned and walked away to the bedroom. Our conversation was over. Suited me just fine. As long as she booked the contract I didn't care if she got mad. She was obviously upset about the words we'd exchanged, but she seemed even more upset about not getting her way. Maybe it was a female thing. For the moment I had a lot bigger things to worry about than her feelings.

During the ride downtown, I broke it down to Bubby that I was having a little work related drama. He wasn't really concerned with any of the "why's" and I was glad not to have to get into details. Eventually the subject changed and we got to talking about women. I told him about Chaine. He laughed at me about it and joked that she must have my nose wide open for me to even mention her. Bubby recounted an endless steam of early a.m. pick-ups from overnight hotel stays with nameless women. This wasn't that. I suppose from talking to me he could tell.

By the time I got home the stress of the day's events had yet to dissipate, and I had a case of Chaine on the brain. It was unfathomable to me that my mind could go from wrestling with the double booking situation to drifting on a memory with her. There was obviously something special between us, but inside I'd begun to worry that it was too much, too fast. Thus far my life had been insulated and precise, and then all of a sudden I was caught up in a whirlwind romance. Funny thing was that despite the unpredictability of it, I was happy about it. I never thought I'd see the day when I'd be happy about my life spiraling out of control toward a destination unknown.

After shedding my suit and throwing on some comfortable sweats, I anxiously picked up my cell phone. I dialed my voice mail and was delighted to hear I had three new messages. One had to be from Chaine because there weren't three people that had that number. The first message was from Nana Helen. Although I'd only left her an hour ago, she already had a line on an overseas contract. I was surprised that she found something so quickly, but I was glad to find out she wasn't letting our argument get in the way of business. The folder would be ready on Monday, which meant I'd have a few days to relax.

Deleting her message, I moved on. Both of the other two messages were from Chaine. On the first she spoke, hesitantly at first, saying she missed me and wanted me to call her as soon as I got free. On the second message, she realized I didn't have the number to her cell, so she left it. She joked that I better not turn out to be a stalker and giggled for a few moments before hanging up. Her laughter soothed my soul. It was like clear water flowing in a babbling brook. It washed over me, making me feel good from the inside out. I knew I was falling for her.

I hung up from my voice mail and called her. The phone rang four times and I was just about to hang up when her voice came on the line, "Hey, Daddy! What took you so long to call me?"

"I just got in and got your message. I had a really tough day at the office," I explained.

"Awwww. You poor thing," she cooed. "I've got just the thing to make you feel better."

"I'll bet you do. I could definitely use some of that."

"You so nasty! That ain't even what I was talking about."

"Oh, my fault. It's hard for me to keep my mind off sex. I got some freaky chick that keep sendin' soft-core porn to my phone," I replied laughing.

"Well, maybe you need to just go on and give her some."

"Nah, never works. You give it up and they just gonna want more and more."

"Oh yeah? So, you got it like that?" she asked.

"Yeah. Just like that. But only for the right woman. For the right woman I am ready, willing and able," I said in my best sexy baritone voice.

"Ummm," she purred. "Sounds tempting, but I'm a good girl. Premarital sex is a no no."

The cat and mouse game was turning me on, but I was getting frustrated. I wanted her in the worst way. I fought to stay patient. Steering the conversation I asked, "If it ain't sexual healing, what were you talking about making me feel better?"

"Oh yeah, I got you a present," she replied.

"You know my born day ain't till January, right?"

"I know it's not your birthday. I treated myself to a shopping spree and I picked you up a little something."

"Damn! A shopping spree, huh? It must be nice," I joked.

"Lex, I know you not hating. What's the matter? Can't handle a sistah who gets her own?" she laughed.

"Nah, it's cool with me. I'm all for independent women. That is, provided I'ma see your independent ass some time this evening."

"Well, I worked hard today, now I'm ready to play hard. Can you meet me at Barcode in an hour?" she asked.

"You didn't strike me as the Barcode type."

"Hmph! Never judge a book by its cover. Bring your 'A' game." She abruptly hung up so that her last words lingered like a threat. I smiled at her creativity. A date had never taken me to a video game arcade. Maybe playing video games would make a good end to a bad day. Chaine was totally unpredictable. On jobs I hated unpredictability, but it seemed that in relationships it had the opposite effect. I got up, showered, and got dressed, all the while wondering what other tricks she had up her sleeve.

I walked a few blocks from my place to catch a cab. Dressed plainly in sweats, sneakers, and a Yankee fitted, I grew frustrated at not being able to catch one. It's crazy but in New York, cab drivers, mostly immigrant minorities, use racial profiling in picking up fares. Then again, I wasn't exactly the one who should be complaining because I was young, Black, and strapped. So, maybe the cabbies were just using a combination of the law of averages and common sense. After twenty minutes of struggling, a Pakistani Muslim finally had pity on me. When he dropped me off, Chaine was already standing out front.

"Damn, it took you long enough," she said smiling as we shared a tight hug and a quick kiss.

"It ain't exactly easy for a Black man to catch a cab in this town at night."

"Well, I hope you don't have a bunch of excuses for when I start whuppin' on you," she said.

I stepped aside, and she led the way. We went inside, and I was kind of surprised to see there were just as many adults as kids in the place. Holding my hand and practically dragging me, she went through the restaurant section and headed for the video games. Her eyes swept the room and as soon as she saw the VR motorcycle racing game she made a bee line for it. She had no idea what she was in for. Maybe on a fighting game or something she stood a chance, but she couldn't be serious trying me on the bikes.

We ended up going at it on that game for over an hour. The girl had skills. Apparently she'd been serious when she asked to take my Fireblade for a ride. By the time we finished the score was tied at five games a piece. We only stopped playing because some kids had grown impatient waiting on their turn.

All the other games we played were first-person shooter games like Doom, Halo, and Rainbow 6. She surprised me even more on the shooting games than the VR motorcycles. We pretty much deadlocked on all those too. With my line of work you'd figure I had some type of advantage. Nope. Chaine could ride and shoot with the best of them. With not much left to lose I decided to call her out some laser-tag. She hadn't actually been beating me so far, but it was too close for comfort. My pride was slightly injured, and a couple of kids had even joked that I was getting my ass kicked by a girl.

I could tell that later on she would be talking up a storm. A thorough beat down at laser-tag would take the wind out of her sails. Or so I thought. When I brought up the idea of playing she surprised me by saying, "I thought you'd never ask." We went to the upper floor of the complex and signed up. I'd never played this type of futuristic laser tag before. The visor in the helmet made it seem like we were really inside a computer game. They gave me a gun and told me to shoot people. I figured, "How hard could it be?"

The game format was a race to ten, the first one to "kill" their opponent ten times won. We chose a "combat zone" theme and the instant we hit the start button it seemed like we were in the middle of a real war zone. It took Chaine a moment to get oriented and figure out how to make her character move. While she familiarized herself with the controls, I shot her in the back.

She got a little frustrated, but by the time I got behind a barricade she had begun to move effortlessly. She took cover behind some sandbags. I tried to just bum rush her, but she shot me. It surprised me because she hit me as soon as I came out of my hiding spot. I guess she either had fairly decent aim or really good luck. We ducked and dodged, running and shooting with neither of us giving the other any clear shots. As she eluded me, and nearly shot me a number of times, I started thinking she had to have played the game before.

The one hour session we paid for wound down. We had two minutes left when I finally got her pinned down behind a bunker. I swore I had her. I crept up ready to fire, expecting her to give up. Somehow she had gotten from behind the bunker and when I came along side it, she was gone. It was a trap. Before I could take cover she caught me with a headshot just as time expired. I never saw it coming.

I can't front, at first I was mad. Beat by a girl at the thing I was best at. But then her comment about judging a book by its cover rang in my head. This was really one of those "free" life lessons. I'd slept on her because she was a girl, and I was a professional. One thing for sure, I wouldn't get caught slipping again. This time it was a game, next time it might not be. I made a mental note while Chaine got her gloat on. She teased me, but I didn't really let it bother me. Besides, she definitely had something to be proud of. She didn't know it, but she had just gotten the drop on someone who got the drop on people for a living. I was completely confused how she'd done it, but I let it ride. Over all I'd had a good time and by the time we left my work problems had faded away.

Out in front of Barcode, I let Chaine hail us a cab. She got one in thirty seconds as opposed to the thirty minutes it would have taken me. On the way back to my loft we sat snuggled closely together the way lovers do. I twirled a few loose strands of her hair around my index finger wondering where she had been all my life. I had the notion to ask her, but she preempted my question with a question of her own, "So Mr. Man...what happened at your job that had you all stressed out today?"

I sighed heavily at the arrival of a moment I'd been dreading. It was only a matter of time before she started asking about my work. I'd been able to skirt the issue so far, but it appeared my time was up. "I lost a client," I somberly replied.

"...And your boss chewed you out, huh?"

"No," my voice rose slightly. It was one thing masquerading as a working stiff, but the thought of being someone's flunky like she was insinuating, offended me, "actually, I'm self-employed."

"Oh?" she wondered out loud, "And exactly what do you employ yourself at?" She eased away from me a bit and eyed me curiously. I moved uneasily under her scrutiny. "I meant to ask you a few times, but we always get...you know, busy."

I stared out the window searching the city streets for the answer. I had a repertoire of fake background info, but something in me made me want to tell her the truth. Of course I couldn't, but I settled on something that resembled reality. I'm an...I'm an independent contractor," I answered.

"What kind?" she asked.

"My company specializes in demolition. We get rid of unwanted properties. They want it gone, I make it gone."

She laughed that laugh.

"What's so funny?" I asked.

"To tell the truth I was worried that maybe I was falling for a drug dealer."

"So, you saying I fit the description. Why if a Black man live in a nice pad he gotta be a dope dealer?" I asked becoming indignant.

"Well, there is that, and that you've been strapped both times we've gone out," she coolly replied.

She stunned me with that one. She was absolutely correct, but how'd she know I had a gun on me? I started to ask but she spoke first.

"Lex, the same way a man looks at a woman's curves is the same way a woman checks out a man. We women just aren't as obvious about it. I noticed a bulge in the wrong place on you just as easily as you would on me."

"Oh." It made sense.

"But don't worry; I don't care one way or the other. My daddy always said it was better to get caught with one than without one."

I liked that. Her father sounded like my kind of guy. I started to ask about him, but I could tell by the way she spoke about him that he was no longer with us. My mind locked in on something else she said. "I'm glad to hear you're a fan of the 2nd Amendment. But what was the other thing you said about 'falling for a drug dealer?'"

She blushed as she realized her slight slip of the tongue. I didn't think she intended to expose her hand, but once it was said she just went with it. "It is what it is. Ever since we met in Miami I feel you getting deeper and deeper under my skin. You scare me. When I'm with you nothing else matters. I've never been like this with anyone."

She was saying what I felt. It seemed like there was this window into my soul that only she could see into. "Would it help you to know we both felt that way?" I asked.

"Promise you won't hurt me," she whispered.

"Never. Not ever," I said. Then we shared a long deep kiss that made everything slip away. With her soft lips on mine we floated. The back of the taxi may as well have been a cloud. We existed for those moments in our own personal heaven. The sound of the driver blowing the horn to get our attention brought us back to reality. I looked and was surprised that we made it to my place already. We paid the driver and went inside.

Coming into my apartment together with her just felt right. In so little time we'd become so comfortable together. I deactivated the alarm and went to use the bathroom. I checked my voice mail, and by the time I was done, Chaine was in the kitchen. She'd already changed into one of my oversized white tees, and was fixing us something to eat. Seeing her in the kitchen brought back memories of our first episode. As I approached her I noticed a small rectangular box sitting on the counter. It was white and bore that unmistakable sun-face Versace emblem. She saw me checking it out and said, "Go ahead open it. It's yours."

I walked over slowly and picked the box up. My movements seemed deliberate and calculated. I was actually just trying to contain my surprise. My heart raced as I carefully opened the box. Every inch of my body trembled when I looked inside. In my mind I was prepared for a pleasant surprise; what I saw blew me away. Nestled inside on a satin pillow was a white ceramic Versace watch with 18k gold accents. It was beautiful. I had seen the same watch while out shopping a few weeks earlier. The only reason I hadn't bought it was because I'd already spent most of my cash that day and I didn't have $8,500 left to buy it. I'd meant to go back for it, but then things started getting crazy. And now here the watch was looking at me. The light glistened on the gold bezel and the smooth ceramic texture hypnotized me. It was like I was staring at a work of art. With my senses overwhelmed, I stood speechless.

"Say something... If you don't like it, I got the receipt. You can exchange it for something else," she said with a concerned expression on her face.

I willed my brain to send the signal to my mouth to speak, but I couldn't. The combination of the surprise, the elation I felt at Chaine's gesture, plus how much I was feeling that watch, held me captive. It was crazy. On jobs I'd seen and done it all and never missed a beat. Now here I was incapacitated by a woman and a watch.

I did the only thing I could. I smiled ear to ear, and hugged her.

"I guess that means you like it," she said, out of breath.

I came to my senses realizing I was hugging her much too tightly. I finally spoke, "Yeah, I really do like it, but maybe it's too much."

"Well, if it is, or if it isn't, it's yours. You stuck with it. If you want to take it back that's on you, but I suggest you wear it. Try it on."

Carefully removing it from the box, I slipped the watch onto my wrist. She fastened the clasp for me, and we both stood a moment admiring the contrast of the white watch against my dark skin. To say it looked good on me was an understatement. I already owned a Rolex, a Bristling, and a Cartier. None of them looked as perfect on me as this one. There was no way it was going back, but I still felt a little uncomfortable accepting such a "big gift."

Noticing the conflicted look on my face she said, "C'mon Lex, I see that look. It's a new millennium; a woman is allowed to buy her man nice things." As it slipped out she caught herself a moment too late. She winced and closed her eyes hoping I didn't notice what she said.

"Does this watch mean we boyfriend and girlfriend now?" I asked, laughing.

Her face reddened with embarrassment. "No, that's not what I meant. I wasn't trying to say..."

"Cause if that's what you was saying, I think that would be a good look," I said, smiling as I cut her off.

This time she was the one speechless. All she could do was smile. She wrapped her arms around my waist and buried her head in my chest. I kissed the top of her head and hugged her. I heard her sniffle, and I felt wetness on my shirt. I couldn't see, but I was pretty sure she was crying. Lightening the mood I said, "You coulda saved some cash, though, and just wrote me a note like back in the days. 'Do you wanna go with me? Check one: Yes, No, Maybe.'"

In response to my smart ass comment she pinched me on my waist, hard! On instinct I reacted by grabbing her wrist and pinning her against the counter. She struggled, bringing her free hand up and pinching me on the other side. I grabbed that hand too and held them both at her sides, laughing as she squirmed to escape. She looked up at me, giving me a condescending smile right before biting me on my chest. That shit hurt. I hollered "Owww," and instantly turned her loose.

The moment she was free, she broke into a barefoot sprint across the room. She wanted me to chase her. I chased her. Laughing, she evaded me, running circles around the couch. After a few times around, I leapt over the couch and tackled her to the floor. We rolled around on the floor wrestling. I had to give it to her, she fought kinda hard. As we struggled we gradually started bumping and grinding. I knew she could feel me becoming excited through my clothes. I pinned her down, holding her hands above her head. She crossed her legs tightly and turned her head to the side when I tried to kiss her.

"Are you gonna take it, Lex? You gonna take what you want?" she seductively whispered.

"No," I replied as I began to kiss her neck, "I'm gonna make you give it to me."

In that moment I recalled two things. One was Nana Helen telling me that no woman could resist a man who took his time and paid attention to her entire body, and the other was Lil' Kim hollering that she wanted "a man with a big ass dick and a hurricane tongue." Both of those I could do and that rough sex foreplay had me horny as hell.

I grabbed the stereo's remote off the couch and pressed a few buttons. By the time I lifted Chaine from the floor and carried her to the bed, the apartment was flooded with the sound of Prince singing "Purple Rain." Somehow the Purple One seemed to have a way of bringing that inner freak out of people. I fell victim.

At first she laid there pouting and uncooperative. I knew it was a game, and I played it with her. I began to massage her feet and suck each of her dainty manicured toes. Her moans were muffled as she fought to resist me. Although she didn't physically struggle, she tried to fight the pleasure. I moved up to her calves, and as I licked and sucked her smooth legs, I could feel her becoming more and more relaxed. Still, she wasn't exactly cooperative. I took my time running my tongue up her leg to her inner thigh and back down, tracing circles at the back of her knees. Her whole body trembled, but when I tried to take off her lacy black panties, she resisted.

I decided on a different approach, figuring I'd start at the top and work my way down. Placing long slow kisses on her neck, I gradually went further south to her breasts. She let me slip the t-shirt over her head. I was getting somewhere, but it was a slow go. While undoing the clasp of her bra, I ran my tongue over every inch of her succulent breasts and took extra care to lick, suck, nibble, and bite her nipples. I felt her hips gyrating under me as she gasped and bit her bottom lip. Her little game was proving effective. I was more aroused than I'd ever been, but she was forcing me to stay patient and take it slow.

An almost imperceptible look of confusion came across her face when I got up and left her lying there on the bed. I crossed the room to the kitchen shedding my clothes piece by piece along the way. I came back to the bed carrying a tray of ice cubes. Chaine peered at me through the dimly lit room trying to watch my little strip show and see what I was getting. When she figured out what it was, a soft giggle escaped her. I set the tray on the nightstand and lay down beside her. She turned away from me reverting to her cat and mouse game.

While she lay on her stomach I massaged her back. I kneaded the tight muscles of her shoulders, lower back, and legs. When I got through, her body was totally relaxed. I put an ice cube in my mouth and slid the cold tip of my tongue down the small of her back. Goose bumps raised on her smooth skin. Seeing her hold out for so long surprised me and aroused me even further. The ice cube in my mouth melted away to nothing, and I turned her over. Laying there with her eyes closed and that blissful expression on her face, she looked like an angel. I held another ice cube between my fingertips and slid it all over her breasts. Her nipples hardened at the cold touch. She licked her lips real slow and sexy. I slid the ice cube down her flat stomach and teasingly licked around her navel.

That was when she cracked. She subconsciously put her hands on my head and gave me a gentle nudge down south. Now, I've been around the block a couple times, I knew what that meant. Problem was, I'd never really been big on giving oral sex. I tried it on a few occasions, and it just wasn't really my thing. The ice cubes and rubdown/kiss down was as ambitious as I usually got. This time I might have gotten in over my head. I slowly slid her underwear off contemplating my next move. As I drank the sight of her beautiful naked body with my eyes, I wondered how I had fallen so deeply for her so fast.

I took the plunge.

With my eyes closed and my face screwed up like a kid preparing for cough syrup, I put my face between her legs. At first I gently kissed her inner thighs, spreading her legs apart. Surprisingly, I was greeted by a heavenly aroma. Her pleasant scent was like a cross between raindrops on roses and a summer breeze. My main problems with oral sex were the smell and the taste. Her essence made me 50% more willing to give it a try.

When I worked my way closer I found she was already soaking wet. Her moans grew louder and louder the closer I got. I drew a deep breath, pausing before I finally tasted her. My senses must have been playing tricks on me. She tasted like honey. With each lick I became more enthralled. I kissed her lips like a long lost lover. She thrashed about in ecstasy and I had to take a firm grip on her hips to keep her still. Her screaming became so loud I could barely hear that the music had changed from Prince to R. Kelly's "12 Play." Juices flowed freely from her and I was so caught up in the rapture that I barely noticed her body quivering until she tightly squeezed my head in a vise-like grip between her legs. Chaine came hard. Then she lay there, perfectly still except for her breathing heavily like she'd just run a race.

I got up and went to get her a glass of water. The cold air from the refrigerator reminded me that I was still harder than a roll of quarters. The love scene I'd just made with her was more sensual than anything I'd ever done or seen and I hadn't even entered her.

Chaine sprung back to life as she downed the entire glass of water. Setting the empty glass on the nightstand, she sat on the edge of the bed eyeing my chiseled body and throbbing erection hungrily. She looked up at me standing in front of her and locked me in an intimate gaze. Without breaking eye contact she took me in her mouth, working me slowly at first. In an act of "deep throat" prowess that defied the laws of physics, she swallowed all nine inches of me, paused at the bottom, and did this little trick with her throat. Then she came up real slow licking around the tip. She repeated the whole process. I called her name. Never did that before, but it was apparent that Chaine would be my first at a lot of things. My vocal participation encouraged her and she blessed my jewel with ravenous enthusiasm. She quickened her pace and I was almost to the highest of heights when she stopped. She stood up in front of me, and before I could even look disappointed, she aggressively pushed me onto the bed.

I really dug the way she could take charge in the bedroom sometimes but be submissive at others. She crawled on top of me with a look in her eyes that reminded me of a tigress stalking its prey. As she straddled me she gave me a long deep kiss while guiding me inside her. On top she took control, working her hips until she broke into a sweat. Her walls gripped me tightly. She rode me with a sexual appetite that seemed insatiable. I sat up and held her body close to mine with her legs wrapped around me. She screamed loudly, and a tear began to run down her face. I almost stopped, but her body told me not to. We climaxed together in the lotus position. I came deep inside her. It wasn't something I planned on; it just happened. The moment I released my mind toyed with the possibilities and/or consequences. Still, it was the greatest sex I'd ever had. Quite possibly it was my first time actually making love.

After a couple more episodes we were exhausted. We passed out together in my bed with the sheets rooted up. I slept peacefully with her there in my arms. Usually I was a light sleeper, but that night I slept deeply. I dreamt this vivid dream where I was riding my motorcycle across a painted desert under a crayola sky. There was an AR—15 strapped to my back and I was riding either away from or toward something. I came to this huge canyon, and on the other side was Chaine. We called out, but couldn't hear each other. The distance between us was too great. She waved her arms frantically. I felt helpless. Finally, in desperation I turned the bike around and doubled back to gather speed to try to jump. I knew I'd never make it, but I was compelled to try, willing to risk my life just to be with her. I gunned it and the bike's motor whined as the tires left the ground. Not even halfway across, I began to plummet to the earth hundreds of feet below. In the distance I heard the sound of a drum beating. The drum beat, I fell, and Chaine just stood there on the other side with a placid expression on her face.

The beat of the drum grew louder as I fell. As it grew louder, the entire dreamscape evaporated away to nothing. The sound drew me back to consciousness and I awoke realizing the sound had been real. Before my instincts and reflexes could kick in, I realized what the noise came from. When I sat up opening my eyes, the first thing I saw was Chaine running on the treadmill. In a pair of my boxers and a white tee, she ran at a pace that was almost a sprint. The slap of her bare feet on the machine created the rhythmic drumming that had manifested in my dream. It was only six a.m. and we'd had a late night, but I figured "if you can't beat 'em, join 'em."

I got up and walked across to go drain the vein. As I passed her on the machine she blew me a kiss but never broke stride nor did the focused expression leave her face. I came back and did some light stretching before climbing on the pull-up bar and taking off into ten sets of pull-ups, push-ups, and dips. We worked out in silence. She ran at about a seven minute mile pace for 20 more minutes. She came off the treadmill sweating hard, and went to beating the shit out of my heavy bag. I was impressed at what I saw. Sister girl must have invested in some Tae Bo tapes or something because she could really handle herself. When I finished my sets I went and held the bag for her. She landed a series of roundhouse kicks that I didn't think they taught in Tae Bo. That tired her out and she quit, but it was a hell of a workout.

Chaine had an athletic figure; that she worked out and was in good shape didn't come as much of a surprise. Her having martial arts skills, however, came as a total shock. I realized that although I was already intimately very familiar with her, there were still a lot of things about her that I didn't know.

Pushing the thought to the back of my mind, I went and started a pot of coffee. I checked my cell phone and saw I had a text message from Nana Helen. Her message said she had info for me but it came with a "code 808" attached, which meant it wasn't exactly urgent. The message cut through the euphoria I was feeling from a combination of Chaine and the work-out. It brought the stress of the double-booking fiasco and the money situation back to the forefront of my mind. I wanted the situation to work itself out, but that approach hadn't been worth a damn so far. Truthfully, thus far my entire career as a hitter had been a cake walk. I was good at what I did, and I followed a strict set of rules. Rolling like that had kept problems off my plate or at least to a manageable minimum. But I'd grown too comfortable, and now when I was least prepared, the game had changed.

I could think of a million ways that two contractors working the same job could inadvertently kill each other. Not to mention that once the competition got to be too much, they would invariably turn on each other. The predators would become the prey. My best bet was to get out soon.

Something moving across the apartment snapped me out of my silent contemplation. I looked up and saw it was Chaine. After her workout she had done some cool-down stretches and now she was taking off her sweaty T-shirt and shorts. Naked, she gracefully strode across the floor stopping at the stereo to cue up some tunes. In another life she could have been a dancer. As I watched her, I was captivated. She stood a moment thinking of what to play and smiled to herself as she made a selection. Then she walked over to my big antique tub and ran the shower as Jill Scott's "Whatever,

Whatever," came on. She looked over at me and smiled, letting me know it was an ode to the previous night's performance. I smiled back at how effortless she made it seem to be so sexy. I watched her as she stepped into the shower and drew the translucent curtain. Just before I looked away she stuck her arm out and beckoned to me with her index finger. Taking off my clothes on the way over, I went and joined her in the shower. We had soapy sex in the a.m... Chaine was definitely my kind of girl.

Chapter 6

After our morning escapade we dressed and had breakfast. We talked for a long while and then got to watching T.V. on the couch. I was comfortable and had fun doing "nothing" with her. I fell asleep with my head in her lap while she watched soap operas. When I woke up later that afternoon, I saw she had made us lunch. While we kicked it and ate lunch I remembered that I'd have to shoot up to Nana Helen's sometime during the day. I felt conflicted because spending time with Chaine was something I didn't want to stop doing unless I had too. It was just a quick errand so I decided to ask her to join me, figuring she could just wait outside a minute for me.

As she cleaned up after we ate, I asked her, "I have to run uptown real quick, would you care to join me?"

"Ummmmm," she hesitated, "not really."

I was surprised and disappointed. I didn't want her to leave, and it seemed like it was a mutual vibe. "I'm gonna take the bike. C'mon it's nice outside," I was trying to convince her.

"Well, in that case, hell no!"

"Hell no?" I repeated, perplexed.

"Lex, I never ride on the 'bitch seat.' I can't stand being a passenger on a bike, and I'm sure you don't want to take your race bike out in NYC traffic."

She had two good points. I wouldn't ride on the back of anyone's bike for love nor money, and my Fireblade was not coming out in traffic.

"Good point," I said, "but I gotta go and it was gonna be quick. I was really enjoying spending time with you."

"Well, if it's okay with you, I'll be right here when you get back. I promise not to steal anything, if you promise to bring me back some Skittles," she said laughing.

That laugh and smile just had this power over me. In that moment all I wanted was to be with her and it was all I could think of. I gave it no thought that before her I'd never even had company, let alone had someone in my place while I wasn't home. It wasn't a step, it was a leap, but without the least hesitation I smiled back at her and said, "That's a bet. When I get back we can go out for dinner... you pick the place."

"Sounds like a plan. In the meantime I'll just clean up since I'm in a cleaning mood. But don't be all day... I guess without your keys I'll be your hostage here," she said.

"Not a hostage, more like a willing captive. It'll be romantic. You'll be like the princess trapped in the tower, and when I come back, I'll rescue you," I laughed.

She gave me a sarcastic grin and went back to cleaning up the kitchen. I went to gather my helmet, keys, phone, and some money preparing to leave. After her comment I realized that she would, in effect, be locked in without my keys to the elevator and doors. For a split second I started to leave them with her, but decided not to. I wondered "what if the place caught fire," but thought better of it. If there was an emergency, she had my cell number. Her attitude was nonchalant about it, so I followed suit. I was feeling her something terrible, but there was still the possibility that she could clean my place out. In NYC it was not out of the question, and I'd heard of it happening on more than one occasion.

On my way out the door Chaine paused at doing the dishes and gave me a quick kiss. I squeezed her ass and she warned me not to start something I couldn't finish. As I wheeled my motorcycle out to the elevator, I took notice of how domestic we were. We worked well together. During the quick ride up to Nana Helen's, I wondered about how things between her and me would play out. For the first time in my life I was thinking about my future with a woman. Whether she was "the one" or wasn't, I still needed to focus on my exit strategy from the murder for hire game. By the time I parked my bike on the sidewalk in front of Nana Helen's building that was the only thing on my mind.

As soon as I saw her I knew she was still mad at me. Her posture told the whole story. When she partly opened the door, she stood there in the way, giving me the distinct impression she didn't want me to come in. With her arms crossed in front of her she clutched two manila folders against her chest. Her face was set in a stern expression. I didn't try to force the issue by trying to reconcile or make small talk. Instead I figured I'd just give her time she needed to cool off. There was no point in apologizing because I'd already said what I said, and I wasn't sorry. Opting to keep it strictly business, I stayed in the doorway.

"I got your message," I said, stating the obvious.

Her cold reply came in a business-like tone as she handed me the two folders. "I found what you asked me to. It's a familiar locale, that should make it easier, but it looks like it's still gonna be a tough nut to crack."

"Why two jackets?" I asked.

"The other one has the specs on 47th Street." She paused, and I did my best to hold off an annoyed expression. She ignored me continuing on, "Maybe you change your mind about it. You got two options. I don't have anything else to say to you about it."

I started to respond, but held my tongue. No sense in stressing things between us any further. She seemed resolute and I had a habit of being more flippant and flamboyant the angrier a person became. It didn't seem that she was about to let me do much responding anyway. After her words hung there in the silence for a minute she said, "Nice watch," and slowly closed the door, giving me time to step out of the way. I let the whole thing ride and just stepped off.

I started to post up in the stairway and do my reading but I decided not to. I needed to put some much needed space between Helena Vasquez and me. I folded the folders lengthwise and tucked them in the inside pocket of my Vanson. Jumping on my horse I realized I couldn't go straight home because Chaine might be curious about what I was reading so intently. A few quick turns on back streets put me in Mt. Vernon. Tearing across East Third Street, I pulled up in front of the Third Rail a few minutes later. It was a safe haven and I figured I'd give Mila and Big Tee a holla.

On my way into the bar I paused in the vestibule. I looked up at the corner of the ceiling where I new a pinhole camera was mounted. Throwing up a peace sign I mouthed the words, "What up Big Homie." The single light bulb in the small space flickered twice. Big Tee and I had just swapped greetings.

I strolled into the barroom and saw Mila behind the bar. She wore a black T-shirt that said "I'm A Hustler" which she had tied in a knot in the back to make it fit tight, and she had on some low cut Frankie B jeans. Her hair was swept up in a bun, and Chanel shades sat perched on her head. I'm sure there were plenty of customers who came in just to see her. It had to be because ambitious and aggressive intimidated most men that kept her single, because her looks were her strong suit. She looked like a fashion model on her day off. The words "What's a girl like you doing in a place like this?" came to mind. When she noticed me coming in her lips curled into a devilish grin.

"Hey sis, how you livin'?"

"Obviously not good as you baby boy...I see you shining," she said, gesturing at my new watch.

"Oh, I forgot I had this joint on." I lied.

"Yeah, it's like that when you big ballin'," she said.

"Ballin'? Nah Mila, this was a gift. Right now all shopping is suspended 'til I get this paper right."

"Lex, you need to stop. Some people are financially stable, you financially able. It's hard for me to believe your bread ain't right. Lemme look at your watch," she said, reaching over the bar and grabbing my wrist, "That's nice. That's real nice. If that was a gift, somebody must love you. I saw that in Vibe magazine. It cost some chips."

"I was surprised when she gave it to me," I said.

"Oooooh! Sound like somebody getting paid to play. Now I know why I ain't seen you in a month of Sundays. You too busy playing American Gigolo to spend time with your homegirl."

"C'mon Mila, you know I ain't on that type of time. I just started seeing shorty, but it's different. Me and her got this fire and I'm just trying to see what it leads to."

"I feel you. I'm happy for you. She must really like you. She must be rich too 'cause that Versace is damn near ten stacks...Just be careful, it's a cold world out there. Make sure you know what you're getting into and with who."

"True dat," I replied. After hearing her say that I began to wonder if all of the "consulting" Chaine did was above board. I reasoned that a good job could afford a single woman the type of lifestyle that included shopping sprees and big ticket gifts. It wasn't impossible for her to be legit. In relation to all the other issues I had on my plate, how she made her money was of minor concern.

"Right now I gotta look over some things. I gotta work on securing my future," I said, removing the folders from my jacket.

"Well, just holla when you need me 'cause my future could use some securing too."

I went to the far corner of the bar and took a booth to myself. With both folders lying in front of me I couldn't make up my mind which one to read first. Now that Nana Helen was no longer pressing me about her diamond district caper, I was suddenly more curious about the details of it. What I'd heard so far had been sketchy at best, and with the $5m payday attached, it made it seem too good to be true. On the other hand, I was slightly more curious about where the hit would require me to go, and more importantly how much closer the job would put me to retirement. My mind was already made up about taking on some overseas contracts so that took precedence over a heist that I may or may not do.

Pushing the 47 Street folder aside, I opened the job description for the hit and began studying it. The first thing that caught my eye was the price tag. At $750k it was the biggest contract I'd ever worked. Had to be something high profile. As I read on, I found out just how high. Nana Helen had been right; it was a familiar locale. The hit would go down in Jamaica. My family was from Jamaica, and I'd spent some summers on the island. I had some people down there, one in particular, that I was pretty sure would be able to line up some hardware for me. So, the good part was that I would be working on somewhat familiar ground…but that was the extent of my good fortune. The more I read the more I realized exactly how "tough a nut it would be to crack," as she had so aptly put it.

Besides being overseas, my next target was in fact high profile. My mark's name was Winston "Wolf" Parks, a reputed drug kingpin said to be one of the richest dealers in the Caribbean. He ran a posse known as the Darkheart Massive, and they boasted operation on five continents. Wolf's net worth was estimated to be in the billions. Most recently I'd heard Wolf and entourage had been apprehended by the U.S. Coast Guard while sailing a yacht in the Gulf of Mexico that was loaded with 20 tons of high grade marijuana. You would have thought that was the end of him, but he never even saw the inside of a jail cell. It turned out that the boat belonged to Jamaica's Prime Minister. The Coast Guard turned Winston Parks and his crew loose with an apology. I'm not sure if they even confiscated the dope! He was well connected. In Jamaica especially, it seemed those connections reached up into some high places indeed. Most Third World nation's governments are riddled with corruption and apparently Jamaica was not exempt.

The more I read, it only got worse. During the weekdays Wolf holed up at his compound on the outskirts of Mandeville, a city in one of Jamaica's 13 close knit parishes. The outer perimeter of his estate was patrolled by Jamaican Army regulars. On the interior there would be no less than 50 crew members, family, and staff at any given time. He had security in layers, and I didn't ever hear of a Jamaican posse that didn't keep guns galore. On occasion I'd heard of the Darkheart Massive putting in work in NYC and Miami, and them boys was no joke.

113

Every other weekend however, Wolf came out like clockwork. Usually he ventured into Kingston, the nation's capital, to visit ghetto strongholds and tear the club up. He particularly favored a club called "Asylum" that was one of Kingston's hottest night spots. His public appearances and the steady flow of cash he pumped into the community had him on national hero status. The people loved him. They would most likely protect him. It was no surprise that no one down there had taken this contract. But they weren't me, and when Wolf emerged from his den, I would take him.

I studied Wolf's case committing every aspect of his life to my memory bit by bit. In half an hour I had it locked. Even his drink of choice was stored away in my mind. I tore up the file, put it in the ashtray, and set it on fire. As it burned Mila gave me a strange look from the bar, but didn't come investigate. I sat staring at the other folder realizing I'd already been gone over an hour and Chaine might be getting restless. She would have to wait. My curiosity about Nana Helen's heist consumed me.

The first page of the file was a picture of the Imperial Diamond Jewelry Company store front. From the looks of it, it was like any of the other Russian or Jewish owned stores on Jeweler's Row. Every Wednesday morning between ten and eleven a.m. a traditionally dressed Hasidic Jew entered the store carrying a black satchel. Not long after he arrived another man would arrive at the jewelry shop carrying a bag. That was the money man. The place was a regular pick up and cash drop for the biggest Ecstasy ring in the city. The black satchel would contain upwards of half a million pills. They had a street value of $1m at wholesale.

From what I read I learned they had drops and pick ups all through the week, but Wednesday was the heaviest day and the only day with a drop off and pick up right around the same time. It made sense to hit them then. There really was no telling how much cash they'd have on hand. For a great big cherry on top, Imperial also wholesaled raw diamonds to other jewelry stores. They were sure to have $1m to $2m in easy to move uncut diamonds on hand. The file said there would only be 3 to 4 men in the shop, the two bagmen and one or two other employees. If pulled off properly this heist would be a trifecta; money, diamonds, and ecstasy, all easily liquidated, all very untraceable.

I closed the folder realizing it was all how Nana Helen had said, an easy job with a payday around $5m. In front of my face were photos, diagrams, and intel confirming everything. All this time I could have just trusted the person I claimed to trust the most and everything would have worked out. I can't lie. As I sat there with it laid out in front of me, I felt stupid. I wanted to take down this score, but after all I'd said, I had to literally stick to my guns. All Nan Helen had ever done was look out for me, and I'd treated her like shit.

My pride wouldn't let me back out of the contract. All my problems with the double booking mess were the result of people not playing by the rules. I decided I had to stay true to the game Up till now, the game had been good to me. As for Nana Helen, I could square things with her later. After I got Wolf, I could take down the Imperial score and ride off into the sunset. Seemed everything would work out after all. If Nana Helen wasn't happy with her $75k cut of the Jamaica job, and her cut of the take from Imperial, then she never would be.

Even though robbery had never been my thing, I already had an idea of how I wanted to play it. If done right, no one had to die. Jewish people are usually close knit and rarely very trusting, so just waltzing in and out with all that loot wouldn't be simple. A "smash and grab" type of move was out because police response times to Jeweler's Row would be better than to anywhere in the city. I knew that right off top. However, these Jewish cats were men, and nine times out of ten if you wanted to get over on men, your best bet was to use a woman. I still had to sort through the details, but I was willing to wager that Jewish or not, they would fall victim to Mila's charm.

For the moment, though, my focus had to be on the task at hand, catching a wolf. I needed a couple of sets of ID's to get in and out of Jamaica, and although Big Tee couldn't do much for me on hardware, he could hook up my credentials. I would need one set to travel on and another for just in case. I tucked all the papers back in the folder, and on the way back to see Big Tee, I stopped off by Mila at the bar. I waited for her to finish serving someone and then she walked over to me. Laying the folder on the bar in front of her I said, "This is that move I mentioned to you. Your cut will be a Mil' ticket. If the take is bigger than expect I'll look out for you, but the ticket is guaranteed. Study this, and keep it in a safe place for your eyes only."

"When?" she asked.

"I got a piece of work to handle first. We gonna move on this in about two weeks. By then, I'll have the play all mapped out."

"I'm waiting on you then, ready when you are."

I looked her over and the look in her eye told me she was serious about success. In response I gave her a slow approving head nod and said, "Aiight then," and walked away heading in back to Big Tee's office. Mila was a ride or die chick, and I couldn't help but to wonder if maybe her being white hadn't made it hard for me to see that all along. The way things were looking she would definitely have a chance to prove herself.

Big Tee and I chopped it up in his office for half an hour before getting down to business. He told me he'd have my ID's ready in a couple of days and assured me they'd be good enough to get through customs. This go around they would have to be because international travel drew more scrutiny than domestic. That was another part of the reason my work had yet to extend across the water.

He asked me how things were going with Chaine and me, and I told him the truth. Things were getting serious. He gave me a warning much like the one Mila had given me, and I wondered if they hadn't maybe previously discussed it. Talking about her reminded me I still had her hostage at my place. I made some lame excuse to leave, but somehow he knew it was bullshit. On my way out he joked that I was too young too be locked down.

I got my ass back downtown in record time, but it was still almost three hours later. An hour and a half longer than I'd told her I'd be. In an effort not to piss her off any more than she might already be, I stopped at the corner store and picked her up some Skittles. On the way up in the elevator I crossed my fingers hoping she didn't flip the script on me for leaving her stranded. I had some days to spare before I had to start getting ready for Jamaica and was hoping to spend them with her.

When I turned the key in the front door it felt awkward, yet at the same time comforting, to know someone was on the other side waiting for me. The first thing I noticed was that the apartment was spotless, hospital clean. Chaine was for real when she said she'd clean up. As I walked in awestruck at the cleanliness, something else strange hit me. She was gone. I couldn't believe it as my eyes swept back and forth across the room looking for her. I started to panic when I looked behind the Chinese screen and she wasn't on the toilet. I set her Skittles and my helmet on the counter, and took out my cell phone. My hand shook a little bit, but I couldn't be sure if it was anxiety over thinking something happened to her or thinking she'd be furious at me.

I dialed her number and after four rings I was about to hang up when I heard something. I could faintly hear her ring tone, some Beyonce "girl power" anthem or another, coming from somewhere in the apartment. Crossing the room it grew louder with each step I took. I'll admit, I almost looked under the bed before I realized it had to be coming from up in the loft. I mounted the narrow spiral staircase, taking the stairs two by two and nearly breaking my neck in the process. At the top of the stairs, I found Chaine curled up in the recliner reading a book. She paid her ringing phone no never mind and only glanced up at me when she finished her page.

"Hey baby! Some rescue. The dragon got me an hour ago," she said smiling, as the ringing stopped.

A wave of relief swept over me as I realized she wasn't mad. "Sorry I took so long, I got a little caught up. When I came in I thought you…"

"Left?" she asked quizzically. "So, lemme guess you didn't see me and tried my phone?"

"Yeah, but why you ain't answer if you knew it was me?"

"I heard you come in. There's only two people who have my number, and I just got off the phone with the other one 15 minutes ago," she simply stated.

"Oh, I was worried you were mad at me for taking so long."

"Nah, Lex. I missed you and all that, but you're a grown man. I know I can't have you all to myself all day long. I ain't one of them possessive chicks."

118

When she said that, it was like music to my ears. Where had this woman been all my life? I walked over to her, leaned down, and gave her an intense lingering kiss on the lips. One thing every man is searching for is a woman who understands she has to give him room to breathe sometimes.

"What was that for?"

"'Cause I missed you," I replied.

"Well, sorry to say, you gonna have to miss me just a little more."

"Why?" I protested, a little more vigorously than I meant to. "I thought we were going out for dinner. I'm hungry. Not to mention I had my heart set on my favorite dessert," I added, trying to entice her.

"For starters, I need to swing by my place to get some clothes. Plus I got a quick errand to run. They both shouldn't take much more than an hour...or at least they'll only take an hour if I'm moving fast."

I knew what time it was, she wanted to take my bike. Every man knows that vibe his woman gives him when she wants to hold the keys to his ride. Here it was as Chaine made a clever little play designed to make me think it was my idea. Had it been a Benz she wanted to take out it would have been slightly easier. I did need her gone for a little while so I could make a phone call or two, and she had kept it so player about me being late. Not to mention she was as fine as frog hair. I wasn't gonna say no, but I worried a little bit if she could handle a 1000cc motorcycle. NYC traffic was not a video game.

As I kicked the idea around in my head, she sat looking at me with her head cocked to one side and a seductive smile on her face. There was no question I was going to cave, it was just a matter of how long till I did.

"Well I guess you better get moving then...You need me to call you a cab?" I asked teasing her.

119

"It's like that, huh? You don't rust me with your ride." Her face said she didn't find it funny.

"Nope." I let a few moments pass, letting her get a little mad. Her face reddened with each second until finally I said, "Nah, I'm just playing. Do you. But do me a favor...be careful." I handed her the keys.

"Thank you, daddy!" she squealed like an ecstatic child. She bounded down the stairs and got dressed. Before following her downstairs, I picked up the book she'd been reading, F. Scott Fitzgerald's The Great Gatsby, an American classic about a man who didn't know who his real friends were. As I replaced it in the bookcase, I thought for a moment to check my stash. I chastised myself for thinking that. Chaine hadn't given me any reason not to trust her thus far, and from what I could tell, she had her own dough. My heart told me to just trust her.

When I got downstairs, she was ready to go. She asked me for a scarf to tie up her hair, and I gave her a bandana. I also grabbed an old sock and gave it to her. It was a test of sorts. She took it without questioning why and pulled it halfway over her left sneaker. She passed. So far it seemed she knew what she was doing. She rolled the bike into the hallway, and I rode down in the elevator with her. We got down to the alley, and she gave me a kiss and started up the bike revving the motor as it growled to life. She looked sexy with her long legs straddling the powerful machine, and as I looked her over, I noticed she'd forgotten to grab a helmet.

"Damn! You forgot to grab a lid. Lemme run back up and grab you one," I yelled over her revving the motor.

"I don't do helmets," she said.

Before I could protest, she put the bike in gear and red-lined the motor while holding the front brake. The back tire spun producing a cloud of smoke as she looked at me and winked. She slowly released the brake and eased the bike slowly to the end of the alley with the back tire screaming in a burn out. At the end of the alley she brought the bike to a stop by jerking the front brake a couple of times which made her ass bounce on the seat. Over her shoulder she shot me an air kiss before pulling out into traffic. I just stood there at the other end of the alley with my mouth hanging open. That was the sexiest shit I ever saw. Seeing her handle a motorcycle that way, I was no longer worried about if she could ride. Not in the least.

I went back upstairs and plopped down on the couch. Getting Wolf hinged on my being able to get a hold of hardware down in Jamaica. Once I'd read that he came out regularly, I knew I could take him. For all the paper he had, he obviously didn't have anyone dealing with his security who was worth a damn. An experienced security detail, the kind any high profile target needed in order to stay alive, would never allow him to expose himself on schedule. Or perhaps he did have good security and they'd just grown complacent. Either way they were slipping, and if they were slipping I could get by them. For me to do that, I needed help from an old friend.

Surprisingly, all it took was one phone call. The phone rang three times and then as clear as a bell on the other end came Bizzie. In the background I could hear what sounded like a domino game and men arguing in the Jamaican broken English known as patois. He was glad to hear me and complained he hadn't heard from me in a minute. We talked shit and joked about old times. Almost seemed like it hadn't been seven years since I'd seen him last. He was ecstatic when I told him I'd be down in a week's time. His excitement was dulled when I told him I'd be down on business and not pleasure.

In coded patois I asked him if he'd be able to straighten out my hardware situation when I got there. Like the quintessential laid back Jamaican he assured me it would be "No problem." Hearing that took a lot of the pressure off me. Only thing left was for me to do what I do. On this job I'd just have to play it by ear once I got down there. That was cool with me because that was how I did some of my best work. Before hanging up, Bizzie made me promise to give him my flight info when I got it later in the week so he could scoop me from the airport.

After hanging up, I started to call Nana Helen. I dialed six of the seven digits of her number but just couldn't make the call. Part of me wanted to square things with her and tell her she had been right. Even though I was taking the Jamaica job, I knew she'd probably be happy I was gonna take her advice and do the "Imperial" heist. Then again, she'd probably try to talk me out of going to Jamaica. I wasn't trying to hear her try to manipulate me into breaking a contract. Despite all she'd taught me, she and I played by a different set of rules when it came to handling business. Not to mention that my pride wouldn't let me tell her I was wrong. As I set my phone aside, it didn't occur to me that my unwillingness to communicate my intentions to her only made our already bad situation even worse.

An hour and some change after she had left, Chaine rang my phone telling me she was downstairs. I went downstairs to get her and when I saw her I was blown away. When she said she was going home to change I thought she'd just throw on a little something simple. This was far from simple. She had on black leather pants that laced up with strings at the hips, and a black leather halter top to match. The outfit clung to her body like a second skin, and the Dianese motorcycle jacket she wore complemented it perfectly. Everything she wore looked like it was custom made with the exception of the Issac Mizrahi slingbacks on her feet. I laughed when I saw she'd put the same sock I gave her on her left shoe to protect if from the gearshift. She slowly climbed off the bike and twirled around so I could get the full effect. The pants hugged low on her hips and her ass looked picture perfect. The top was barely sufficient for her cleavage. It was obvious that she wasn't wearing any underwear. That was fine by me.

I was so caught up in staring that I barely noticed she also had a knapsack with her. We shared a hug and a kiss, and while I held her I ran my hands over all her curves. Truth be told, standing next to my bike all "sexy-ed" up like that, she looked like something out of my fantasy.

I slung her bag over my shoulder and wheeled the bike into the elevator.

"What you got in here? This bag damn near heavier than the bike," I said, noticing the knapsack's weight.

"I got some clothes and some of my stuff in case you take me hostage again."

"Don't you think you're assuming a bit much? How you know if I was even gonna ask you to stay over?" I asked, teasing her.

"Stop playing, Lex. I got a couple days off from work and I thought I was gonna spend time with you…but if you don't want me to…," she paused, letting her threat linger.

"Well, I wouldn't want you to have to tote this heavy ass bag back home, so I guess you can stay." I laughed like I was laughing at her, but in reality, it was sheer elation I felt at knowing I wouldn't have to part with her any time soon.

When we got upstairs I had to fight off the urge to seduce her. I was sure she would have been game, but

I wanted to take her out. I didn't want us to be one of those couples that stayed in having sex all the time. Not that a whole bunch of sex wasn't good but I wanted us to have a functional relationship where we did more than that. So, while I found something to wear she took a flat iron from her bag and did her hair. Her outfit was a show stopper, but her windblown hair didn't quite go with the look.

I eventually settled on some black Ralph Lauren slacks with a thin charcoal gray colored cashmere sweater. She finished her hair not long after I was dressed. Now she looked perfect. Before leaving, we stood giving each other an approving once over. We both had the same look in our eyes that said later that night it would be on.

Out on the town that evening we had a ball. We talked, laughed, and kissed our way through dinner at an upscale restaurant. Seemed like all eyes were on us, and people even commented on what a nice couple we made. We barely took notice of the attention. For us, the time just slipped away as we enjoyed each other. After dinner we went and got our grown and sexy on at a trendy night spot downtown. The men in the place couldn't keep their eyes off Chaine, and some of the women made eyes at me that I didn't have to pretend to ignore. I was wrapped up in my lady, and she was wrapped up in me. With her I found a level of comfort I'd never known could even exist between a man and a woman, let alone someone in my profession. I even had a few drinks which was a huge step for me because before I met her I never drank and this would make two times in as many weeks.

We danced like Fred and Ginger to old school grooves. By the time we were ready to leave we weren't drunk, but we weren't fit to drive either. Despite the short cab ride back to my apartment, the cab driver threatened to put us out three times if we didn't "behave."

We were at each other on the way upstairs and had the elevator ride taken any longer, it would have been fine with us to make it happen right there. Instead we settled for the kitchen counter as soon as we came in. Somewhere in there Chaine found her unopened pack of Skittles, and when we adjourned to the bed, she put on a Nine Inch Nails CD and showed me a use for Skittles I'm sure the manufacturer never intended. Nothing out of bounds of course, but adventurous enough. We went at it all night, and slept in the next day.

The next couple of days passed in a blur. We had sex a lot, but we talked a lot, too. She didn't have a lot of the complexes that most women had. We shared intimate details about ourselves. Chaine told me more about what it was like when she was first on her own. Despite her beauty she'd actually had a hard life. I admired her toughness, and it endeared her to me even more. I told her about my father, or rather lack thereof and how his absence had created coldness inside me that I couldn't seem to shake loose. I found myself feeling guilty that I couldn't tell her the whole truth. I'd probably never be able to tell her, but I felt like if I could just close that chapter of my life, everything would be okay. Some things she just didn't need to know.

After everything she had already told me about her desires, dreams, and fears, I couldn't escape the feeling that some of the simple things, like where she lived and worked, that I didn't know were the important things that I should know. I was just so caught up between the newness of my first real relationship and our powerful emotional and physical connection that I overlooked a lot. Through all I'd done and seen, falling for a woman was something that up to then, my lifestyle had never permitted. Now that I had finally been struck by Cupid's arrow, I wasn't turning back.

Before we knew it Wednesday rolled around. That evening we sat across from each other in silence, having dinner at a little Chinese spot up the block from my place. We were both in a somber mood, and it was as though a dark cloud hung over us. Neither of us wanted our time together to end no matter if it was for a couple of days or not. It was like we had to sit and watch the tide coming in to destroy our castle in the sand.

Thankfully, it wasn't all my fault. I told her I had a job on the weekend, and she was welcome to stay until I got back, but she said she had to get a presentation ready for an important client. At least while we were apart she'd have her work to keep her occupied, and when I got back in work mode I'd be so focused that I wouldn't notice how much I missed her. Once I got back to town, I had that one other piece of work to deal with, and I could call it quits. I had no doubt that I could convince Chaine that we should spend all our time together. Especially once my money situation was straight.

While I paid the check after dinner, Chaine thumbed some keys on her phone. Tears welled up in her eyes but didn't fall. I wondered if she was on the brink of crying because of our impending separation or if it had something to do with her phone. We walked slowly and quietly up the block to my place holding hands. My mood picked up a little bit as I began to hope maybe we'd have some "sayonara sex" before she left. When we came to the alley that led to my building, she stopped short. I playfully pulled her by the hand, but she held fast and then snatched her hand away. When I tried to look her in the eye she looked away.

"What's wrong?" I asked.

"I can't go back upstairs with you. If I do, it's gonna be a lot harder for me to leave...I might not leave."

"What about your stuff? You gotta come get your stuff," I said, grasping for a reason to make her stay.

"I'll get it next time," she said, as she barely kept from crying.

"Easy for you to say, you got panties hanging in my shower. If I ain't know no better I'd say you was marking your territory," I joked, trying to lift her spirits.

A smile creased her face. Strangely enough it made me happy to see her happy, and suddenly I wasn't as concerned if she came upstairs or not. While she laughed I pulled her by the hand trying to physically convince her to come up. Looking back on it, I realize it may have looked to a passerby as though a large black man was trying to drag her into a dark alley. We playfully struggled for a moment.

All of a sudden the same black sedan that picked her up on our first date, or one just like it, came to a screeching halt at the curb in front of us. I tried to move Chaine out of the way and reach for my heat in a single motion. The move was awkward at best. My movements had never included a second party before. I managed to get her out of the line of fire, but I was slow on the draw. By the time I was in hand and ready to operate the tall black baldheaded dude driving the car had already gotten out. He stood glaring at me for a moment before Chaine made a subtle hand gesture, and he silently climbed back in his vehicle. If he'd really wanted to make a move he would've had the drop on me. I was slipping. The fun and games ceased and I was suddenly very, very pissed. As far as signs went, that happening right then was like a flashing red light before a cliff.

"That's my ride. I better get going," she said.

"I don't like the way your boy hopped out like he was 'bout to do something. Getting' in my business he like to get dealt with." I shot an ice cold stare through the tinted windows as I said it, but the damage was already done.

She hugged me and laughed like it was cute that I was mad. "Lex, don't pay that no mind. That's my driver, Bruce. He's just looking out for me." She held my face in her hands and locked me in that gaze. "Now, can I have a kiss before I go?"

I was mad and on the brink of transforming, yet somehow just looking at her face warmed me from the inside out. This was the singular moment that stood out to me and let me know I was in trouble. In a situation when I could have needed to be a killer, I was a docile love struck puppy. If I'd needed to I couldn't have squeezed a grape, much less a trigger. To make matters worse, I justified it by telling myself that maybe falling in love was just another indication that I needed to call the murder for hire game quits. I looked at her pretty face with its poetic features and I realized for the first time just how deeply I was in love. As she kissed me softly I could feel every inch of my body tingle. The second our lips parted I started missing her. I watched her sexy strut to the sedan and as she grabbed the door I called after her.

"Chaine."

She looked back.

"I...I...ummm," I searched for the words.

She smiled as I struggled.

"Chaine, I wanna tell you I..." Somehow I just couldn't say what I was trying to say. It was my first time ever saying it to anyone.

She sauntered back over to me and pressed her finger to my lips. Wrapping her arms around my neck she put her lips right on my earlobe and whispered the two single most beautiful words my soul ever heard, "Me, too."

Later that night I made my rounds before leaving. I stopped by Big Tee's place and as promised the ID's he got me were flawless. I kicked it with Mila before leaving, and she seemed real excited about the job. She said she even had a few ideas about how we could handle it, but since it was my lick she was leaving that part up to me. I was glad she was down for it. Had I realized she was so thorough, we could have taken Imperial down months ago. I promised to get up with her as soon as I got back.

After that I went and met up with Bubby at a pool hall he hung out at over on Boston Road called the "Cue Lounge." In the evenings, he liked to spend his time trimming the fat off of old pimps and retired number men at 8-ball. I asked him to pick up my two sets of tickets and phone from Nana Helen. She had been right, but be that as it may, I wasn't quite ready to see her yet. Bubby didn't protest because she always gave him a handful of Cuban cigars. I think he might have had the hots for her but never made a move because she was like a mother to me.

The following morning I stood in front of my place sipping a cup of piss-warm black coffee. I probably cut an odd picture in the olive green Armani safari suit and brown Wallabee Clarks I had on, but when I touched down in Jamaica, I'd blend right in. The small bag I had with me held more clothes than I needed for the trip. If I couldn't do this job in a couple of days, it probably couldn't be done.

The very second my watch said 5:30 I saw Bubby come around the corner. Today he drove a black '83 Monte Carlo identical to the one Denzel Washington was pushing in the movie "Training Day." He coasted to a smooth stop in front of me and gave me a small head nod that said not only did he know he was riding clean, he also knew he was right on time. I gave the care the requisite couple seconds of admiration. It was on point. Looked like someone even took the time to polish the chrome tips of the dual exhaust pipes. I threw my bag in the back seat and we rode out into the pre-dawn city streets.

We got to the airport a few minutes early, and we sat in the ride kicking it for a while. Bubby commented that he hadn't seen me much lately besides for work, and he asked me if it had anything to do with this new lady I'd been seeing. I gave him the rundown and he listened intently, nodding in approval at some of what I said. He pulled a Cuban from the visor and lit it as I spoke. When I finished talking, he exhaled a plume of purple grayish smoke and said, "Well, Lex, sounds like you got a winner on your hands. Question is, are you gonna keep her? Good ones ain't hard to come by; they hard to keep."

"I think she one I wanna keep. Problem is, it's like she make it real hard for me to focus on my work when I'm with her. Bub, she making me sloppy," I matter-of-factly stated.

He paused for a minute staring at the stream of smoke emanating from the tip of his smoldering cigar. Seemed like he gave his words a lot of thought before he finally responded, "You love her?" he asked.

I hesitated, but I decided to keep it real. "I... I think I do," I tentatively replied.

"Either you do or you don't," he demanded.

"Yeah, I do."

"Alright then I'm gon' tell you like this... I ain't never asked you your business, but you know ole' Bub is far from stupid. Rolling how you roll you don't got a big margin for error. The game will show you love if you make her your wife, but if you put her to the rear, she

130

can be a jealous mistress. A jealous mistress ain't gon' do nothing but fuck you over. Seems to me you need to decide which lady you wanna be faithful to because you can't be true to both."

"If I choose the girl, then what? I 'pose to be a square? Get a job?" I asked.

"Now I didn't say all that, but you definitely gonna have to reevaluate your lifestyle and probably make some changes."

"Man, it sound like you tryin' to tell me to be some type of full time sucker for love," I said, becoming frustrated.

"See, Lex, that's the problem with ya'll young cats today. Ya'll see love like it's some type of disgusting virus. It ain't like that. It's nothing wrong with love. I was in your position years ago and I chose the wrong route. All I'm tryin' to school you to is that love is a gift. If it's given to you, you need to cherish it. Beyond that, you a grown ass man; you make your own decisions. Just be careful because the way you running right now, your two worlds is bound to collide... and if that happens, I assure you it won't be nothing nice." He leaned back and puffed his cigar letting his words marinate.

I sat there pondering what he said and I realized it was just that simple. I had a choice to make. It was about surrendering to what I was feeling for Chaine and allowing our relationship to really grow. There was no way I could do that living a double life. Bubby's statement about my worlds colliding rang in my head like the peals of a church bell.

I thanked him for his insight and promised to give it some serious thought. As I grabbed my bag and was about to hop out he wished me "Good luck." In all the time he had been driving me he had never said those words to me. I stopped for a minute, confused as to whether he meant on the job or with Chaine. There was no way for me to tell, and I didn't bother to ask. I figured I could use some luck on both. I gave him a pound and promised to find some time to kick it with him when I got back. Walking away from the ride I tried hard to push aside all he'd said and put on my game face, but I just couldn't escape the sinking feeling that the bottom was about to fall out.

Chapter 7

I spent the three and some change hour flight staring out the window trying to get my mind right for the task at hand. Flying in over the island's picturesque north coast dotted with brightly colored resorts and pristine white sandy beaches, I fought the urge to think of what it would be like to be here with Chaine. To keep my brain busy, I recounted all the details I'd memorized about Winston "Wolf" Parks. Gradually I drifted into that zone where I did my best work, and by the time the plane's wheels touched down I was ready. As the other passengers applauded the pilot's safe landing, a tradition on Air Jamaica flights, I gathered my things. I barely let the plane stop before making a bee line for the exit door from first class. I was one of the first people off the plane.

I was welcomed back to Jamaica by tropical sweltering September heat the moment I stepped off the plane. The air was hot and thick. It had to have rained sometime in the last 24 hours. The soupy air was only ameliorated by the occasional cool breeze that swept across the island.

Inside the terminal I saw that Norman Manley International had gotten slightly more modern in the four years since I'd seen it last . As I cleared customs I noticed that arriving passengers were barely scrutinized. Made sense for a country in the "export" business. I by-passed the group of island beauties welcoming visitors to Jamaica in song and strolled right by baggage claim. Numerous taxi drivers offered me their services, but I ignored them. Activating my phone I keyed in a text message to Nana Helen letting her know that I'd touched down. Even though we had yet to resolve our personal issues, I still maintained professional courtesy.

The closer I got to the exit the harder I looked around. Bizzie was supposed to meet me, and I figured I would have spotted him already. He had my arrival information, but he was nowhere in sight. As I came to the exit, I wondered what could have happened to him. I walked through the sliding glass doors and scanned the row of idling taxis. Just as I was about to select one, I saw a tinted out black Ford F-150 pick-up pulling up. I immediately knew it was Bizzie because the truck had a pair of Honda CBR 600 motorcycles in the back. He hopped out coming around to the passenger side. At a slim 6'2" he stood in the classic "rude bwoy" pose, leaned back with his arms crossed and one foot out front. His hair was in short plaits. He had on a green mesh tank top, some Iceberg jeans I knew for sure had just come out, and Boston Celtics custom Air Force 1's. His light skin was bronze from the sun, and I couldn't see his hazel eyes behind his shades, but I was certain he still had those unmistakable "cat eyes."

"Whap'n, Lexus?" he greeted me smiling, as he took my bag and threw it in the truck.

"I see you still move fast but never on time," I said.

"It's hard to get free when you're a G like me," he replied. He spoke in a unique combination of New York and Jamaican accents.

"Nice ride," I said, as we climbed in. "You moving fast and furious...Maybe I been doing my thing on the wrong side of the water."

"Nah, rude bwoy. Up top is what's good. Mi miss de Apple...mi miss it bad," he responded shaking his head. I could tell he really did miss N.Y.

134

"Well, I'm glad to see you, and I'm glad to see you doing it big down here."

"No doubt. Can't say I didn't have help, though," he said as he started the truck.

"Say no more homie. It's nothin'. I just did what you woulda done for me."

"Fa' shizzle my nizzle," he hollered, as he turned up the stereo. A hard hitting Beanie Man rhythm thumped from the speakers as he mashed the gas, and we peeled out into traffic. From the way the music bumped and the truck accelerated, I could tell he'd tricked out both. I leaned back in the air conditioning and relaxed as he weaved through traffic. I'd gotten use to his erratic driving a long time ago, and as he merged onto the highway, I found myself reminiscing on our days coming up together back in the Bronx.

I first met Bizzie when I was in the fifth grade going to P.S. 109. His family had just moved from Jamaica to the Bronx, and he was the new kid in school. The other kids were particularly hard on him because he spoke with a heavy accent. To make matters worse, on his third day of school, he pops up with a pair of brightly colored Pro-Wings on his feet. At that age that was fashion suicide, and the mean kids cut into him something terrible. Anything less than Nikes, Reeboks, or Adidas (in that order) was unacceptable.

At recess a group of kids surrounded him on the playground taunting him, calling him "wing-wing" and all types of other names. He tried to fight back verbally, but he was out-gunned. Kids in the Bronx can be real mean and talk as slick as they come. Me and my little crew sat across the yard watching from the bleachers. Some of the fellas were even betting on how long before

135

he started crying. Eventually Bizzie got frustrated and caught the biggest boy in the face with a two-piece. The other boys jumped on him in a heartbeat, and they commenced to beating the brakes off him. After school they caught him again and punished him some more. Both times he fought hard, but five on one is horrible odds. It went on like that for about a week, but he never stopped fighting and he never told.

One day at lunch when it was about to go down, I decided enough was enough. My boys wanted nothing to do with it. I felt like it could have easily been me since my family was Jamaican. Plus, I liked something about Bizzie. He had that "go hard" type of spirit and I was drawn to it at a young age. So, that day when they surrounded him, I came to his aid. At first I talked shit to the kids, but they weren't trying to play the dozens. I made a last ditch effort to get one of them to just fight Bizzie head-up; they wanted no parts of him in a fair one. That day Bizzie and I got our asses beat, but it wasn't nearly as bad as the beatdowns he'd been getting. My "friends" didn't lift a finger to help, and I didn't speak to any of them ever again.

I went and got Bizzie a half an hour before school let out and we snuck out early. All the boys who'd jumped us were from the neighborhood, and I knew where most of them lived. That afternoon we ambushed them one by one when they split up. We got three out of five of them. With the odds in our favor we beat those three so badly that they didn't show up for school the following day. The remaining two did come. We ran down on them first thing in the morning and aired them out in front of everybody. We ended up getting kicked out of school for two weeks a piece, but nobody in school so much as looked at either of us wrong ever again. From then on Bizzie and I were inseparable. We went to the same schools and ran the streets together. He was a quick study and picked up on all the music and fashion really fast. By the time we hit high school his accent was a lot less noticeable. At that point it was cooler to be Jamaican anyway, and with his hazel eyes the girls were all on him. The ladies were an added bonus, but for the most part I stayed rolling with him because I knew what he was made of. We got into a lot of sticky situations and never once did he let me down. Instead of kicking it with a bunch of jokers who weren't road tested, I just stuck with what I knew.

Facing teenage pressure to stay fly, we both started hustling around the same time. My career didn't take off as such, but Bizzie blew up with a weed spot on White Plains Road. He was connected to some of the moves and shakers in the 'hood and got some good ass weed at a nice price. I have to admit he was more of a born hustler than me. Beside slinging weed, he just had that talent for using money to make more money. Hence the name "Bizzie." He stayed busy, and he was about his business.

One summer Bizzie comes flying through the block on a brand new Kawasaki Ninja ZX-9 he had just copped. Before then I never even knew how to ride a motorcycle. He spun by my crib later that day showing off his new toy. I sat on the bike, and I was hooked. He offered to let me ride, but I confessed that I didn't know how. He was appalled. He took me that instant to a desolate block and taught me how to ride. I caught on real quick, and by the end of that session I wanted a bike of my own. From the moment I got off the bike I was fienin' to ride again. An insatiable passion was awakened inside me. I became very depressed, however, when during the following weeks, I realized I didn't have nearly enough money to buy a bike of my own.

I scrambled for a month straight and got nowhere fast. It was making me sick seeing all the bikes coming through and not having one of my own. That summer it seemed like there was an influx of motorcycles and just about everybody had one. Around the way there were even girls doing burn-outs at the stoplights. My torture ended one day when Bizzie called me over to his crib. We went in the backyard, and as we walked back he gave me a set of keys. In the backyard parked next to his Ninja was a slightly used, but in good condition, Suzuki GSX-R 750. I flipped my lid when he told me it was mine. That was by far, one of the happiest moments of my life. When I offered to pay him for the joint in installments he refused me and told me it was a gift. For the rest of the summer we balled on the bikes, hitting up everything in the tri-state area. Before long, we learned to do tricks and came through putting it down everywhere we went. For a while there it was like heaven.

The wheels literally fell off around Labor Day as the summer drew to a close. We went to the huge West Indian Day parade out in Brooklyn on Eastern Parkway. The parade was off the chain! It was better than all the cook outs, bike rallies, and Greek fests we had been to put together. We met hundreds of beautiful women and partied until the parade was over. Two Trinidadian dime pieces had even invited us back to their place, but we fell back because it could've been a set-up. In N.Y. it was just bad business to go home with women you just met. There were about a thousand ways it could go bad. So, with that in mind, we hit the road.

We chose to ride back through downtown Brooklyn and come over the Brooklyn Bridge into Manhattan. From there we took the FDR up to the Major Deegan Expressway up to the Bronx. Just as we merged onto the Deegan was when we saw the lights. We hadn't been speeding, stunting, or anything like that, but still, there behind us were the flashing lights of a police car.

138

On closer examination we saw it was a "Highway One" unit, one of NYC's relentless highway patrol cars. Highway One had a reputation that once the initiated a chase they never gave up. That day they had their hands full because Bizzie and I had a standing rule that we never pulled over for cops. It didn't make sense to pull over and take a ticket, or worse get your bike towed, when you could just burn the road up. Most times cops didn't even try us, but we did have a couple of occasions when we had to give them the business.

We were both nasty on the bikes, weaving through traffic sometimes at 100-plus miles an hour. One time we got chased we did some daredevil maneuvers, manipulating traffic so we ended up behind the cop car! As he watched helplessly in his rearview, we got off the exit behind the poor fool waving goodbye to him. It wasn't like he could turn around on the highway.

I looked over to Bizzie in the far right lane just as he looked back from seeing we had company. He had his helmet on, but I knew he was laughing underneath it. When he looked at me, he gave me a 'go ahead' nod, and I knew it was on. Without hesitation I cracked the throttle and took off like a rocket. At first I had a lead on him, but in a few seconds he caught up to me because his 900cc motor was more powerful than my 750. Together we darted from lane to lane in between cars, criss-crossing the highway like some type of well choreographed ballet. We rode at high speed together so often that each of us knew what the other was going to do. To onlookers in traffic it looked like poetry in motion. Sometimes a motorist would get frightened and invariably tap his brake. That helped our cause because by the time they reacted to us we'd already blown by, and they only slowed down the cops pursuing us.

139

When we came up on the Fordham Road exit we slowed down a little and looked back to see if the cop was still chasing us. To our surprise, this persistent bastard was on the shoulder doing about a buck, and coming right up behind us. To make matters worse, the traffic had thinned out, so now there was nothing slowing him down. I couldn't believe he hadn't given up. We ripped the throttles and took off again, opening up a huge gap s our speeds climbed over 140mph. The exits whizzed by one after another even though they were each miles apart. The cop was nowhere close behind, but as we flew past the Van Cortland Park exit, two more units shot around the on-ramp joining the chase. Apparently we couldn't outrun the first cop's radio.

At the 233rd St. exit fast approached I considered getting off and losing the cops on the back streets and familiar one ways around our neighborhood. It was risky because it was close to home, and traffic was a lot more unpredictable. The other option was to stay on the Deegan. Problem with that was the highway crossed into the adjoining Westchester County, and crossing to there we might have county and state police joining the chase. Then we'd have to worry about the chase growing so long it ran us out of gas. It was slightly less risky, though, because more cops might not be there at all, and the NYC cops couldn't pursue us in another jurisdiction.

When I pulled in beside Bizzie I found he had already done the math and made a decision. He waved me on, indicating to me that we would press forward and take our chances on the open road. The highway straightened out and I twisted the throttle back, holding it wide open. My speeds climbed towards 170 mph, and everything fell silent as though I'd broken the sound barrier. For a moment Bizzie was right beside me, but just as we came up on the 233 Street exit he slowed down. At that speed he looked like he had thrown his bike in reverse when he broke the clutch down, and then locked his brakes up going into a graceful controlled skid, known as a power slide, just in time to turn off the exit. It all happened in seconds, and there was nothing I could do even if I'd tried to. We split up, and I pressed on. In my rearview I saw that all three of the police cars chose to follow him and give up on me. He had drawn them off me. At the county line I found no police welcome reception waiting on me. I broke my speed down to a respectable 80mph and took the Yonkers Avenue exit. As I made my way from Yonkers back to the 'hood via back streets, I silently hoped Bizzie had a similarly easy time getting rid of his police escort.

Turned out that he didn't, though. In addition to the highway patrol cars, some local units joined in as soon as he came off the exit. He gave them the blues, taking them all through the 'hood. Zipping up one ways and running red lights he caused five separate accidents, three of which involved police cars. No matter how many he made wreck though, they just kept coming like agents in "The Matix." It became a chase the cops refused to lose. Bizzie tried everything, but he just couldn't shake them. They added cars and cut off streets until there was nowhere for him to run to.

When they boxed him in on Bronx Boulevard he rode on the sidewalk and shot right past them. He was doing about 60 and almost home free. As he passed the exit of a car wash his rear tire lost traction on the invisible coating of Armor-All residue that was all over the sidewalk. The exit of a car wash, where they sprayed on Armor-All for an extra buck, had to be the most dangerous spot in America for someone on a motorcycle. When Bizzie hit that patch it was like he hit an oil slick. The back tire slid out from under him, and the bike went tumbling end over end for 30 yards before hitting a parked car and damn near disintegrating. I guess you could call him lucky because he flew off the bike in a trajectory that landed him in some bushes. He ended up with a concussion, a broken rib, some mean road rash, but worst of all a pair of NYPD custom silver bracelets.

Later on that night I found out Bizzie was locked up and charged with multiple counts of 'you name it.' The cops were mad at him, so they charged him with everything but the kitchen sink. When he was arraigned, the prosecutor told the judge that he was here in the U.S. illegally, and he was ordered held without bond. I was sick over what happened to him, but when I visited him on Riker's Island he told me not to beat myself up about it because at least they didn't get us both. Facing three to nine years in state prison plus deportation, my partner stood strong and even cracked jokes about how bad he did the po-po before they caught him.

When Bizzie got locked up he had a lot of his money in the streets. I wasn't a pro yet, but I was just starting collections then, so I hit the ground running and collected as much for him as I could. Usually a guy got knocked off and lost everything, but with me on the case I got $100K of what he had floating, which wasn't bad at all. He was surprised I got that much, even though it was only about a third of what he had out there. We used $25K and got him a good lawyer who pled the case down and got him one to three, but couldn't get the deportation thrown out. Bizzie ended up doing a year and a half upstate and then got shipped back to Jamaica. While he was in prison I held on to his money for him, kept money on his books, and even sent chicks to visit him. I would have gone myself, but he refused to see me. Pride, I guess.

Touching back down in Jamaica with $75K wasn't much for a guy use to living the way Bizzie had been in N.Y. It wasn't long before his money ran thin. Luckily, while he was on the way down, I was on the way up, so I just looked out for him sending him money as my figures increased. When I made my first million I shot him $100K. From there the hustler in him took over, and he opened a clothing store in Kingston. He kept all the latest fashions, courtesy of some Africans out of Queens that I plugged him in with. The clothes blew him up in Jamaica, and before long he was the man to see for all types of merchandise from electronics, to cars, to c.d.'s, to whatever. Before I knew it, he was ballin' again, and my career had taken off. We kept in touch, but I never got tight with anyone after him. I threw myself into my work and stayed focused.

Chapter 8

I stared out the window of the truck watching the island's lush scenery fly by. At first glance Jamaica looked like paradise, but upon closer examination, one came face to face with the gritty subculture that lay beneath the beautiful surface. It said a lot about Bizzie's character that he'd been able to make his way down here. As he navigated the winding roads while simultaneously playing the i-pod wired to the truck's stereo, I wondered if he would ever come back up top.

Bizzie had been confused when I told him I was flying in to Montego Bay which was practically on the other side of the island from Kingston where my business was. As we rode I explained to him that I wanted to stop in Mandeville to check on some things. I wanted to see first hand if Wolf's compound really was as impenetrable as it seemed on paper. When I told him about the detour I could see the wheels turning in his head. He didn't say anything, but I knew he was curious. He was the one person I didn't need to keep secrets from, so I gave him the full rundown. I told him who I was there to see, and about what. On hearing the information he abruptly whipped the truck onto the side of the road, and came to a grinding halt on the gravel.

"Yuh mad?" he yelled incredulously, as he gawked at me like I was the kid in the class caught eating glue. "Might as well mek this a vacation 'cause Wolf cyan't be touched inna' Jamaica."

"Aw man. Bizzie, don't tell me he your hero too."

"I'mon nuh worship mon," he said in thick patois. "Anybody else yuh woulda had a chance, but tryin' him is a Kamikaze mission."

"It's been a long time…we come a long way from P.S. 109 homie. I wouldn't be here if I couldn't do it."

"I know yuh big time now Lex. I might be down here, but I got mi ear to the ground. I know your work." Something about the way he said it made me not even bother to ask how he knew what I was into. He continued, "Yuh probably 'av a betta chance fi try the Prime Minister!"

"Homie, he could get it, too, if his name was on the contract. I'm just gonna have to ask you to trust me."

"Trust yuh?" he replied looking at me sideways. "Mi trust yuh wid' mi life. But yuh nuh understand…"

"He got personal bodyguards, the Army at the crib, any police got his back, and folks in the street gonna go hard for him," I said, cutting him off and finishing his sentence.

"Then how yuh plan fi get pass dat? Yuh a magician now?" he asked laughing.

"You got them things I asked for, right?"

"Yuh know I did."

"Then I got all I need. All I can say is, 'I'll show you better than I can tell you,'" I matter-of-factly stated.

"I got yuh back; whenevah, whatevah. Jus' be careful."

I resisted the urge to reiterate how much of a pro I was. Instead I nodded, silently accepting his cautionary advice as he pulled back onto the road.

The road to Mandeville took us through winding hills. To the sides of the road were gullies that plunged hundreds of feet into rich green seas of plants fit to rival the rain forest. In places the road narrowed to a degree that it barely seemed passable by two vehicles at one time. Somehow they fit, though. In all my trips to the island it still amazed me that not only did two cars pass on the treacherous roads, they often did it at speeds in excess of 80mph. Bizzie fit right in here, careening around sharp curves like it was nothing. At one point he barely had his eyes on the road as he fiddled with his phone while taking a hairpin turn. I just told him that whoever he was texting I hoped she was worth us going over a cliff. He shook his head like I just didn't know, and mumbled something about me soon finding out.

Instead of taking the turn-off that led to the sprawling outskirts of Mandeville, Bizzie drove us straight into the city's bustling center. The children in their various khaki or gingham school uniforms were even more beautiful than I remembered, as they made their way home in the city streets. Each time we came to a stop another scent wafted inside the truck, and I found myself fienin' for another island delicacy. Vendors in the street got their hustle on pushing fresh nuts, sky juice, tamarind balls, and all types of other things that made my mouth water. People gave head nods as we passed through. I couldn't quite figure if it was because Bizzie was so well known. It could have been that they were just acknowledging that he was doing it big in the new truck with the twin bikes in the back.

The sights, sounds, and smells had me hungry as a refugee. I thought Bizzie was reading my mind when he pulled into the small dirt lot in front of a restaurant and bar. As soon as he parked, I hopped out of the truck and dashed inside to get my grub on. The mixture of aromas in the place made it smell like heaven. I could detect the distinct scents of nutmeg, curry, scotch bonnet peppers, and a number of other things lingering in the air. The sparsely furnished place had a long bar that doubled as a lunch counter and a few tables that were presently unoccupied. Playing on a small T.V. behind

146

the bar was a cricket match that had the counter man's undivided attention.

I anxiously awaited a break in play before laying a couple of euros on the counter. The man was instantly responsive, and scooped up the few bills as he disappeared into the back to fill my order. I had converted $5K from dollars to euros for walking around money. Euros because the locals loved whatever foreign currency was the hottest at the time. The dollar and the pound had both had their run, but right now the euro was running shit. With the instability of the Jamaican dollar people felt better holding onto a foreign currency that would invariably be worth more later. And of course I would obviously get pegged as a foreigner, but spending euros would throw some shade on where I was from.

In a flash, the man emerged from the rear with a steaming Styrofoam plate of ackee and salt (cod) fish, calaloo, and fried dumplings. He popped the top on my Ting grapefruit soda as I dug in. Then he went back to watching T.V. as I relentlessly punished the delicious food. It wasn't that I was really that hungry, and I wasn't exactly longing for Jamaican food because in the North Bronx you could throw a rock and hit three Jamaican restaurants. Maybe it was all the fresh ingredients, but something just made island food taste better on the island.

I finished my food and walked out sipping my Ting, leaving the counter man behind in his trance. When I came out I found Bizzie had unloaded the bikes and was posted up against the truck talking to two tall, dark, curvy Carla Campbell look alikes. As I came closer I saw that they were twins and that the model Carla Cambell had nothing on them. One of them had on a black mini dress that was too short but punctuated her sexy figure, with some Jimmy Choo pumps that made her long legs look like perfection. The other twin had on

147

low rise jeans and a cut off tank top that struggled to keep Victoria's Secret a secret. Since there were two of them I'd have to say they were a perfect 20. Judging from the way they were all up on my homie I figured he hadn't just met them...although that wasn't impossible.

"Whass'up, homie? I see you got company," I said.

"Yuh jus' in time, rude bwoy. This mi girlfriend Maxine," he said, gesturing to the tank top twin on his right, "and this is mi girlfriend Marlene," he said, indicating the one in the Jimmy Choo's.

"Hi," the twins said in unison.

I shot Bizzie a puzzled look wondering what the deal was.

"What cyan I say, homie? Yuh done know how tings run. I cyan't choose one...I gotta be fair to both. The two of dem is mi girl."

"Okay. That make sense," I replied.

"He loves me the best," chimed Maxine, in the Jimmy Choo's, in a saccharine voice.

In response Marlene rolled her eyes. She drew closer to Bizzie and started pouting. He whispered something to her and gave her a quick kiss that seemed to comfort her.

"What's the deal?" I asked, gesturing at the bikes.

"The girls gonna take the truck. We gonna ride...Yuh still 'member how?"

"You the one that laid it down," I laughed. "I'm still waiting for you to catch up!"

"Alright killa yout'. Jus' don't ask me fi slow down."

While Bizzie kissed his girlfriends goodbye, I grabbed some shades and a bandana from my bag. He started up the bikes and the twins hopped in the truck. Looking at the bikes I almost couldn't believe it was about to be me and my road dog riding again. Inside, I wished it had been a pleasure trip and not business. The twins pulled out of the parking lot kicking up a cloud of dust as we got on the bikes. We sat for a couple of minutes giving the motors time to warm up. The anticipation seemed to be mutual.

We set out under the early afternoon sun. I rode easy, following Bizzie's lead. Being on the bike made me feel even closer to the sights and sounds of Mandeville. We back tracked through the city to the turn-off that led us into the surrounding hills. With its towering coconut and lush fruit trees, the scenery looked like something out of a postcard from paradise. The further out of the city we rode, the larger and more opulent the colorful homes along the road became.

No sooner than we turned onto the road bordering the south end of Wolf's property did we see an army patrol riding in a jeep. They slowed down scoping us hard as we rolled by. It was an intimidation tactic. We took the hint and kept it moving. I didn't get to see much other than some fields. Next, we tried riding the road that led to the east gate. There were two jeeps parked there with a bunch of soldiers milling around smoking and kicking it. They didn't look to be very well trained, but the AR-15's strapped over their backs made them serious business. With nothing doing on that end, we rode on. I was frustrated, but Bizzie smiled, and it let me know he knew something.

Up the road a ways he took a sharp turn onto a road that I could barely call paved. The neglected road was a steep incline, and with all its twists and turns, it seemed to meander away from the estate. For a minute I thought he had given up on our little reconnaissance mission. I pulled up beside him just as he turned off the road into a field. He stopped and hopped off his bike, and I pulled next to him looking around. There was nothing around us but some mango trees and fragrant hibiscus plants. It was a pretty little field with a nice view. For a moment I was confused as to why we were there, until I noticed that from up there you could see clear to the ocean. By the time I had fully caught on, Bizzie was climbing up into a tree. I parked the bike and followed him.

From up in the tree I could see everything for miles around. He had brought me to the one spot where I had a bird's eye view of the entire compound. What I saw was not good. Although we were a ways off, I could see that Wolf's home was very heavily guarded. Besides the one's we'd already seen, form my new vantage point I could see that there were army patrols on all the access roads around the estate. On top of that, I could make out dozens of people going about their business inside the grounds. I didn't need binoculars to see that bum rushing this dude at the crib would be out of the question. It was highly unlikely that I'd even be able to get into the place, much less get close enough to hit him *and* get away undetected. I'd already known that my chances of getting Wolf at his home were slim to none, but I had to see first hand to be sure. Looked like my only chance would be at the club.

We made our way out of the hills and headed to Kingston. Along the way we passed through May Pen and Spanish Town. As much as I wanted to tear through the cities with Bizzie, I couldn't. We had to keep it low key because I wasn't certain how things would play out. After I left I didn't want whatever work I put in to come back to haunt him. The Darkheart Massive had long reach, and a memory that went even further. We rode easy, trying to keep it nonchalant and nondescript.

It was 5 p.m. on the dot when we got to Kingston. The air in the capital city had a different texture than in the country where we'd just come from.

The green jungle seemed to lose its battle, giving way to the concrete one. The jerk chicken stands and small restaurants became KFC's and McDonald's. As we passed through the poorer sections of the city, ghetto youths ran alongside us with outstretched hands trying to make a quick come up. I was tempted to stop and pass out some money, but that wouldn't exactly have been a low key move. We made a quick stop at Bizzie's store, and I was instantly impressed when I saw the place. Centrally located in a small plaza with a law office, a recording studio, and a record shop, I could see the spot was a money maker. Inside I saw that he was pushing all the same merchandise that was currently hot in NYC. Not to mention there was a line at the register and a good amount of customers, mostly women, shopping.

While I peeped the scene, he went in the back. He came back out a few minutes later with a yellow North Face knapsack. As he passed by the woman working the register, she asked him something that he responded to by shrugging his shoulders and laughing. As we walked out he told me that the woman at the register had asked him if I was married. I saw why he'd laughed. She was a decent looking chick, but she had to have been at least twice my age. We got back on the bikes joking about "Milf's" and 40-something actresses who could get it, like Angela Basset. For some reason, whenever Black men got on that topic, Angela Basset always came up.

Bizzie's house was a short ride from the store on Kingston's south side. As we drove up to the house the door on the garage automatically went up. The truck was already parked inside. From the outside the house looked like all the rest on the block. When we went inside, however, I saw he had the spot laid out fit for a king; marble floors, central air, and beautiful furniture. He had the perfect hiding spot, living lavishly in a working class neighborhood.

The air in the crib smelled like somebody was cooking up a storm. We heard giggles coming from the kitchen, and we found the twins in there doing the damn thing! They had fried fish, curried chicken, and rice and peas. They had also changed clothes and were now in some short shorts and tank tops. Between the food and the beautiful girls I had to say my boy was doing quite well for himself.

He showed me to one of the three bedrooms off the hall. I found my bag sitting in there on the bed. I figured I'd wash up and throw on some sweats before dinner. As I unpacked Bizzie came in and threw the yellow knapsack onto the bed.

"Try on these, see if dem fit yuh," he said.

He went back to his girls in the kitchen before I had a chance to answer. I opened the bag, and inside wrapped in some clothes, I found two pistols. One was a Smith & Wesson .38 snub nosed revolver with an ankle holster, the other was a Glock 40 fit with a silencer and a hip holster. Plus way more bullets than I would need. I smelled the barrels of both weapons, and they had either never been fired or had recently been cleaned. They were perfect. More than I'd expected really. For most jobs I really only needed one pistol, but it didn't hurt to tote a back-up. As for the bullets, all it took was one. If I popped off even half of what was there, it would mean all the bullets in the world couldn't help me.

After a quick change and a shower I sat down for dinner with Bizzie and the Wonder Twins. They served us a delicious meal that tasted every bit as good as it smelled. Since the girls had changed I couldn't tell them apart. Best I could figure, Maxine was the one with the diamond stud ice cubes on her ears, and Marlene was the one that clung to Bizzie most. After dinner the twins cleared the table while we talked. When they were done straightening up they came back and joined us with Marlene sitting on Bizzie's lap, and Maxine coming and sitting on mine. It threw me at first, but my homie's demeanor let me know it was all good at his show. Of course I didn't protest to having this Jamaican Goddess sitting on me.

"So, the clothes dem fit yuh, rude bwoy?"

"Yeah, Biz. They nice...they real nice! Perfect fit."

"Sorry I couldn't find yuh a top hat, a cape, and a magic wand," he said laughing.

The twins exchanged confused glances missing the joke.

"Nah, playa, I'm cool right there. If I pop up at Asylum in the top hat, they might send me to the asylum for real."

He raised his eyebrows as he recognized what the play was. He sat back nodding his head, realizing that the club was a good look. Heads in the 'hood knew Wolf went to the club every couple of weeks. He said, "So, yuh plannin' fi tear de club up? Might jus' work."

"I don't make it do what it do, homie...I just help it happen."

"Mi 'av a 'bredrin' work security. Won't be a problem gett'n in that piece. Sampson gonna 'av us front row inna' de V.I.P."

"No, no, no," interrupted Marlene, "Bizzie, you promised, no more clubbing."

The girls both pouted in a way that let me know it was hard for a man not to let them have their way. Responding to the confused look on my face, Maxine explained to me, "See ummmmm...What's your name again?"

"Call 'im Lexus, like de coup, baby," said Bizzie.

153

"Okay. Well, Lexus, Bizzie promised us he didn't want to be a player anymore. We keep him well entertained here at home."

"Plus, there's two of us! What more could you want?" Marlene added, grinding seductively against Bizzie.

"But, baby...we goin' on a business run," he pleaded.

"Only business at Asylum is 'ho' business," countered Maxine.

I noted that the twins had a slight accent, but still spoke very properly. It almost made them sound British. I figured them for either college girls or society types. Bizzie had made a good catch and was having it his way. I didn't want to rock his boat so I said, "Homie, it'd probably be better if I flew solo on this joint. I know you could go if I had needed you, but let's not upset the ladies."

"Dem no call it Asylum fi nothin'. It get crazy in there...It betta' if mi roll wid' yuh."

"Bizzie," whined the twins in unison.

He waved them off. They settled down, defeated.

"I appreciate all your help, B...but on the real, I got it from here," I said.

"Yuh sure?"

His eyes said he was hungry to do whatever he could to help. I knew it was genuine. The bond him and me shared form childhood was strong. I decided to ask him one more favor. "Well, now that you mention it...I could use a clean set of wheels and a plug with your security connect to get me in V.I.P."

"No problem!" he replied, and we all laughed at the irony of him closing the deal with the national slogan.

154

With that settled, we adjourned to the living room. We stretched out on the plush leather sofas watching "Man on Fire" on the plasma screen. At first the girls complained about watching it for the umpteenth time, but Bizzie rolled up some premium Jamaican weed and smoked it with them, and that seemed to ease their pain. I didn't smoke with them, never touched the stuff, but just from sitting in the room I caught a mean contact high. We all got real cozy snuggled up in pairs, me with Maxine, and Bizzie with Marlene. When the flick was over my head was spinning from the weed, so I got up and got ready to call it a night.

As I walked to my room Bizzie called after me, "Lexus, Maxine say she wan' come tuck yuh in!"

I heard some laughter from him and the girls after he said it, so I figured it was a joke. "Whatever's clever, playboy. Sound like your girl ready to leave the wimp and choose the pimp!" I shot back to a response of heavy laughter. On that note I went to my room and started changing for bed.

I was shirtless in my sweat pants when I heard a faint knock at the door. Before I could say "Come in," Maxine stepped in the door. I was surprised partly because she had actually come to my room, but even more because she was wearing a chemise that came to her mid thighs. Baby girl had a body that wouldn't quit. I stood speechless ogling what seemed like miles of bare flesh and curves.

"See something you like?" she asked, smiling.

"Maxine, you put the 'PH' in phat, but what's good?" I felt kinda guilty standing half naked in a room with my man's half naked girlfriend. We shared everything growing up, but I wasn't sure if that extended to his women.

"Bizzie said you might be confused. He said just tell you 'whenever, whatever.'"

155

"Oh! Okay, then it's all good if we hang out...But lemme ask you, how does this sit with you?" I asked.

"As far as..." She didn't catch on to what I was getting at.

"Well, I just mean you don't have to be in here if you don't want to."

She said, "I'm not Bizzie's whore, if that's what you mean."

"That's not what I meant. Sorry you took it that way. I just meant there's no pressure."

"Oh...Well, my sister's sleeping in Bizzie's room tonight, and three's a crowd if you get my meaning."

She had solved a puzzle I had in the back of my head all day. Jamaican men are notorious for being anti-oral sex, and my homie was no exception. So, ever since he'd introduced me to his "two" girlfriends I'd been wondering how he held it down. No oral sex had to make it pretty hard to have a threesome. Apparently the twins took turns.

"In that case, you're more than welcome to stay in here with me," I said.

"Actually, this is my room."

"Then I guess that makes me your guest," I smiled.

She laughed. "I like you; you're cute."

"I aim to please." I flirted.

"I'm very pleased looking at your body." She came closer to me and ran her fingertips lightly across my ice hard chest.

We stood there exchanging sexual innuendos for a little while. Our minds were on the same thing. We turned down the covers and climbed in bed. I think the weed had us both feeling ambitious. There was a vibe between us, but when we started fooling around under the covers, I knew where things were headed and my thoughts went to Chaine. I'd be lying if I said I didn't want Maxine, because I did. At the same time I didn't. I felt conflicted. There I was, in bed with a top flight island princess, and unable to close the deal. Maxine took notice that I'd suddenly become apprehensive.

"What's the matter?" she asked.

"I can't do this."

"They won't hear us if that's what you're worried about. God knows, they probably doing..." She didn't finish her sentence, and a slightly pained expression crept onto her face.

"It bothers you that he's with her?" I asked cautiously. I was aware I was on a slippery slope, and I didn't want to throw salt in my man's game.

"No," she lied. "I know where I fit in. I'm the third wheel in this relationship."

"I thought twins were supposed to share everything?" I joked.

"Ha, ha, ha," she mock laughed. Then she got serious again. "Right now AIDS is running rampant in Jamaica. These men are not to be trusted. At least this way is safe. Bizzie is only sleeping with me and my sister. Not to mention, he's good to us."

"Ya'll got a good thing going. It's safe and it's smart...Don't let it bother you too much. Look at it like this, at least when he sleeps with someone else she looks just like you. That might not even be considered cheating," I explained.

"You men have no clue," she laughed, shaking her head. Little did she know I did. She longed for that one on one emotional connection. I knew exactly what she was missing because it was the very thing I had found with Chaine. What they had going on really was good for a temporary arrangement, and I was reluctant to make waves. Their three-way wouldn't last forever, but I wasn't going to be what broke it up.

"So, what's your problem?" she asked, remembering that I was the one stutter stepping. "Are you suddenly allergic to pretty girls? I told you, Bizzie is cool. He must think very highly of you."

"Actually it's not that. I really want to, but I can't. See...I'm with someone, and for once in my life I'm pretty sure she's the one I wanna be with."

"Tall, dark, handsome, <u>and</u> faithful! Some girls have all the luck. I understand, and I envy her," she smiled.

"Don't get it twisted, Maxine," I said, playfully feeling on her butt, "if I was gonna wander, I'd surely want you to be the one to lead me astray!"

She laughed, slapping my hand away. I was glad her feelings weren't hurt. We snuggled up together and pretty soon the Sandman came for the both of us. Before I drifted off I wondered where Chaine was, and if she was thinking of me right then.

158

Chapter 9

The following morning Bizzie woke me up at the crack of dawn. He took me for a ride to see the lay of the land around the club. We talked on the way, but he never brought up whatever went down with Maxine and me. Either he didn't care, or somehow knew there was nothing to tell. We rode around all the streets near the spot so that when I got ready to get gone I would know where I was going. From a parking space across the street he pointed out all the club's entrances and exits. He also described the entire layout down to where it got particularly crowded when something popped off. I already knew the basics from a schematic of the building Nana Helen added to the file, but his extra input was the icing on the cake that made it like I'd already been inside.

We were back in the house before the twins ever even woke up. I spent the day lounging around the house with Bizzie and the girls. Usually before a job I liked to strategize, but this job had so many variables that I just had to play it by ear and wait for the opportunity to present itself. Other than that, I was ready. I just had to hope that all the jobs before this one had prepared me well enough for what I hoped would be my last piece of work…At least my last piece of work as far as hits for hire went.

Around nine that evening Bizzie sent the twins to pick up my ride. While I dressed he told me he'd called his man Sampson, and he'd be expecting me. He also made one last offer to roll with me, but I told him I was better off flying solo. He accepted it and wished me luck. When he said it, I got a tingle. Twice in two days on this same job someone had wished me luck. I shook it off as I smoothed a few wrinkles from the linen cream colored Helmut Lang suit I wore over a white button down shirt and tan lizard Bally's. With my top two buttons undone I had the trendy Caribbean night life look down cold. I strapped on my two pistols and I was good to go. Bizzie looked me over and nodded his approval.

We walked out front just in time to see Marlene pulling up in the truck. I looked at Bizzie wondering why he'd want me to use his truck on my mission. Before he spoke we were interrupted by the sound of tires squealing around the corner. The driver downshifted, and went from flying to an impossibly smooth stop right in front of us. Bizzie smiled like a Cheshire cat as Maxine stepped out of a brand new Alpine white BMW M6 coupe. My jaw dropped looking at one of the most impressive sports cars known to man.

"You might as well 'av a magic carpet fi go wid' yuh act," he said.

"True dat, homie," were all the words I could muster. I hugged the twins, and gave Bizzie a pound before hopping in the Beamer and firing it up. As I pulled off I could only hope I'd get to touch all seven gears between there and the club.

I had hoped to arrive early, but judging from the traffic and the swollen crowd, Asylum was already jumping by 10. I pulled up real slow bumping a Maxi Priest groove. The gawkers gawked, and heads in the long line in front of the club craned their necks to see who I was. A security guard saw the ride and moved some orange cones, waving me into a V.I.P. parking lot around the side. Another crowd of more well dressed club goers milled around a separate V.I.P. entrance. They seemed less impressed with me than the people in front. I stepped out of the ride and handed the valet my keys and five euros. When I asked he pointed out the dude who had moved the cones as Sampson. He was already walking over to me.

I scanned the lot that was filled with Lexes, Beamers, and Benzes and saw nothing a dude on Wolf's level would be riding. Sampson introduced himself and was just about to escort me in past security when Wolf's motorcade arrived. In front were two men on motorcycles armed with sub-machine guns who pulled up first, parked, and took up positions near the door. All the action outside the club froze as two black Humvees rolled into the lot escorting a tinted out ice blue Rolls Royce Phantom. The men in the Hummers in front and in back of the Phantom jumped out. The eight men formed a tight perimeter around the man getting out of the Phantom with two women on his arms. The men studied the crowd cautiously, and I recognized their formation as a "double diamond" perimeter. It was smart, effective, and professional. They had him protected at every angle. I never even got a clean look at the man or his companions, but I was certain it was Wolf. Their entire entourage was swiftly whisked inside, leaving the first two guards standing post outside. When they'd gone inside the crowd instantly came back to life as if someone had pressed the play button setting things back into motion.

Wolf's security was tight so far. If I'd even so much as reached for my heat I would have been dead as Dillinger. Had JFK's security been so thorough, he'd have never eaten a bullet. As soon as the fanfare died down, Sampson took me inside. We by-passed the metal detector arcs and wands that all the patrons were subjected to. I had no doubt that Wolf and his crew had skipped that part too. So, now it was just him and them versus me. We took a corridor that brought us into the back of the V.I.P. I tried to hand Sampson some euros, but he waved the money off and kept it moving. Now it was up to me.

The club was jumping. Things were already in full swing in V.I.P., so I knew the main floor had to be equally, if not more, crazy. Players drinking champagne straight from the bottles had scantily clad women on the dance floor doing dances that looked like sex with clothes on! Strobe lights pulsated and lasers flashed in syncopation with heavy bass driven dance hall rhythms.

I two-stepped my way through the crowd peeping the scene. On the floor I spotted six of the eight men from Wolf's entourage getting up close and personal with women. I was glad to see that they'd let their guard down already, and I began scanning the room for my mark. He was nowhere to be seen on the dance floor or at the bar. At the other end of the room were a half dozen or so booths. Three of them were occupied, but only one had the thick red velvet curtain drawn. One of the adjacent two had a crew of dreads popping bottles. The other had some reggae artist I didn't recognize, profiling with a couple of women. That meant that tonight's lucky contestant had to be behind door number two.

I resisted the urge to just pull the heat out and dump 16 hot ones through the curtain. There was a good chance I'd get him, but a fair chance I could miss him too; not to mention the two women and two security guards who were no doubt in the booth with him. They weren't on the contract, but I'd be willing to forget that if they got in the way later. Within 20 minutes of arriving Wolf's boys were already slipping. Before the night was over they'd probably only get more lax. With that in mind, I adjourned to the bar where I had a direct line of sight to the booth. From there I could chill and not appear to be studying what I was studying.

The curtain on the booth stayed closed. I tried to steal the occasional glance inside when a waitress brought drinks by the bottle, but I couldn't get much of a look. After a while I started chatting up this caramel complexioned Amazon so as not to seem the suspicious lonely stranger. She had to have been every bit of six feet tall, slim but curvy, and she was wearing a fishnet bodysuit with a bikini underneath. I had watched her on the dance floor, for a while and it seemed like every jam was her jam. She danced vigorously to every cut the D.J. spun. After she'd worked up a sweat to an Elephant Man track, I caught her by the bar and bought her a drink. From talking to her I gleaned that she came to the club every weekend. Her name was Shonda, Shalonda, Sharonda or some shit like that. She was what you'd call a dance hall queen. As long as the music kept pumping and the drinks kept flowing, I had her full attention.

Just after midnight the curtain came back on Wolf's booth, and I actually saw him across the crowded room for the first time. I wasn't close enough to see detailed features other than his jet black skin that looked navy blue in the low light. His two guards sat on the ends of the semi-circular leather couch, and his two female companions sat on either side of him. Best I could tell, one girl looked to be an Asian chick with long black hair and a Chinese dress. A China doll. The other woman's hair had to be a dye job. It was bright fuchsia. She had some type of body glitter on her skin that made her sparkle. The poor lighting made it hard to discern her race from a distance. Both women snuggled up close to Wolf whispering things in his ear that made him smile periodically. If they played him that close all night, they very well might end up joining him on his trip.

Most of the bottles on their table looked empty. There was a haze around them that looked like it was left behind by weed smoke. I wasn't sure if the guards had been smoking and drinking, but even just a little contact high would slow them down enough for me to get the drop on them. I decided to make my move before my small tactical advantage wore off.

I took "What's-her-face" by the hand and gestured at the dance floor to which she happily obliged. She was tipsy and wild, which worked well for my play. We blended in perfectly with all the other revelers. The remainder of Wolf's clique was all on the dance floor or posted up in dark corners with the women they'd met. When we got on the floor, I saw one of Wolf's two guards get up and head to the restroom, leaving him behind with just one guard and two women. Big mistake. It was now or never.

I danced "What's-her-face" through the thick crowd over toward the edge of the dance floor that faced the booth. I intended to keep it simple. My plan was to ease her as close to the edge of the crowd as possible, and when she got to 'dropping it like it's hot', I would drop two hot ones off in Wolf. Then I'd just dip off through the crowd. Hopefully people would take time from partying to notice he was hit, and the momentum of the crowd's mad dash for the exits would sweep me right out the door.

I maneuvered into position. Wolf and company were oblivious to my presence as I wrapped my hand around the pistol's rubber grip. I stood behind my party girl as she "backed that thang up" on me. Timing her movements, I began to draw as she started to "dip it low." When she bent over I was just about to fire, but the girl with the bright ass hair was kissing Wolf. I hesitated only for a moment; that kiss saved his life. I held the gun down at my side waiting for them to finish the oral exam.

Their kiss ended, and while the fuchsia-haired girl slowly pulled away I got ready to make it happen.

164

For some reason my attention stayed on her for an extra couple of seconds, and I got a good look at her for the first time. Beyond the hair, my eyes locked onto her face. My heart pounded triple time, as though trying to beat its way out of my chest. I recognized her, but my mind and my common sense were in conflict. I stood still in a daze trying to process what I was seeing; trying to make sense of reality. Things went black for a moment as my eyes closed involuntarily, trying to reset. Maybe I'd closed them hoping to open them and waken from a bad dream, but the picture was the same. Sitting right next to Wolf, the woman who had just been kissing him…was Chaine.

I was so shocked that my muscles relaxed for a split second and I dropped my pistol. Before it hit the ground I regained some of my senses and quickly bent to catch it, bobbling it for a second before getting hold of it. At that instant "Sha-ra-londa" was coming up from "dropping it like it's hot." Our bodies collided, and she flew forward to the floor. I hadn't been drinking, so I maintained my balance. When she went down the crowd parted and people looked at her like she was crazy. Everyone was so focused on her that no one saw me tuck the pistol. We had everyone's attention as she cursed me out in staccato patois while I helped her up. I looked up and saw that included Chaine. Our eyes met, and I saw the flicker of recognition in her. I was a small ship tossed violently on a stormy sea of emotion.

She stared.

I stared.

The pulsating strobe lights set the scene in slow motion. The music was gone, and only the heavy bass line remained. The look on her face said she was very confused. The look on my face said I was confused and furious. She had been kissing another man.

All thoughts of the job at hand left my mind. My blood boiled at 500°. Had I been a cartoon I would have had smoke coming out of my ears. It was surreal that I went from cold and calculating to heated and irrational in a heartbeat. I left "What's-her-name" standing there yelling at herself and walked toward the booth, toward Chaine.

I'd made it to ten feet away when I was intercepted by the guard who was returning from the bathroom. He was a lightweight. I shifted him off balance, shoved him out of the way, and kept walking. The second guard stood up and reached for his heat. Without taking my eyes off of Chaine, I put my hands out at my sides so dude could see I wasn't holding or reaching. He paused, giving me a moment to state my business. Wolf leaned forward, looking me over with a scowl. Chaine shook her head "no" ever so slightly, with a look in her eyes that begged me not to blow up the spot.

"Whass'up, Skittles?" I addressed Chaine. "You think your friends would mind if I borrowed you for a dance."

She looked relieved.

"Find somewhere else fi beg a dance," Wolf coolly stated.

"I don't do no beggin' brotha…And if I'm not mistaken I asked her, not you," I arrogantly replied.

"Bwoy, you know who mi is?" he roared.

"I don't give a fu…"

"I'll dance with him," Chaine said, cutting me off. Then she whispered something in Wolf's ear. Whatever she said seemed to put him at ease and diffuse the tension between us.

As I turned and headed to the dance floor I saw Wolf's entire goon squad was behind me. They were mean mugging me something terrible. The one I'd

166

pushed reached in his waistband, but Wolf gave them some type of signal and they parted. I walked through with Chaine close behind me. I'd never even seen that they'd mobbed up behind me seven deep. My emotions had me oblivious to the danger.

Gregory Isaac's "Night Nurse" slowed the tempo in the packed V.I.P. area. While all the other couples swayed closely grinding to the music, Chaine and I danced with an awkward space between us.

"So, what you tell ole' boy to save him from getting his head busted?" I asked, breaking the silence between us.

She rolled her eyes knowing she'd actually saved me. "I told him you were my cousin...Lex, what the hell are you doing here?"

"What am I doing here?" I repeated. "I'm here on business. You need to tell me what you're doing here. I just seen you all up in homeboy's mouth...you told me you had to work."

She paused, caught out there. She chose her words carefully before speaking. "Look, I can explain. That was business; I swear."

"Business?" I looked at her crazy.

"Yeah, Parks is a client."

"Ooohhhh! I get it now." It was all crystal clear. All the pieces suddenly fit together. She looked at me hopeful that I understood. I laughed at the irony of the situation. "So, Wolf is your client, and that, what I saw, was business?"

"Basically, yes."

"Bomb ass pussy...nice clothes...expensive gifts. I guess it's my fault for not figuring it out sooner."

"What?" A bewildered look came across her face.

"Guess they wasn't bullshittin' when they told me 'the only business at Asylum is ho business.'"

167

"Hold the fuck up!" She stopped dancing, or pretending to dance, and her face got bright red. First time I'd ever heard her curse. "Sweetie, you got it twisted. I'm not some fucking hooker! I know you're confused and upset, but if you let me..."

"You right. I am confused," I said, cutting her off, "Maybe you can enlighten me. I'm tryna' figure out why you ain't charge me?"

"Charge you?" Her lower lip quivered, and tears welled up in her eyes. She struggled to maintain her composure.

"Matter of fact...I always pay my bills. What I owe you?" I asked as I pulled a thick wad of euros from my pocket.

"Lex, you acting a damn fool right now. I know you're mad about what you saw, but there's a good explanation."

"A good explanation? A good explanation why you said you had to work, and I catch you in the Caribbean kissing another man?"

"Yes."

"G'head explain." This, I had to hear.

"I can't...At least not here," she said, as she scanned the room to see if we were being watched.

"Why, 'cause your boy and his crew is here?" I said, crossing my arms. I was pretty much fed up with her games. I was furious, but I just had to hear this "good explanation." If there were some words that could make sense of what I'd seen, I needed to hear them.

"It's complicated."

"Well un-complicate it," I demanded.

"Alright," she sighed, "Did you drive here?"

"Yeah."

"Can you meet me by the main entrance in five minutes?

"I'm not really sure it's worth my time," I responded scornfully.

"I don't deserve that," she protested. "When I explain it all to you, you'll understand."

"I'm gone in five minutes, "I said, walking away.

She was just coming out the front door when I pulled up. I flicked my headlights twice, and she quickly hopped in. As I pulled away from the club she looked over her shoulder, checking to see if she'd been followed. I made a series of quick turns and that seemed to ease her nervousness.

"Nice car," she said, getting comfortable in the cushy leather seat.

"Do you have something to tell me or not?" I demanded, cutting the small talk short.

"Turn here," she said, directing me onto the highway. "I'm gonna tell you the truth, but I need to know I can trust you."

"Come on with all the games already, Chaine." I accelerated boldly on the dark stretch of highway leading out of Kingston.

"Oh, it's 'Chaine' again, now," she smiled. "How'd you know not to call me by my name back at the club?"

"Just a hunch"

"Very perceptive."

"I been 'incognegro' a time or two before. Just 'cause you made a fool of me, don't make me stupid," I spat.

"That's what you think?"

I didn't respond, just kept pushing the powerful whip deeper into the darkness.

"Alright, this is the deal..." she bit her bottom lip nervously, which made me nervous. I knew she was about to drop a bomb on me. I braced for impact. "You did see me kissing Parks. And he is my client, in a way…but I swear I wasn't sleeping with him."

"You told me that already. That's your good explanation?" I yelled. I violently brought the car to an abrupt stop, pulling to the side of the road. "I ain't for the bullshit, you can tell that story walkin'. Now or never, tell the truth, or we part ways right here!"

My threat to put her out of the car was a serious one, and she took it as such. I was that mad and frustrated. She exhaled long and deeply. I turned off my lights and the car's interior became pitch black. Alone in the dark it was just me, her, and the truth I had yet to meet. I sat anxiously waiting on her to make the introduction.

The privacy of the darkness was like a confessional, and it helped her confession flow freely. "I'm not down here to sleep with Winston Parks…I came here… to kill him. That's what I do, Lex. This is who I am."

In the darkness I saw white flashes, and I realized that for a few moments I'd forgotten to breathe. My brain worked overtime trying to make sense of what I'd heard. Beside me I heard Chaine fidgeting nervously waiting on me to make some type of response. There were so many thoughts and emotions flying around inside me that I couldn't' grab hold of just one. Each moment of silence tortured her. As my mind cleared and my boiling blood came down to a simmer, I finally found one emotion that I could take hold of…I felt relief. I was in love with her, and what she'd told me was something I could deal with. My real problem was how she would react when I told her I was in the same game.

"Say something," she said, her voice almost a whisper.

I turned the headlights on and pulled back onto the road. When I finally made it to 7th gear, I spoke. "You don't gotta worry about me telling. Your secret is safe. I ain't no rat."

"I know you're not gonna tell. I was never worried about that."

"You know, you coulda just told me."

"I never had the chance."

"Guess not," I replied, smirking as I recalled how often we'd made love.

"So, you're not mad?"

"Don't get it fucked up, Chaine. I'm real mad I saw you kissing Wolf...but as far as the other part, I can't be mad what you do. Long as it ain't ho'in!" We shared a brief laugh. "That doesn't necessarily make you who you are."

I could tell she was very surprised at my reaction. In the moments she'd spent waiting for me to reply she seemed tortured. Now that I was telling her it was alright, she was so relieved. After thinking she was a high end call girl, finding out she was a hitter was definitely a relief for me. She said, "You're taking all this really well, considering..."

"Still a lot you don't know about me," I exhaled.

"Yeah, like what you're doing here," she demanded.

"I told you, I'm here on business."

"You came all the way to the Caribbean to tear down buildings? Nobody on this whole island can do that? You must think I'm stupid. Please tell me you're not down here on a 're-up' mission."

"Re-up?" I repeated.

"You know, 're-up', as in buying drugs. Jamaica is known for...well, you know what they known for," she said, as she studied my face for tells.

"No!" I practically shouted. "I told you. I don't sell no dope...Funny, you ain't have no problem kissing all on the dope man in the club."

She released a frustrated sigh. "Are you fucking that giraffe I saw you dancing with...Wait a minute, how do you know Winston Parks is a dope man? Better yet, you called him 'Wolf' before, how'd you know his handle? I never called him by that name." She eyed me suspiciously.

"I'm aware of my surroundings." I shrugged.

"Now you're the one playing games. I was straight up with you, now you need to be straight up with me."

"It's complicated."

"Well un-complicate it," she said, throwing my own line back at me. She leaned back waiting on my response. I could tell there was no room for manipulation or well crafted tales. The only break in her no-nonsense demeanor came when she saw a sign she recognized. She said, "You should probably take this next turn-off," and went right back to waiting on my explanation.

I didn't protest because in truth I'd just been driving without a particular destination in mind. She seemed to know where she was going, so I followed her directions. I realized I'd driven quite a ways from Kingston. For a moment I thought about the job, but it was obvious which one I'd chosen as more important. There was no way I'd get another crack at Wolf. Now him and his people knew my face, so I couldn't even get close. The job was a wash.

"You were saying..." she pressed, reminding me that she was still impatiently awaiting my response.

"Chaine, what if I told you we were both here for the same thing?"

"What?" she asked, clearly puzzled.

I exhaled, and out came the truth, "I'm a contract killer. Wolf was my mark." There it was. I had shot it to her straight with no chaser. I really didn't know what to expect as a response. In my mind I'd only considered best case scenarios, but there were a lot of ways it could end badly. We were after all, two predators. There wasn't much I could do besides watch it unfold.

Her laughter startled me. I studied her in disbelief trying to make sure she really was laughing. Laughter was just about the last thing I'd expected as a response. In Jamaica they say, "The truth can often pass as a joke," and as she laughed that pretty laugh that I was so in love with, I realized the saying was true. When her laughter finally abated I said, "It's your turn to say something."

"Take the next right," she replied.

We'd driven to an area near Hellshire Beach that was developed but purposely left looking rural to maintain ambience. Back from the narrow road were multi-million dollar homes and villas. The playground of the rich. A long dirt road bordered by manicured shrubs and flowers led us to a charming secluded villa by the water. I pulled up and parked behind a cherry red Porche Cayenne SUV that was sitting in the driveway.

"This is your place?" I asked, impressed with the island hideaway.

"A friend's."

"So, what now?" I asked.

"Well, we've pretty much ruined this job for each other. Neither of us'll be able to get near Parks again."

"Probably not."

"I figured I'd go inside and make love to my man...no sense wasting a beautiful moonlit night in paradise."

She stepped out of the car and closed the door. A motion sensor triggered interior lights and sconces along the walkway. After walking a few feet she paused. As if she knew I was watching, she seductively bent over to take off the strappy Via Spiga pumps she was wearing. Her Dolce dress clung to her and in the low light I could almost tell she wasn't wearing panties. That was more invitation than I needed. A few days prior I'd never have imagined things playing out the way they did, but as it unfolded I was happy it had. Having the truth out in the open between her and me felt like a huge weight had been taken off my shoulders.

I grabbed my phone and typed a simple text message to Bizzie. It simply read, "working late." It let him know I was still on the job and probably wouldn't be back anytime soon. It was a lie, but the truth would have been too much to type, especially considering that I had yet to even tell him about Chaine.

With checking in taken care of, I followed her inside. I was already aroused at the prospect of making love to her again. When I walked through the door, she was standing naked in the foyer. She'd let down her fuchsia dyed hair and her slinky Dolce dress was a ring at her feet. It was like being in a role playing fantasy. This Chaine was one that I had yet to meet. She stood there in front of me, nipples becoming erect in the evening air, with a look on her face that challenged me to take her. Before I approached her, I smiled ever so slightly at a thought that crossed my mind. I was about to make love at a cost of $750K. This certainly had to be some of the most expensive pussy in history. I intended to enjoy it for all it was worth.

For each step I took toward her, she took a step away from me, leading me into the spacious villa with a sly come hither stare. The villa was rustic with elegant appointments, like wicker furniture alongside expensive sculptures. As I followed her into the living area I saw a glass cabinet with three Grammy awards in it. There was also a white Steinway grand piano in the corner that I hadn't noticed until Chaine backed into it ending my pursuit. Whoever owned the place was obviously someone in the music industry and probably someone I'd heard of.

"Now that I caught you, what do I win?" I asked, as I eliminated the last bit of space between us.

"Whatever you want," she replied.

I leaned in and deeply inhaled the fragrance emanating from her neck. She smelled like warm vanilla sugar. She leaned her head back, inviting me as she undid my shirt buttons and began to remove my suit jacket. As she slid my jacket off, her hand brushed against the butt of my pistol. She tensed up and a frown eased onto her face.

"What's wrong?" I asked.

After a long slow sigh she said, "Just wondered what happens to 'us' after this."

"Nothing has to change."

"We both know we got a problem."

"Not both of us," I said, as I took both of my pistols and laid them on the piano. "This shit is over for me. I'm retiring; this was supposed to be my last job."

"It must be nice to be able to just up and quit."

I put my arms around her and pulled her close to me. "You could quit, too. We could leave this game behind together. Start fresh."

"It's not that simple, Lex. I got money saved, but not nearly enough to retire."

"Fuck the money! We can make it. Be like normal folks." I resisted the urge to tell her my financial situation or about the heist I had lined up. I wanted to see where she stood minus the money.

"I love you...and I wanna be with you, but I can't work a 9 to 5. Maybe if I finished this job, then we could..."

"Chaine, you talkin' crazy! The spot is blown with Wolf. Leave that shit alone. Going after him you gonna fuck around and end up with your name on a contract."

"There's still a way I could..."

"Leave it alone!" I shouted, cutting her off. "Ain't no amount of money worth your life."

"You're right," she whispered. On the floor she traced small circles on the hardwood surface with her toe. Her demeanor was like an admonished child. I'd never seen her in such a delicate state.

I felt bad for yelling at her. I sat on the piano bench and she sat on my lap. I put my arms around her and said, "Look, I know you probably a good contractor. Maybe even better than me," I lied, "but I couldn't stand to see anything bad happen to you. Let me get us out of this and we can both close this chapter...start fresh somewhere, and do 'us.'"

With glossy eyes she sniffled and preempted a falling tear with the back of her hand. "You promise?" she asked.

"I promise."

I held her face in my hands and kissed her. It's funny how high emotion and unbridled passion seem to live right next door to each other. After a few moments of kissing, she was straddling me on the bench and rocking her hips against mine. I explored her body with my hands as she slid my shirt off. I cupped her breasts and alternated licking each of her erect nipples. It felt so good to be that connected to her again. My tongue danced on her tender flesh. As she felt my erection swelling beneath her she reached down undoing my belt and my pants, releasing me from the captivity of my clothes. She adjusted so that I wasn't penetrating her, but my hardness rubbed against her moistening flesh. Pushing my shoulders back against the piano, she gave me an intimate lap dance.

When she was satisfied I was thoroughly aroused, she stood up. I rose thinking she wanted to adjourn to a bedroom. My pants fell to my ankles, so I stepped out of them and my shoes. I looked at her curiously as she sat back down on the piano bench. She said, "Lights...Music," and for a second I thought she was talking to me, but then all the lights dimmed. From a stereo system I couldn't see, Bob Marley and Lauryn Hill began to have verbal posthumous intercourse on the track "Turn Your Lights Down Low." The sultry island groove surrounded us. It was incredible how perfect a mood she'd set. She looked at me and smiled like she knew what I was thinking, and then she reached out and grabbed my hips, pulling me closer to her.

She took me in her mouth, working me slowly at first, but she gradually increased her pace as the act excited her. She devoured me with fantastic enthusiasm. Felt like not only did my toes curl, but every bone in my body curled. She took the hand that I didn't have bracing myself against the piano and guided it to the top of her head. I grabbed a handful of her fuchsia locks. Don't ask me how she knew I'd wanted to do that, she just did. It's a guy thing, but she let me have it my way. I leaned my head back and watched the ceiling fan slowly twirling above us. Watching it spin made me feel like I was climbing a spiral stairway to heaven. As she got me closer and closer to ecstasy I called her name. Sprung wasn't an adequate word for how open she had me.

Before I came, I stopped her. I wanted to be inside her, to feel her. When I tried to lift her onto the piano, she resisted. She took me by the hand and led me through a set of French doors onto the patio. The view was spectacular. The back of the property sat on a secluded cove, and sitting low out over the ocean was a nearly full moon that looked close enough to take a bite of. In the moonlight with the body glitter on, Chaine sparkled like a gem. She leaned over the wrought iron railing that encircled the patio and looked out at the view.

"Beautiful, isn't it?" she asked.

I looked at her leaned on that railing in her slightly bowlegged stance and I said, "Perfect." Chaine was my ocean and my moon, and she was perfect. The view paled in comparison.

I went and stood behind her. She parted her legs slightly and let me enter her from behind. I kissed her neck and massaged her breasts while I stroked her slowly. There wasn't a more perfect setting or a more perfect woman that I could imagine. I was living a dream, and at that moment it was worth every penny it was costing me. She gripped the railing tightly and pushed her hips back so I could go deeper. I obliged. She screamed out in pleasure loud enough for the thousands of stars that dotted the night sky to hear her. She thrashed wildly nearing climax. Before letting go she slowed our pace to a stop with me deep inside of her. We lingered like that for a few moments, just connected.

We moved over to a chaise lounge that was on the patio. I lay down and she got on top of me. She took hold of me and gently guided me inside her wetness. She closed the distance between us slowly, lowering herself onto me. Her pace was slow at first. She made it so that every trip I took inside of her was long and deliberate. I watched her over me sexily bite on her bottom lip. Looking up at her with a backdrop of stars she looked like an angel descending upon me from heaven. For the first time in my life, making love was a spiritual experience. I took hold of her hips and held tightly

178

matching her pace. She maintained control for most of the way, but when I saw her face and her chest redden I knew she was close. I thrust my hips beneath her, driving her to orgasm. The contraction of her walls and her flowing juices took me over the edge right behind her. We lay together in that position kissing passionately. I closed my eyes, but I still saw stars.

That night we made love again in the master suite. We explored each other until the wee hours of the morning. I fell asleep holding her, and we slept comfortably in a bed that faced a picture window with a view as breathtaking as the one from the patio.

Chapter 10

Chaine put that 'thang' on me something fierce! I slept like a baby until almost noon the following day. A strange noise brought me back from dreamland. The first thing I noticed when I woke up was that she wasn't in bed, but I figured she was probably in the kitchen fixing us brunch in paradise. Stood to reason she'd be hungry after the previous night's demonstration. I walked through the villa calling her name and got no response. I looked out front and saw only the M6. She was gone.

In the living room I found my clothes neatly folded on the piano bench. I finally identified the strange noise I'd heard as my phone that had vibrated its way off the coffee table and onto the floor. It still vibrated periodically indicating that I had a message. I dressed while I checked my message. It was a text from Bizzie. When I read it I was so shocked that the phone slid from my fingers and clattered across the floor. It read: "U R a magician! Hole in one. Let's celebrate!"

My mind knew what the message meant, but my heart had a hard time validating it. The room spun. When I regained my focus I was looking at the piano. There on top of it was my .38, still in the holster. My other pistol, the Glock with the silencer, was gone. In its place was a small yellow post-it note with seven words scrawled in Chaine's bubbly handwriting, "I'm sorry…This is who I am."

In front of my face I had a clear picture, but the reality of it burned my soul. Chaine had taken my pistol and gone after Wolf. Judging from Bizzie's message, she had apparently succeeded, and my homie thought it was my work. She had chosen the game over me. The woman I was in love with was in love with the same game I was trying to be done with. Strangely enough, it dawned on me that it was far less painful when I'd thought she was a high priced hooker.

For a few minutes I sat there half dressed trying to come to terms with the big mistake I'd made, and how much it hurt. The first woman I had fallen in love with had deceived and betrayed me. It wasn't so much that she had gone after Wolf, what was killing me was that she had chosen to do that over being with me. All the rules I'd followed before her had protected me from something like this ever happening, and now breaking those rules had proven to be a costly mistake. Not only was my heart broken, but I was out of $750K. Not nearly a "cheap lesson."

After five minutes I willed myself out of my dazed and confused state. My survival instincts kicked in and told me it was time to get gone. I couldn't even imagine how Chaine had pulled it off after leaving Wolf high and dry at the club. The words "hole in one" in Bizzie's message meant he'd been taken down with a headshot. After seeing Wolf's crib and how he rolled at the club, the technician in me was curious and impressed with Chaine's work. I had to push that aside. My first and only priority was to burn the road up. Wolf's people would be out in force looking for the shooter. At the top of their list of suspects would be any and every new face they'd seen hanging around. That list would most likely include the stranger he'd had words with the night before, and would most certainly include his new girlfriend with the bright red hair. If Chaine was as smart as I thought she was, she was already off the island.

When I hit the road I was grateful Bizzie had gotten me something fast. In my mad dash for Kingston's airport I almost wrecked while calling him to

181

tell him to meet me with my things and pick up the Beamer. The airport in Kingston was my closest shot to the next thing smoking. Originally, if the job had gone smoothly I'd planned to spend a few days kicking it with Bizzie afterwards and just fly back out of Montego Bay. On the off chance that sugar turned to shit, I had my second set of I.D.'s and an open ticket out of Kingston. Things were pretty shitty, and I just had to hope Wolf's men weren't on point enough to have the airports covered.

I pulled in front of the departure terminal, and I was relieved to see Bizzie's truck parked with him and the twins waiting on me. Their faces had puzzled expressions that begged to know what my rush to leave was. Bizzie no doubt assumed a clean hit didn't require a speedy exit, but he didn't ask questions and the girls followed his lead. I wished I didn't have to bail so fast, but I'd been sloppy and the cost was already too high. I gave him a pound and promised to tell him the "full 'undred" when I got back to N.Y.

I hugged the twins and as I handed Maxine the keys she held on to my hand. I walked her to the Beamer and opened the door for her. She put a foot inside and looked at me with dreamy rueful eyes. I already had an idea what she was thinking. She said, "Guess all the good ones really are taken...Maybe in another time, another place..."

"I wouldn't hope so fast."

She raised an eyebrow reminding me, "Your girlfriend?"

I exhaled, trying not to wear my heart on my sleeve. "Max, I got a good feeling she wasn't into me as much as I was into her."

"Her loss...Does that mean I maybe won't have to wait till next lifetime?"

Prey For Love

I smiled at her Erykah Badu reference. Perhaps she and I were kindred spirits. I wondered if I'd ever get a chance to really find out. "We'll see," I responded. My future was uncertain and that's all the answer I could give. The sound of a plane's engines reminded me I didn't have time for loafing. "Gotta fly," I said regretfully.

I leaned to place a goodbye kiss on her cheek. She turned her head at the last second, and we shared a brief, but wet and passionate kiss. Caught me by surprise, but I needed it. My pride was hurt after being tossed aside and her kiss reminded me I was wanted. I smiled as I walked away tasting her strawberry lip gloss. When I passed Bizzie sitting in the truck, he grinned, giving me a head nod and a thumbs up. As I walked through the automated glass doors, he and Maxine burned tires pulling out from the terminal.

Once inside I cautiously looked around for anyone who seemed to be looking for me. I checked in for the 1:30 direct flight to JFK. I kept the .38 on my hip all the way to the metal detectors where I ditched it and my phone in the bathroom. There were no henchmen on the prowl looking for me, and even if there had been it dawned on me that they probably weren't prepared to light up an airport. I boarded my flight and got out of Dodge. On one hand I was thankful to be leaving unscathed, but on the other, the whole trip had been a tremendous loss.

Since I'd had to leave Jamaica in such a hurry, there was no Bubby waiting to meet me when I flew into JFK. I could have called him and he would have been there despite the short notice, but I was in the mood to be alone. I needed time to think. There was no doubt in my mind that some of what I was going through was written all over my face, and anyone who knew me would see it. With my usual poker face failing me I cleared customs as fast as I could and caught a cab for home.

Coming into my empty place was strange after everything that had happened. I felt like an alien in my own space. Like I was a character, a fake "Lex" who'd somehow transcended the confines of a bad dream, and usurped the real Lex's life. The real Lex was a smooth, calculating professional with all his shit together, while the other was a square; a passenger on the emotional rollercoaster. A mark.

After turning off the alarm I grabbed my phone and sent a text to Nana Helen telling her the gig was a wash. She called back a few moments after I sent the message. I was sure she was curious about the how's and the why's, but I didn't feel like explaining or lying, so I let her call roll over to my voice mail. I held the phone for a few minutes contemplating checking my voice messages, but I didn't because I knew that was the other Lex, the sucker for love, wanting to know if Chaine had called. I was out of the murder for hire game, but I assigned myself one last contract. My lovesick alter-ego, the part of me that had risked life, limb, and big money for a beautiful woman, had to die. In essence, I was my last mark.

I spent the next few days holed up in my loft. I worked out, read, and even caught a little television. Gradually the hurt and the underlying feeling of longing I was feeling for Chaine started to dissipate, leaving behind just a dull aching hurt. When the hurt finally did start to wear off it was replaced by a deep distinct feeling of regret. I could tell the regret was going nowhere fast. Perhaps that was for the best, and maybe it was something I could build a foundation on to keep me from ever making the same mistakes ever again.

Iyanla Vanzant said, "The way to move forward was often with a broken heart," and I now understood what that meant. There was a piece of me that Chaine had taken with her when she left, and as the days rolled by it became apparent to me that I was just going to have to live with that.

On Tuesday night I was all but fed up with Toni Braxton singing about love and loss while I sat around feeling sorry for myself. The job at Imperial needed to get done, and I figured that securing my future would be an appropriate end to that part of my life. My come-up would be my closure. I decided that the following morning I would get up early and go case the spot. If things looked good, Mila and I could take them down the following week.

I called Bubby to see about some wheels. It was short notice, but he promised he'd have something for me. He was glad to hear from me and offered to do whatever driving I needed done, but I told him I was straight. For a moment I could tell he was about to ask me about Jamaica. He paused and left it alone knowing that business remained unspoken. I was glad he left it alone.

The following morning I got up at the crack of dawn, dressed and went downstairs. Parked directly across from my place I found a black Chrysler 300C with dark tinted windows. The keys were over the visor and it had a full tank of gas. The car was clean and inconspicuous, just like Bubby had promised. I fired it up and took the short ride up to 47th street, stopping off to grab a tall cup of coffee and a bagel on the way.

It was a little after 6 a.m. when I parked a couple doors down and across the street from the Imperial Diamond Jewelry Co. I was early and still had a good hour before merchants on Jeweler's Row started preparing to open their doors at 8 a.m. I eased my seat back and chilled out, patiently waiting and watching the scene.

The first to arrive was Micah, the co-owner of the spot. In his plain black suit, long jacket, hat, and traditional beard with locks flowing from his temples, he was indistinguishable from his cousin and co-owner Isaac. I knew it was Micah because Isaac was supposed to arrive later on a Wednesday carrying the bag I was there to collect.

Not long after Micah got there a younger, more stylishly dressed Jewish man arrived at the shop and joined him in preparing to open for business. That was Adam, their shop's manager and their weakest link. Adam was the charismatic salesman who handled the counter. He was known for building relationships with all their high profile clientele, especially female clients. The owners stayed out of sight in the back of the shop and let their front man do his thing while they took care of more pressing matters.

The only had two customers the entire morning. The file said their main customers came in by appointment. That meant less chance for potential bystanders, and that was a good thing. Not having to worry about some square playing hero was one less thing to worry about.

At a few minutes to eleven, Isaac came strolling down the block carrying a black satchel. No one on the street paid him the least bit of attention. It was gangsta' how easily he strolled toting a million dollars in drugs. Ten minutes after he arrived, a young white guy with a baseball cap on backwards hopped out of a taxi carrying a small black leather duffel bag. He walked into the shop and disappeared into the rear.

It all unfolded like clockwork. Taking down this score was a golden opportunity with just a few small hurdles to overcome. The place had eyes all over, but every camera in the place was on a closed circuit system. It was a common mistake. What was the use of a video feed that went no further than the place that was getting knocked over? I suppose under no circumstances did Imperial jewelers want the business they did transmitted off-site. Their efforts to secure their legit business were nullified by their need for privacy in their illegal affairs. My main concern was that they had switches for the alarms behind every counter and in the back. The first and only priority had to be keeping them off the alarms, at least until we were well on our way. After that, it was like taking candy from a baby. There weren't too many hang-ups I could imagine once I had them at gunpoint...and gunpoint was the one part of the job I knew best.

Chapter 11

"**D**amn, Lex, that sound like some Hollywood shit straight out the movies."

"Who you tellin'," I replied.

"So...when you woke up and seen the bitch had skated, you just went on and handled your biz, right?"

"Nah...," I paused. I had spent the past half hour in Big Tee's office giving him the full rundown on my trip, but I had yet to tell him Chaine had hit the mark. I sat for a second debating on if the truth would make me sound like a bit time sucker. "After I seen she was gone, I flew the coop."

"What?" That surprised him. He continued cautiously, "I know you was feelin' her and all that, but homie once I woulda found out I woulda off'd that bitch. She done seen where you lay your head and all that...Bitch woulda had to go." He was adamant and I understood why. Where you slept nights was privileged information. That, plus the deception, should have been adequate grounds for a dirt nap.

"Never crossed my mind, we was talking about retiring and riding out."

He leaned back and took a small palm sized brush from his desk. He began brushing his waves, more out of habit than necessity. "Young gunna', I hate to bust your bubble but ole' girl ain't the type you ride out with. Ya'll both predators. It don't mix. Broad like her need to hook up with a computer programmer, or some type of square like that, so she can hide her true self."

"You probably right."

188

"That love shit is complicated homie, especially when it coincides with the game," he said. I could tell he was trying to ease my wounded pride.

"I shoulda just took my shot when I had one." I shook my head, deeply regretting my missed opportunity.

"Hold up!" He leaned forward. "If you ain't handle the business…I heard dog took two in his bean."

"I'm assuming it was her work. If it was, she 'bout her business. I was by his house, security tight as fish pussy."

We shared a laugh and he lit a cigar. He puffed out two perfect rings of smoke and then blew a narrow stream that went straight through the middle of them. "I'm kinda glad it wasn't you who got him…Word is, them Jamaicans givin' up half a mil' for the shooter. You know them Darkheart boys is no joke. Say, they got a line on somebody out this way."

"Yeah?" I tried to restrain my anxiety.

"Just heard this morning. I was gon' holla at you, put you up on game. Didn't sound like you to leave much a trail."

"Nah, you know how I roll," I mumbled. Despite trying hard not to, I wondered if Chaine was alright.

"I hope your girl really part chameleon like you say, 'cause when the rude boys catch her it's a wrap."

I didn't respond. I just sat there pulling on my bottom lip thinking. There was still a part of me that worried for Chaine's well being.

After a brief silence he said, "So, what you thinking 'bout? You gon' try and fill the contract on baby girl?"

The thought hadn't crossed my mind. I had sacrificed $750K to be with her. Not to mention that I didn't even know how to find her, much less kill her. Still, I took the opportunity to salvage my image with

Big Tee somewhat, "Yeah, I think I may just try to recoup my losses on this fiasco. Somebody gon' get paid if she go down, might as well be me." I left as we shared a few moments of laughter.

I walked up front to the barroom from his office and I was glad I'd told him. The way he reacted let me feel like it could have happened to anyone. They say confession is good for the soul, and somehow I did feel just a little better having told someone. Plus, I knew big Tee would keep it to himself. Usually it would have been Nana Helen I divulged that type of information to, but with the way things had left off between us, I wasn't ready to go crawling back to her admitting my mistakes. A lot of the shit that had happened had transpired because I went against her advice. If I'd taken down the heist and left the murder for hire game alone like she'd been pushing me to, I could have avoided most of my present headache. I knew it, but I was in no mood to hear it.

Up front I found Mila at the bar pouring drinks for a few regulars who came in on Saturday afternoons to watch college football while they drank. When she looked at me I nodded toward the booth in the back. I'd been sitting for no more than two minutes when she came over with two glasses of orange juice. She set one in front of me and slid into the booth across from me.

"Whass'up, Playboy? Long time no see. I thought you was gonna come and go without speaking."

"Nah…jus' had to put a bug in Big Tee's ear. You know you my friend to the end like Chucky," I replied.

"So, what's good? You been M.I.A. for like two weeks."

"Jus' been tying up some loose ends. Bizzie told me to tell you 'what up' and that he miss you."

"Bizzie was up here and didn't come see me? I can't believe that mutha...," her voice raised an octave as she nearly leapt from her seat.

"He wasn't up here," I interrupted. "He's doing good, though, 'cept that he really miss the town.

"Then how'd you...oooohhh! Damn Lex, you get around."

"Kicking it wit' him brought back a lot of memories."

"Remember that truant officer who use to chase us when we cut school?"

"Fat ass Barnes...I hated that dude." I recalled the guy instantly.

"He didn't give us no more problems after Bizzie started giving him that good green...that shit had his big ass stretched out on a bench in the park!"

We both bust out laughing at the funny image from a faded memory. Mila had rolled with Bizzie and me a lot in high school. The two of them were even tighter than her and me. Through her laughter I could see sadness. I could tell she missed him a lot. We picked up our glasses and touched them in a toast to our absent comrade.

"It's about time for us to make that other move. You ready?" I asked.

"I been waiting on you. I thought maybe you had changed your mind."

For the next 15 minutes I walked her through what I had seen watching the place. She filled in names as I went along, letting me know that she had been thorough in studying the information. It kind of surprised her that the file was so accurate. After a few years of working with Nana Helen, I was use to it. Although we weren't getting along at the moment I knew that her thoroughly informing me was why we'd seen so much success doing hits for hire.

Once I finished giving her the layout, I explained the game plan. I also gave her some suggestions about what to wear, but I doubted she needed my help there. When I was done, she smiled ear to ear at the simplicity of it.

"Just like that, huh?"

"Pretty much homie. It ain't rocket science...no need to make it all complicated," I replied.

"What about the alarms?" she asked.

It was a very good question. An informed question and I wasn't mad at her for asking. The alarms were the only significant potential problem. She was on point. "I'm gonna make sure nobody trips the alarms," I said, looking at her eye to eye to reassure her.

"Can you do that without anyone getting shot?" she asked matter of factly.

"Probably not." I kept it real.

"Well, if you wanna hear it, I got an idea that should get us around that..."

I leaned back in the booth and listened as she filled in the final piece of the plan I'd been missing. It surprised me that I hadn't thought of it, but I'd had a lot on my mind lately. When she finished, I agreed that we should do it her way. We finished our orange juice sealing the deal. If things worked out as planned, she would be a millionaire come next weekend...and I would be retired.

The following Wednesday I got up early again. I threw on some sweats and drove up to 47th street. I had to be sure to get a spot directly in front of Imperial, and in the early morning that was no problem. I had my choice of parking on the empty block. I used the way back home as an opportunity to get some exercise. Jogging was always a good way to clear my head. As I ran along the Hudson River, Chaine gradually crept into my thoughts from the corners of my mind. I wondered if she'd made use of her chameleon-like ability to change her appearance and left town. Pulling up stakes was hard to do, but with $750K in her pocket she should have been able to get away clean. Smart money was, she knew they were on to her. With a crew as deep and as determined as the Darkheart Massive on your heels you didn't get low, you ran as fast as your legs and your money could carry you. I hoped on hopes that Chaine was that smart.

At a quarter to eleven I was standing in front of the pretzel cart at the corner of 47th Street and 8th Avenue. I brought a pretzel, a hot dog, and a soda and posted up. In a simple black Hugo Boss suit I looked like any one of the working stiffs in the mid-day Manhattan stream of six million. From behind dark tinted shades I didn't appear to be attentively scoping the block. My keen eye picked up Isaac emerging from the 47th Street subway station before he even cleared the stairway. As he walked right by me I glanced at the bag he carried, but he remained oblivious to my presence.

It would be cliché for me to type the guy as cheap just because he was Jewish, but as he casually strolled down the block to his shop I wondered how a guy could be toting millions of dollars worth of dope and be too cheap to spring for a taxi.

He'd only been inside for five minutes when a taxi pulled up out front. I noticed that it was a different bagman from the previous week. This one was a white guy too, but taller and more neatly dressed. That was trivial. My main concern was the black leather bag he had slung over his shoulder. I grabbed my phone and texted the word "GO" to Mila.

I walked down the block slowly on the opposite side of the street from the spot, feigning the utmost interest in my hot dog. When I was almost directly across from the store front I spotted Mila coming up on the other side of the street. Even from a distance I could see she was in rare form. She was wearing a dress almost identical to the white one Sharon Stone had made famous in "Basic Instinct." This one was slightly shorter, showcasing her legs. Her body took it to a level that would have made Sharon Stone blush. She had a long white cashmere overcoat draped over one arm, and she clutched a white leather Burkin bag under the other. The diamond stud earrings and matching pendant she wore sparkled in the sunlight. Her hair was up in a neatly styled ponytail that accentuated her face and neck. Every man she passed craned their necks for a second peek as she click clacked down Jeweler's Row in Max Azria stilettos. She gave off that aloof super model vibe as she ignored the world absentmindedly peeking in the stores' window display cases. I smirked at how well she pimped the role.

As she passed by the Imperial Diamond Jewelry Company's display case nothing seemed to catch her eye. At the very last second she pretended something had grabbed her attention and stopped. From inside the store, Adam, the counter man and manager, got a look at her and was on her like ants on a picnic. Mila ignored him as he rushed over and started tapping on the glass to get her attention. She started to walk off when this mark actually comes out of the store and stops her. Watching her verbal exchange was the equivalent of seeing the fly proposition the spider. After a few moments of conversation she followed him into the store where he started showing her merchandise. The only merchandise old Adam was really interested in showing her he'd had since birth, and it was circumcised.

As planned, she maneuvered him to the far end of the counter close to the door that led to the rear of the store where there was a workshop, an office, and a storage room. I watched as Mila tried on necklaces, flirting and gradually lulling Adam into a docile state. I saw her yawn and stretch giving me the signal for our scripted play. It was imperative that I got straight into the back before the three men in the rear could reach an alarm switch. There was a chance one of them could be watching the front of the store via camera. It had to play out in a fluid motion, but it wasn't like Adam was just gonna buzz me into the back.

I crossed the street purposefully gliding and striding. When I stepped into the shop Mila was letting Adam fasten the clasp of a necklace on her neck. He lingered for a moment savoring the closeness to a beautiful woman. The door chimed as I walked in, and he looked up startled by the noise. Just as he looked at me, Mila reached into her open purse and pulled out a tazer. Before he knew what hit him, she had it right on his chest and gave him a 50,000 volt shock.

He convulsed momentarily and collapsed in a heap behind the counter. I walked right toward Mila, gently lifting her over the counter, and kept moving right for the door. She reached under the counter and hit the switch that buzzed the door open as soon as I got to it. Within six seconds of being inside the shop I had access to the back. The choreography was flawless.

I pushed the door open with my foot, simultaneously drawing my two weapons. As the door swung open, Micah was crossing the hall from the workshop to the office unaware of danger. A panicked expression came over his face the instant he saw me. He turned to make a dash for the alarm. I fired the weapon in my right hand.

Two prongs deployed from the stun gun flying at over a thousand feet per second. They made contact with his skin and dropped him. He was instantly reduced to a quivering mass in the hallway. I stepped over his body and turned the corner entering the workshop just in time to see Isaac moving toward the far wall where an alarm switch was located. I fired the stun gun in my left hand and it froze him mid-stride. He stood quivering on his feet, momentarily paralyzed from the high voltage jolt. He collapsed with foamy spittle flowing from his mouth.

The bagman who'd come in the cab looked from my stone cold expression to the workbench in the center of the room. The two bags sat there wide open. In the large satchel that Isaac had carried I saw more pills than I could count, all shrink wrapped and ready to go. From the leather duffel bag beside it, crisp neat stacks of hundred dollar bills peeked out at me. A couple of stacks littered the table beside a money counting machine. I'd caught them just as they had begun the count.

As I stepped toward the bags, the bag man seemed to take notice that I wasn't presently holding a weapon and stepped toward me. I couldn't believe he tried me. I quickly produced the 9mm Walther PPK from my shoulder holster. I said to him, "They got shocked...you'll get shot. Lay it down, playboy." My words momentarily froze him, and then he did as he was told suddenly more aware of the clear and present danger. With him facedown and the two owners incapacitated I called out to Mila, "How you livin', baby girl?"

"Cool water," she replied.

I stuffed the loose cash into the bag and slung it over my shoulder. I grabbed the bag with the pills and tossed it up the hall by the door I had come through. As I looked around the workshop I saw jewelry fragments and small gems but no significant cache of diamonds like the file said. Without taking my eyes of the men on the floor I backed across the hall into the office. It was my pleasure to find the safe behind the desk sat wide open. The large safe had trays of diamonds of various clarity, color, and cut. Some were raw and looked more like rock salt than precious stones. On the bottom shelf of the safe sat a pleasant unexpected surprise. Wrapped in plastic was a bundle of $100 dollar bills that had to be at least a million dollars. I snatched a black trash bag from the garbage can in the corner and after making sure the hostages were holding still quickly turned and emptied the safe's contents into the bag. The plastic stretched, but didn't burst from the weight of the cash.

Leaving the office, I spied their last line of defense; the digital video recorder that captured the feed from the cameras. I ejected the disk pocketing it on my way out the door. The two owners groaned and moved slightly as I prepared to leave. I picked up the stun guns with prongs still attached to both men and squeezed the triggers delivering a farewell jolt that would keep them down for a while after we left. Although the bagman was lying on the floor perfectly still, I delivered a swift blow to the base of his skull with the butt of my pistol, knocking him out cold.

With bags in tow, I emerged from the rear of the store. Mila smiled at seeing me with the three bags, but she was all business as she kneeled down and gave her friend Adam a jolt with the tazer to keep him still as we departed.

"No wonder you ain't got no man," I joked as I handed her the garbage bag to carry.

We cut an odd picture emerging from the spot carrying bags. Maybe walking out of another business on Jeweler's Row carrying the same bags would have been suspicious, but at Imperial, people came and went with bags on a regular basis. No one seemed to notice as we hopped in the black 300 parked directly out front. I eased the nondescript black sedan into the flowing stream of traffic, and before we ever even made it off the block we had already disappeared.

We rode in excited silence with adrenaline racing to Grand Central Station where I dropped Mila off. She gave me a hug before stepping out of the car. She put on her coat and removed the clips holding her hair up, letting it fall around her shoulders. With her changed look she entered the train station, disappearing amongst the busy mid-day commuters. We weren't hot, but we split up according to the script. With her well on her way, I drove off thinking of how vital a role she'd played in pulling off the job. Her idea for the use of stun guns and tazers had kept the job clean. My way would have had one or maybe even all the men in the place shot. That would have drawn a lot of unwanted heat. We probably would have never made it off the block. Mila must have apparently learned a thing or two from the mistakes her father made and now she saved me from the same headache.

The downstroke was the easy part. I hopped on the FDR Drive and took it up to the 59th Street bridge. Just on the other side of the bridge I ditched the car on a side street in Queens. I grabbed the bags and caught a cab back over to Manhattan. On the ride home I periodically glanced back to see if I was being followed, but it was uncalled for. Taking down scores probably didn't always come off so smoothly, but I couldn't help but think maybe I'd been in the wrong business. I guess Mila and I had just come up on the right lick. I had yet to do a count or liquidate anything, but the take looked good. I was in a position to retire and Mila would have the financial independence she sought. As the cab let me out up the block from my place, I thought about how much I owed Nana Helen a huge debt of gratitude.

Up in the crib I was itching like a dopefiend to do the critical breakdown. I dumped all the cash on my bed and counted that first. The duffel bag portion came in at $1.5m and the plastic wrapped block from the safe was exactly a million, like I'd guessed.

Counting the pills was a little bit trickier. There were five separate shrink wrapped bundles. I opened one, and it took me about 30 minutes to count the hundred thousand pills inside. I assumed that went the same for the other four, but I wasn't about to count. Had it crossed my mind at the time, I'm certain with a gun to his head the bagman would have told me his pick-up was for 500,000 pills. The Jews were giving him a good price at 3 bucks a pop, so I figured I'd probably sell them at two and get them off that much quicker. The pills would turn me a fast million.

As for the stones, I was in no hurry to sell them. After settling up with Mila and Nana Helen I was planning on skipping town and the stones would be a lot more travel friendly than bulky cash. Best I could tell, I was looking at every bit of $2 million in diamonds. I sorted the raw stones from the processed ones placing them in two separate zip-lock bags. I took the diamonds, the pills, and $1m in cash upstairs to the loft, leaving behind the $1.5m in the duffle bag to use to cash out Nana Helen her ten percent and Mila her mil' ticket.

Everything had played out as smooth as glass. After adding the new money and merchandise to the $1.5m I already had on stash, the complexion of my financial situation had changed dramatically. I was sitting on over $5m and it sounded like real nice traveling music. I was ready to change my life,and the best first step I could think of was a change of scenery. Maybe I'd head out west and start up a little private security firm. I had more than enough money to do whatever. Working protection would be a 180° turn, but after all my work helping marks get dead, maybe it would help my karma some to help some marks stay alive. It was legal and I already knew the business.

As I came back downstairs pondering the vast possibilities for my future, my phone vibrated. It was an in-coming text message form Mila that simply said, "Home Safe." She'd made it home okay. I shot back a message that read: "Lunch was great! Who wants to be a millionaire? C U tonite!" I had plenty of time until my meet with her later that evening, and after her, Nana Helen would be my last stop.

I made a few calls and lined up a sale for the pills. I knew they would go quick, but how quick surprised me. They sold like hot bread. In less than 15 minutes I had a meet set up for the following day with some cats out of Queens. I knew them from my hustling days; they knew me and were familiar with some of my work. It was all square biz'.

With that taken care of, my list of things to do in N.Y. had become very short. I planned on keeping my place, the lease was paid up all the way until the spring and I figured it wouldn't hurt to have someplace to lay low just in case. All I was taking with me were some clothes and essentials. There wasn't much else for me to do but start packing.

Chapter 12

I t was around four that afternoon when I took a shower and started getting ready to make my rounds. They say you're not supposed to wear white after Labor Day but seems like nobody pays attention to that anymore. I was glad of it because I had this white Prada suit I had yet to wear, and I figured I may as well go see Mila rocking all white. Fall through the Third Rail like the proverbial White Knight.

After splashing on some Issey and stepping into my white Cole Haan loafers I still felt like my look was missing something. I went to my collection of watches. At first I grabbed my Rolex, but as I fastened the clasp I couldn't take my eyes off the White Versace timepiece Chaine had given me. It was the perfect accent to the all white thing, but I was reluctant to sport it for obvious reasons. With a slight hesitation, I took the Rolex off and slipped the Versace onto my wrist. I figured Chaine was somewhere "doing her" and not thinking about me so for me to allow her to have an influence over what I did or didn't wear was trifling.

When I checked myself out in the mirror I knew I'd made the right choice. I looked and felt like a million bucks, except that the pistol on my hip interrupted the lines of my suit, and the black leather bag contrasted my white vibe. I could tolerate them though, wasn't like I had a choice.

As I rode the elevator downstairs to catch a cab uptown, I was snatched from fantasizing about the day's come up by the sound of my ringing phone. I paused before answering, trying to think of something clever to say to Nana Helen as an ice breaker.

When I looked at the screen I saw that the call came from a number I didn't recognize. I walked up the alley to hail a cab staring at the strange number trying to place it. Figuring it was someone calling a wrong number, I slipped the ringing phone back into my pocket. Just as I stepped to the curb and raised my arm, a familiar voice said from behind me, "You know, it's rude not to answer your phone."

I knew who it was instantly. I responded without turning around, "It's a cold world…they'll get over it." I heard the sound of a phone snapping shut and the ringing in my pocket stopped just as a taxi pulled up. I should have just gotten in and drove off. Instead, I slowly turned around.

Chaine stood casually leaned against the front of my building. Had she not spoken, I'd have walked right past her. My internal response at seeing her surprised me. I felt neither residual love nor the demented rage I imagined I might feel if I ever saw her again. Instead, I felt a cool ambivalence and annoyance at her presence.

She looked good, no use in trying to argue that. Standing there with one foot of her tan suede ankle length Donna Karan boots propped up, she eyed me from behind oversized rose tinted Chloe glasses. She had her hair wrapped in a Burberry gypsy scarf that matched her coat. Her honey colored legs still looked tanned from Jamaica, showcased by her short flannel skirt.

Looking me over from head to toe with a raised eyebrow, she said, "Where you headed looking all GQ…Must be one hell of a hot date."

I could tell she was impressed. It was a good thing I'd decided to get fly. Nothing like looking good when you ran into your ex. "Places to go, people to see," I replied, as I grabbed the taxi door handle.

202

"Can I talk to you for a minute?"

I put one foot inside the taxi and paused as if giving it some thought.

"You had plenty chance to talk. Right now I got shit to do…maybe next lifetime."

"Lex, wait!" she shouted, as I started to close the door. "I know I ruined everything between us, but I really do need to talk to you."

"Why should I care about anything you got to say?"

"Because I love you, and I thought you loved me." She walked over to the cab with a pleading expression. A tear formed in the corner of her eye.

I sat watching her performance. It was unbelievable how good an actress this broad was. I wasn't buying it, but I was slightly curious about what her angle was. With an incredulous look I said, "You can't be serious."

"I am. Please, just lemme talk to you. Please."

The cab driver overheard our brief exchange and looked at me to make a decision. I looked at Chaine with frustration while inside my curiosity grew, and just a hint of compassion seeped to the surface. I grabbed my bag and stepped back out onto the sidewalk. As I slammed the cab door closed the driver sped off resuming his paper chase.

"State your biz," I said sternly.

"Thank you," she sniffled, and tried to hug me.

I raised a hand shutting her down. "Jus' say what you gotta say and keep it moving."

"Why're you being so mean?"

I resisted the urge to fly off the handle. Instead I coolly recited her note, "I'm sorry…This is who I am."

"Guess I deserved that." She got quiet.

Behind her glasses I could see her eyes scanning the pedestrian and vehicle traffic. Even though her look was different, she was still on point watching to see who was coming and going. Sizing up possible threats. She obviously knew she was a wanted woman.

"What are you doing here? Thought you'd be in the wind by now," I said.

"Me? Why?"

"If you gon' play stupid..." I turned to walk away. She grabbed my arm, and I tensed every muscle in my body. She got the hint and let go.

"Alright, alright. Wait. Can we talk inside?"

"Right here is fine."

"Lex, right here is not safe for either of us.

"I'm straight, dem people ain't lookin' for me."

"You think if they run down on me right here they're gonna politely ask you to step out of the way?"

Excellent point. I stepped aside and gestured for her to walk ahead of me. She led the way back. Before I opened the door for us to go inside, I had a thought. "You holdin'?" I asked.

Without a word, she put her hands on the wall, assuming the position for me to check her. Apparently, she knew I didn't trust her word and I was going to pat her down no matter what she said. She mocked me by poking her butt out slightly and standing in that bowlegged stance. I frisked her and found she had a sub-compact .32 caliber pistol tucked at the small of her back. I pocketed it and said, "You can have that back later. You need to think about keeping it where you can reach it better."

She mumbled something imperceptible. I could care less what she'd said. Good thing I'd decided to check her. I knew she wasn't to be trusted. What I was really glad about was that with her out of my system some of my instincts and careful movements seemed to have gotten back on track. I opened the doors and we rode up on the elevator in silence.

Whatever was between her and me was over with. The only reason I was even hearing her out was professional courtesy. As the elevator came to a stop I checked my watch thinking, "I'm giving this chick three minutes." Out of the corner of my eye I saw her peep that I was wearing the watch she bought. She stifled a smile. It was a slip on my part because it slightly bolstered her confidence.

We walked into my place and I gave her a gentle nudge into the kitchen letting her know I didn't want her any further in my space. I went and deactivated the alarm and dropped the leather bag off on the couch. When I came back to the kitchen she'd shed her coat and was sitting up on the counter in the exact same spot I'd first made love to her. The gesture was ironic but intentional. She was wearing a cream silk peasant blouse that was off one shoulder and showing plenty of skin and cleavage. Sexy, but intentional. I saw right through her game as she leaned back on her palms and crossed her legs.

"Did you come to profile, or do you got something to say? You got three minutes, better use 'em wisely."

"You're being real shitty to me, Lex," she complained.

"You shitted first."

"Well, you lied to me. What was I s'pose to do?"

"Is that what you came to discuss?"

"No."

"Tick, tock," I said, glancing at my watch for effect.

"Alright look…" She finally took off her glasses, so I could really see her eyes. They were misty, but I didn't read too much into it. She was an actress and could cut the water on and off at will. "I came to see you

205

because I made a mistake in Jamaica. I know the way I left you was messed up, and you don't have any reason to trust me, but I'm here to ask you to give me another chance."

"Why would I wanna do that?"

"Well, for starters because I risked my life in coming here."

"So, you know there's a contract out on you right now?" I asked, leaning comfortably against my motorcycle and watching her closely to gauge her response.

"Yeah," she exhaled.

"What made you think when you came here I wouldn't just clip you and be done with this whole fiasco?"

There it was, on her face in its purest form...fear. She was suddenly not so concerned with being sexy. She leaned forward and crossed her arms. Defensive posture. There wasn't much she could say, so she just looked at me with helpless eyes waiting on my next move.

Me? I was fronting big time. I hadn't the slightest intention of killing her. For what? I was retired and wealthy. Scaring her just made me feel like I was recovering some of my gangsta' that I'd lost fooling with her. I was like a cat toying with a wounded mouse. After being tossed aside in Jamaica I needed to feel empowered. I let the impregnated silence linger between us for a few moments before I let her off the hook. "Lucky thing for you I say what I mean, and I mean what I say. I told you in Jamaica I'm retired, so whatever's gonna happen to you won't be by my hands."

I could tell she was relieved by the way the color returned to her face and chest. "I guess I deserved that too," she said.

"You deserve more, but personally I don't even think you work $500k."

"Lex, I know we had real love. I never loved anybody the way I love you...Now all I'm getting from you is hurt."

"This whole thing with us was a mistake."

"How can you say that? You weren't the only one who took a risk. I broke all my rules messing with you. Ever since the first time I saw you..."

"Chaine," I interrupted her, "let's not do this."

"Alright, admit you didn't love me and I'll leave."

That froze me for a second because I couldn't truthfully say it. She actually did look sincere. I stared at her and just couldn't tell that lie. Instead I said, "Time's up, Skittles, I got things to do."

"So, all that you asking me to retire and ride off into the sunset with you, that was bullshit?"

"Nah, that was real...it's just no longer possible."

"I really destroyed 'us', huh?"

Before I had a chance to answer she grabbed her coat. Her glasses fell from her hand. She tried to catch them before they fell, but missed. I crouched down and caught them with cat-like reflexes just before they hit the ground. I looked up and saw I was face to face with her smooth bare legs. That close I could tell she'd had them waxed or something. I rose slowly, watching her intently. She had that coy smile on, the one like she knew a secret. When I got halfway up, about eye level with the counter top, that's where I ran into trouble. As I stole a glance at her thighs she spread her knees apart just enough for me to see up her skirt. She wasn't wearing a stitch of underwear and apparently had a hellified wax job. Her passion fruit was bald as Telly Sevalas.

The whole exchange was brief, but the time did that slow motion thing it did while I was with her. I handed her the glasses realizing that they just may not have fallen by accident. When she took them from me she held on to my hand. I halfheartedly tried to pull away. She pulled me toward her. I found myself standing between her legs with my face so close to hers that I could smell her cinnamon scented breath every time she exhaled. In that moment she reintroduced me to a closeness I'd thought was gone, but still existed between us. The warmth I was feeling infuriated me. There does exist a thin line between love and hate. I wasn't near the line...I was the line.

I stared into her eyes, and we were frozen there sharing the look of love. My "Spidey" senses tingled, warning me not to fall in, but as her moist lips parted and she leaned closer closing the distance between us, the passion and rage I felt for her overcame me. Every bit of love I felt for her made me more and more furious. I kissed her, hard. It was one of those neck grabbing, lip biting really aggressive kind of kisses. She submitted to me, becoming docile as I released my frustration kissing her face, chest, and shoulders like I was trying to draw blood.

One thing led to another...The next thing I knew, my fly was undone and I had her legs wrapped around my waist. She was really wet. It was no secret that the rough sex thing turned her on. She hugged onto my neck tightly as I thrust myself inside her as deeply as I could. She sang out in soprano, and I stroked her harder. I quickly became frustrated because the force of my hips made her slide further and further back on the counter like she was trying to run from the punishment I was trying to give her. What I was doing to her wasn't making love, it wasn't make-up sex; it was a grudge fuck.

I got tired of playing around with her. I snatched her down off the counter like a rag doll, and spun her around. I entered her from behind. My hips made loud smacking noises slapping against her butt. As hard as I hit it, though, and as loud as she wailed, I just wasn't satisfied.

Now I know that sexing Chaine in my kitchen was a bad idea, but by the time I realized it was happening, it was already too late. In those moments I learned that not only was my body still weak for her, but I also still had some residual feelings for her. I was mad at myself and at her for those feelings. I may have been a fool, but I wasn't a damned fool! Just in case she was running some type of ploy, the whole time I'd kept my clothes on, and I had my pistol at the small of my back.

I was behind her doing my best imitation of a human jackhammer. Between her flowing juices and the sweat I was working up; my Prada suit was pretty much ruined. I couldn't have cared less and kept working her body like a damned demon. I never did have an orgasm; I just went until my thighs, hamstring, and calves were on fire. I was so winded my lungs felt like I had gargled with broken glass. I steadied myself against the counter, unsatisfied and already angry at myself for the moment of weakness.

Chaine stayed there bent over the counter for a minute recovering. After a quiet moment passed she pulled her skirt back down and grabbed a glass from the dish rack. She half-filled it with tap water and downed it. When she finished, she refilled the same glass. She went to the refrigerator and dropped in a couple of ice cubes before bringing the glass over to me. I accepted it and drank it slowly. I was thankful to have an excuse not to speak. She watched me drinking and I knew she was waiting on me to say something that might validate what had just happened. There was no such validation that was going to pass my lips. We undeniably did have something, but there was just no way possible that it could work between us.

As I neared the bottom of my glass I was just about to tell her to hit the bricks when I noticed something. Chaine had given me tap water, not lemonade or juice, but still I noticed the water had a bit of an acidic flavor, like citrus or something. I looked at the faucet because I thought for a second that the water was running bad, like it did sometimes in NYC. Then as I got near the bottom I encountered a gritty texture, and I realized the bitch had put something in my drink.

I immediately stopped drinking and started spitting, but I knew whatever it was, I'd already ingested way too much. She had already backed away from me and was by the door out of my reach. From a safe distance she gave me a pathetic excuse for an apologetic shoulder shrug. I wanted to wring her neck, but I knew she was fast and there was no way I could catch her if she didn't want to be caught.

I put my head in the sink and stuck two fingers down my throat trying to make myself throw up. There was ipecac in my medicine cabinet, but I'd never make it to that in time. I was frantic thinking of how fucked up a way this was to die. My biggest mistake was letting Chaine in my space and now I was going to pay. An expensive mistake…it was costing me my life.

The room started to spin, rotating slowly at first, but accelerating the more I tried to focus. My vision became blurry. I looked at Chaine and there were about five of her floating around in a circle. For all the marks I'd sent to the upper room, I never thought I'd end up as a mark myself. I had never been the least bit religious, I knew God existed, but we'd been out of touch for a very long time. As my consciousness faded and I desperately clung to life, I found myself slumped over the sink asking God for help. I guess that was something everyone did when they felt their life slipping away. I collapsed, and just as everything got dark, Chaine spoke, "It could've all been so simple...but you'd rather make it hard." Couldn't remember where I'd heard that, and I wanted to respond, but everything went black.

Chapter 13

I woke up six hours later with a splitting headache. Either my afterlife was going to take place in my apartment or Chaine had only given me a sedative. It was better to get slipped a Mickey than be laying down for the big sleep. My small celebration of escaping death was cut short however, as my brain came on-line fully processing what had gone down. I looked around the apartment, but she was obviously long gone. As I wondered what her motives were in having sex with me and then drugging me, I automatically remembered the bag. I ran from the kitchen to the couch as fast as my groggy legs would carry me.

My heart raced.

I breathed a deep sigh of relief at finding the black duffel bag sitting on the couch exactly where I'd left it. She hadn't even touched it. Nana Helen was right about hiding things in plain view.

I checked myself. I still had my money, phone, and watch. She'd taken both pistols and my keys. From the looks of things it seemed my only problem was that I was locked inside my own apartment. That was a small thing, but I was mad about it because I felt violated.

I grabbed my phone and called Bubby. He could tell it was urgent from my tone. By the time I finished asking him to come and get me, he was already en route to Nana Helen's place to grab my other set of keys. Bubby was a good man to have at your side in a clutch. I rested easy knowing I'd be liberated within the hour. I didn't like the idea of my sanctuary becoming my prison, but as I changed clothes I considered just tying up my loose ends and getting in the wind. Chaine wasn't

212

worth me tracking her down for some get back. With the Darheart Massive on her heels, she probably didn't have long to live anyway.

I took off the triple white Prada suit and opted to throw on jeans, a white tee, and construction Tims; the hood uniform. I strapped on my double shoulder holsters and threw my Armani Exchange leather jacket on over that to conceal the heat I'd be holding. After that close call I planned on rolling extra strapped. I mounted the spiral staircase up to the loft to go grab my twin Ruger P-89's from my stash. What I saw at the top of those stairs snatched the breath from my lungs and the ground out from under me.

The bookcases that hid my stash swung wide open, mocking me. After I pinched myself to make sure I was awake, my knees got weak. I fell to the ground despite a feeble attempt to stay on my feet. The bag with the pills and the one with the money and diamonds were gone. All my guns and grenades sat untouched, but offered little in the way of consolation. Chaine had stolen every penny I had. The money in the bag downstairs belonged to Mila and Nana Helen, and I had every intention of paying them. All I had left were my guns and $250K in a safety deposit box. Might as well have been nothing compared to the $5m plus that I was short. For all intents and purposes I was broke and starting from scratch.

I laid there on the floor wishing I could just melt into the floorboards. I hadn't eaten much all day otherwise I surely would have been sick. There was a taste in the back of my throat like rotten fish. In the space of one day I had gone from chasing a goal to retired and independently wealthy, to destroyed. Destroyed at the hands of a conniving woman. I silently wished she would have killed me. She had left me alive, though, and that told me she had no intentions of being caught. A $5 million head start made her hard to catch, but I was going to get the bitch or die trying. I grabbed the twins and a grenade and went downstairs to wait on Bubby.

I paced the floor of my living room sorting out the broken pieces of my existence. It was like trying to make sense of a giant jigsaw puzzle. The first question I answered for myself was how she had known where my stash was. I'd been knocked out for hours, and sure she had plenty of time for a search, but I was even simpler than that. Any woman dating a new guy will invariably search his crib the first chance she gets. I thought back and remembered that my super stupid ass had left her alone in my crib for a couple of hours. When I came back, she was practically sitting on top of my stash spot. Sure my spot was well hid, but a nosey woman has a level of determination that's a freak of nature. The reason Bin Laden has yet to be found is because he doesn't have any women he's sexing looking for him! Anyway, she probably didn't rob me then because she was locked in, and she probably would have gotten caught.

The revelation of how long she'd been playing me put me in a whole new frame of mind. I started going back over all our time together, analyzing things, searching for signs I might have missed, and clues to where I might find her. Tracking her down was something I was going to have to enlist Nana Helen's help in. Finding people wasn't my thing. All my marks had been served up to me on a silver platter. I knew how to use information, but it was Nana Helen who got it for me. She would definitely help me once I told her what had happened, but that full disclosure meant I would have to tell her how I'd broken my rules. I didn't relish the thought of the lecture and the grief she was going to give me over breaking the rules.

Breaking rules…Broken rules…Broke my rules.

The words echoed through my mind. They ricocheted and refracted within my psyche until I started hearing the words in Chaine's voice. They grew louder as I focused in on them, trying to decipher their significance. From the moment I had met her I had been breaking all my rules. I checked the time on my watch, the watch she had given me, and as I stared at its serene whiteness, the puzzle pieces fell into place like falling snowflakes.

When we were talking in the kitchen she had said she "broke all her rules" messing with me…ever since the first time she saw me. Miami? I'd been working and I was way out of pocket kicking it with her the way I had. Broke my rules. She broke her rules. Why hadn't I realized it sooner? We were both in Miami on business…the same business; and in our business socializing was a big no, no. When we saw the news report we were both equally shocked. Me, at learning there was another contractor, her, at seeing her car bomb had come up short.

Fast forward. I go to Virginia, she's got "business." I thought about the hot waitress who conveniently popped up just before the mark went down. I couldn't believe I hadn't spotted her. Looking back I knew it was her. I could picture her walk and her ass clear as day. That was when she came back and bought me the watch. Ain't that a bitch! She snatches a payday right out from under me and turns around and buys me a gift with the loot.

The shoe was finally on the other foot. All the time I had been contracting I was the deceiver. I pulled strings like a puppet master and kept people in the dark. From the moment I'd met her I thought I was in control, but it had all been her show. Everything might not have been crystal clear to me under normal circumstances, but

215

surely I would have done the math and put it together sooner than I did. Loving eyes can never see. I had fallen in love, and the love had blinded me.

The faint hum of the elevator interrupted my thought process. Barely half an hour was fast for Bubby to have gotten downtown already. My pulse raced, and the thrill of the possibility of revenge awakened my killer instincts as I realized that perhaps Chaine had doubled back to finish me off. I drew one of my pistols and slipped my index finger into the pin of the grenade as I took cover behind the bathtub. I had a clear shot at the doorway and adequate cover. Anyone who came through that door didn't stand a chance. As I crouched down waiting, I silently prayed that Chaine had realized that she'd left behind too much of a threat. I trained my sights on the doorframe at headshot level.

The locks clicked.

The door opened slowly.

I tensed the muscles in my forearms preparing to fire. My heart sank as I saw the brim of a black leather Stetson. It was Bubby. My finger relaxed on the trigger as he slowly stepped into the apartment. Chaine was a clever technician, and although I doubted it, there was still a chance she'd intercepted Bubby and used him as bait. I called out to him from behind the tub, "Ay Bubby? How many cigars you bring?"

"One good one, bub," he called out, as he scanned the room looking for me. Anything other than one meant he wasn't alone.

Satisfied he was by himself, I emerged from my spot. I walked over to him holstering my weapon and tucking the grenade in my pocket. Although I was glad to see him I couldn't manage a smile. For a moment I just stood in front of him looking like I'd seen a ghost and lost my best friend at the same time.

"Rough day?" he asked, breaking the silence.

216

Even though I trusted Bubby I stood silent racking my brain about whether to tell him some, most, or all of what had happened to me that day. Trust was a funny thing with me. Somehow, some way I'd developed a pattern of shutting out the people who'd earned and deserved my trust. The woman I'd just met and been willing to trust had snaked me. It was obviously time for a change.

Besides, over the next few days or possibly weeks, I would be in the trenches and on the grind and Bubby would invariably be down for me. The least I could do was let him know what he was getting into.

"Bubby, this day been the coldest."

"I can tell...you locked in your own place and strapped up like Pancho Villas!" He let out a hearty chuckle.

I laughed a little too.

"We ridin'?" he asked.

"Yeah, but first lemme pull your coat to something."

I led him into the living room. He took a seat on the couch beside the leather bag. "This a nice set up you got here, Lex," he commented as he drew a fresh Cuban cigar from his shirt pocket. He didn't light it, just twirled it in his fingers as he waited for me to tell my story.

Pacing back and forth behind the couch, I recounted the details of Chaine's and my whirlwind romance. He already knew most of the story, but I added in all the new parts about her being a contractor. He listened intently and quietly, only making slight grunts at some of the explicit details. I took it slow explaining everything up to and including the job Mila and I had gone on and the take. Finally, I told him how I'd ended up a prisoner in my own home. At hearing the final blow he let out a long smooth whistle.

Giving him a moment to let it all sink in, I went and grabbed a Louis Voitton knapsack and began separating Mila's mil' ticket from Nana Helen's $500k. He held up his cigar, silently asking me if it was okay to light it. I shook my head yes and he dramatically fired it up. He stared at the stream of smoke coming off it as if he were trying to discern my future from some tea leaves. When he finally spoke, he asked me a weighted question.

"So, you think it was a coincidence?"

"Coincidence? What, her showing up today of all days?"

"Nah, bub. The whole thing from front to back," he said, before taking a deep pull of his cigar.

"You mean a set up?"

"Yup."

"Haven't had too much time to think about it. I only just now made her as the contractor on them other jobs."

He broke eye contact with me. I could tell he had something he wanted to say but was reluctant. I waited through his hesitation until he spoke in a husky, smoke laden voice. "Young Lex, I know you a smart man, so you probably would have put this together in your own time...but did you consider that maybe you and this lady been getting ya'll work through the same channels? Seems to me it's leaving a lot to chance to assume ya'll was working the same three contracts on a coincidence. Coulda been she showed up today as a stroke of buzzard luck, but on the jobs...I doubt it."

His words knocked the wind out of me like a sledge hammer to the gut. In that one statement Bubby had opened my eyes to the underlying reality of my situation. I was Neo and he was Morpheus showing me the true nature of the Matix. All the puzzle pieces shattered and reformed before my eyes into a bigger, much clearer picture. In the center of it all I saw Nana Helen's face.

As I mumbled dozens of curse words under my breath, part of my brain rationalized that it just wasn't possible. Nana Helen had been like a mother to me, practically raised me, and now I had every indication that she had crossed me. I tried to concoct a reasonable explanation on her behalf, but when I looked back over the chain of events leading up to them, I knew she'd had more than a benign role in things. I didn't want to believe, couldn't believe, that the one person I truly trusted had turned against me. I sat on the arm of the couch and whispered two words: "Manipulatin' bitch."

We both knew the implications of what he'd just brought to light. Bubby knew Nana Helen, was maybe even attracted to her, but by exposing her he let me know where his loyalties lay. I abruptly grabbed the bags off the couch and headed for the door. There was no need for me to tell him it was time to ride or where we were headed. He knew that, he just didn't know what I intended to do when I got there. Truth was, neither did I, and that scared me. All I knew for sure was that my life had been endangered; I'd been lied to and robbed of a fortune. Somebody or some bodies were going to pay.

When we got downstairs I was surprised that nightfall had overtaken the NYC skyline, but then I remembered I'd lost hours being unconscious. At the curb I discovered just how Bubby had made it downtown so fast. This time he'd come through pushing a pearl yellow '96 Toyota Supra. It looked like something out of "The Fast and the Furious," and I was sure it had to be a Special Edition 6 speed. I barely broke stride admiring the car as I jumped in. I was really just thankful that once again he'd come through in something fast.

We'd barely closed the doors when he fishtailed into the street and rocketed us to the end of the block, taking to the streets like Jeff Gordon. The world outside the windows became a blur, and I used the time to myself to plot my next move.

Chapter 14

The ride was too short. When we pulled up in front of Nana Helen's building I still hadn't come to a decision on what to do or even how to play it. I grabbed the black bag with the $500k and was about to get out when Bubby grabbed my arm. He said, "Bub, don't let your head stop you from using your heart."

I accepted his advice with a curt nod and headed inside. On the way upstairs I was only sure of one thing; Nana Helen had two possible fates, one was in the leather duffel bag, the other was in my holster. It was up to me to decide which one would choose her. In a trillion years I would never have thought I'd be coming over here with murder on my mind.

I drew my pistol before knocking on her door in our knock. When I got to the third knock she snatched the door open. She'd been expecting me. She swung the door open and stood aside. I was momentarily surprised to see she was wearing an elegant coral blue Carolina Herrera evening gown with some matching strappy high heels. With her make-up done she looked radiant. I was curious where she was headed, but I was there on business that was far more urgent.

I walked in sweeping the room with my eyes to see if someone else was there. As I passed her I saw her notice the gun in my hand and a puzzled look came onto her face. Ignoring her, I checked the entire apartment. When I was satisfied we were alone, I came and sat in the chair across form her on the couch. I set my pistol and the bag on the coffee table between us. She took her cigarettes from the table and lit one before speaking.

"How'd you lose your keys?" she asked.

"Didn't lose 'em; they got stolen."

"Stolen?"

"Stolen...You actually look surprised about that," I said.

"Why wouldn't I be? You acting really strange. What's wrong with you?" she asked, looking truly confused.

Her innocent attitude was making me mad, but I played the game a little more. "Wrong with me?" I repeated.

"Yeah. I haven't heard from you in two weeks and now you come in here with your gun drawn like it's Beirut. You're safe here, Lex. This is practically your home."

"So, you haven't heard?" I knew she wasn't gonna just lay her cards on the table. Talking to her when she was hiding something was like a chess match, and she was a grand master. I had to proceed with caution because while I knew she was involved, I didn't know to what degree.

She nonchalantly puffed on her cigarette before speaking. "I heard Jamaica didn't work out. Don't feel bad, though. Wolf was an open contract. A price tag like that is gonna bring a lot of competition.

"I also heard that someone caught Imperial Jewelers with their pants down," she smiled, "So, I suppose congratulations are in order. Does this mean you're officially retired now?"

I was awestruck at how cool she was playing her hand. Most people would have been shaken by the drawn pistol, but her composure was flawless. Either she didn't see me as a threat, or she thought whatever game she was running had to be airtight. A clever fox can only be caught by a clever trap, so I made my move. "Imperial was a good look. It played out just like you said it would, smooth as glass."

222

"I told you it was a good job," she beamed.

"Yeah," I agreed, "the take was five mil', give or take. When I cash out the stones I'll give you the difference." I pushed the bag to her. She took it without looking inside and set it on the couch beside her.

"I'm glad you're finally done with the hit for hire business. I was so worried you might not quit before it was too late." She looked relieved.

"Actually, I'm not retiring yet. I got this one last job I wanna do before I call it quits."

"What?" she practically yelled. "Tu eres loco? Why would you want to do more work? You got more than enough money to do whatever you want."

"This last one should be cake. It's business and personal. Two birds one bullet." I leaned back, relaxing with my fingers interlaced behind my head while watching her placid expression transform to Defcon Five.

"What job could be so important you willing to risk everything?"

"Well...down in Jamaica I was this close to hitting Wolf, and another contractor snatched him right out from under me..."

"What's the big deal?" she asked, cutting me off, "we've been dealing with that type of stuff for over a month now. That's why you wanna quit, remember?"

"Yeah, but this time I got a good look at the other contractor. Turns out the hitter left a trail and now there's a $500k contract out...Just so happens the trail led right back here to New York. Ironic, ain't it?" I smiled.

"Lex, it's not worth it."

"Damn if it ain't! That's half a mil' in my own backyard. I'm not about to let no easy money slide by. I'm out $750k. The $500k don't make it even, but I'll sleep better."

"It's a waste of time, and it's not worth the risk. Word about that contract is probably all over town by now. Anybody who knows they have a contract out on them is gonna be laying low. Finding her will be next to impossible.

And there it was, she had slipped. The master had been trapped. As much as I wanted to think she wasn't involved, now I knew for sure that she was. I snatched my pistol off the coffee table and leveled it between her eyes. She looked confused and agitated, but that was more about me chasing another contract than the gun in her face. "Nana Helen, I never told you the other contractor was a woman, but you just referred to her as a 'her.' How the fuck you know it's a woman?" I stared at her across the gun with a stoic expression.

"You just told me it was a woman," she replied.

"No. I told you I saw the other 'contractor.'."

"Oh," she said calmly, "I thought you said..."

"Come clean," I yelled, as I cocked the hammer.

My no nonsense demeanor and the gravity of the situation seemed to take effect instantly. Suddenly she realized she was caught. She gestured toward her cigarettes and I nodded that it was okay for her to grab one. After lighting a fresh one with the old one she leaned back, casually crossing her legs. Although she was trying hard to appear calm, her foot bounced a mile a minute giving away her whole act. She was scared.

I said, "Before you start speaking I want you to bear in mind that I came here totally prepared to kill you. Only reason you ain't already shot and bleeding out is because you been like a mother to me. I owe it to that relationship to at least try to make sense of this madness."

"Everything I did, I did for you. You were never going to quit. I tried everything from talking to you to dangling millions of dollars in your face. Nothing

224

worked. It's like you were addicted to that shit. I was the one who got you in, so I felt I had to get you out."

"By double booking my jobs?" I asked, puzzled by her logic.

She exhaled and finally admitted, "Yes."

"How the fuck did you figure that was gonna do anything but get me killed?"

"Lex, you have no idea how stubborn you are… Guess maybe that's my fault. I taught you to live life on your own terms. I'm proud of you for that. The only way to make you quit was to make you feel like it was your idea.

"As far as you getting killed, I wasn't worried about that. You're too good. And, that's why I hired a female, one with minimal experience. All she was supposed to do was get in the way a little. I was surprised when she actually filled a contract."

I was livid at how lightly she had taken it all. In her game I was a lowly pawn. My hand tensed on the pistol grip, but I reminded myself that I still needed more information from her. "Minimal experience, huh? That bitch you put on me is the Black Widow incarnate."

"The who?"

"Never mind. I can almost understand your sociopathic reasoning behind that part. What I wanna know is how you knew I'd fall for her in Miami?"

"What?" she looked dumbfounded.

"Okay, better yet, what the fuck was the point of hooking me up with the Imperial gig and then having her rob me? Now I gotta start from scratch hitting marks. That shit basically reversed your plan…if that was your plan." I watched her face keenly as she wrestled with a look of utter confusion.

"Fall for her? Robbed you?" she whispered, silently connecting the dots. "Aye, Dios mio! Lex, are you saying the girl you were telling me about is...and she robbed you..."

I pressed the barrel of my Ruger flush against her forehead as I stood up towering over her. Her head tilted back, and her eyes met mine. "You know I almost believe you didn't know anything about her robbing me..." I eased my finger onto the sensitive trigger.

Tears started to roll down her face. I almost couldn't look at her. As I prepared to squeeze the trigger, she spoke, "Lex, we both know I never meant for all this to happen. There was no way I could have known you'd fall in love with her. If killing me makes us even...then so be it. I feel so bad for what happened, I feel dead already. I know it's too late, but I'm sorry." She closed her eyes and her face looked tranquil as she quietly recited a Spanish prayer.

I stood there contemplating killing the woman who had been like a mother to me. Even though it was her life that was in danger, my life flashed before my eyes. There had been so much love and so many memories between her and me. From the corners of my mind I heard Bubby's advice about not letting my head prevent me from using my heart. I knew in my heart that Nana Helen's deception had started out with good intentions and my meeting and falling for Chaine had simply been a cruel twist of fate. Although she had deceived me, killing her wouldn't solve anything. I holstered my weapon.

She looked up at me through streaming tears and said, "Lex, I'm sorry."

"The deed is done; all you can do now is tell me how to find her."

"All I have is a phone number. I can call her, offer work, have her come here," she plotted.

"First, I think you done enough... Second, she got $5m, she ain't gonna come out for work. Jus gimme the number," I spat, from behind a stone faced expression.

As she scribbled a number on a slip of paper, she said, "Please let me help you. Let me make this right."

I snatched the paper from her hand and headed for the door. She called out, "Lex, wait!"

Over my shoulder I said, "Me and you are done. If you ever see me again, it means I've come to see you on business. I hope the money in that bag was worth it."

I was out the door and in the stairway before she could do or say anything. I never looked back. As I stepped out of the building into the chilly evening air, the door closed behind me reminding me that I had just closed the door on a big part of my life. I took out the slip of paper she'd written the number on. I recognized it as Chaine's answering service. A dead end. I let the paper go and it was carried away on a breeze. I jumped in the ride with Bubby. He knew the next stop.

Bubby received a warm welcome from the crowd in the Third rail. Folks milled around him and hung on his words as he spoke. It was like he was the Mayor of wherever he went. I'd often wondered what it was like to have a lot of friends and be well liked. I sort of envied Bubby that way. Maybe when I left N.Y. and my old lifestyle behind me I could start fresh as a likeable "everyman" type. A cat like Bubby surely would never find himself in the position I was in.

As I lingered in the bar's entryway I realized that I had very few options, and even less chance of finding Chaine. I had dialed her cell number and come up short. It went straight to voice mail. The actual phone was without a doubt resting at the bottom of some body of water or another. Her answering machine and any phones she had were certainly not in her real name anyway. Nana Helen and I had both made the mistake of underestimating Chaine. She was a cold technician. The only hope I had of finding her outside of divine intervention rested with Big Tee.

When Mila caught sight of me from behind the bar her face lit up. I smiled briefly and nodded for her to join me back in Big Tee's office. She left the bar unattended and caught up with me in the hallway slipping an arm around my waist. I couldn't help but smile at how giddy she was.

"Is that mil' ticket in that 'Louie' knapsack or are you just happy to see me?" she asked playfully.

"Yeah, this you," I said, as I handed her the bag. "Make sure you get my bag back to me too…know how you don't like returning stuff," I added.

"Maybe I'll get you a whole Louis Vuitton set to show you my appreciation."

"Think nothing of it. You did great, can't think of nobody I'd rather ride with."

She gave me a big hug. I lingered. After the day I'd had I needed a hug. My smile had faded and she took notice. "Long hug, sad face…lemme guess, you leavin' on a midnight train to Georgia, aren't you?"

I sighed. "Homie, I wish it was that simple."

"What's up?"

"C'mon, I got a story to tell," I replied, as I headed back to the office.

I had decided to tell both her and Big Tee how things had fallen apart on me. I was telling Big Tee because I needed his help, and I just figured Mila deserved to know. She had risked life and limb helping me on that job, so the least I could do was tell her what happened to a large portion of the loot. If anything it would save me from having to tell the same story twice.

"Lemme guess, ya'll finally gon' make it official and jump the broom!" Big Tee joked as we walked in.

"I damn sure ain't getting married no time soon," Mila said, as she smiled at the knapsack holding her fortune and took a seat on the edge of Big Tee's desk. She hugged it like it was a newborn.

"I got too many problems to be the marrying type," I said in a somber tone. I took a seat in the chair in front of the desk and it seemed Big Tee immediately noticed that I had some type of problem with me.

"What's happ'n, young brother?" He pushed aside some papers he had been dealing with and gave me his full attention. Mila eyed me carefully, curious if I was about to give up the goods.

I paused before taking off into my saga. Something in the way Mila looked told me she hadn't told Big Tee or didn't want him to know about the job. At the same time, I wasn't exactly ready to lay all my business on the table as far as hits for hire went either. I decided to tell an edited version of what had happened. Both of them would know I was leaving stuff out, but it was need to know. Mila didn't need to know I was a contract killer, and Big Tee didn't need to know Mila had rode shotgun on the Imperial caper.

They both sat listening intently while I ran through a carefully edited version of the tale. I could tell they had no idea where it was all leading, and as I told the story I realized what an astronomical misfortune it had all been. When I came to the events of the day, they still couldn't tell how it all tied together. I finally got to the part about Chaine making off with my loot plus my stash and their looks of confusion were suddenly replaced by astonishment. Their jaws dropped and they both quietly cursed as I added in the final part about having little or no leads on how to even find her.

When I finished Mila's face was pale, and she covered her gaping mouth with the tips of her neatly manicured fingers. Big Tee neatly folded his hands together, placing them on the desk in front of him. He had a sorry look on his face that looked like it had

229

happened to him. Seemed like he was at a loss for words. I guess seeing $5 million disappear would do that to you.

Mila spoke first. "How are we gonna find this bitch?"

"With her pockets fat she ain't comin' out for work," I replied. I could see Mila hadn't put together what kind of work that was. She was curious, but left it alone.

"Told you you shoulda handled that in Jamaica, homie."

"Spare me the lecture, Big Homie."

"It's gonna' be hard getting that money back if you do manage to catch up with her," Mila said.

"I want the paper, but I really jus' wanna..." I paused, choosing my words carefully, "...let this broad know how I feel about the while thing."

"So, how you suppose we run her down?"

"I was hoping you might have an idea about that."

Big Tee leaned back in his chair thinking. As he pondered my predicament I silently hoped that something would come to him. I'd never found myself in position where I needed anyone's help, and it was awkward for me. I t was the equivalent of sitting in jail waiting on someone to send bail money. I briefly glanced at my watch and was reminded of not only what Chaine and I had shared, but how deep the deception ran. Mila saw me stressing and broke the silence, "You probably don't wanna hear this, but it coulda happened to anybody."

"Fuck that! Miss me with that bullshit, Mila."

"I'm just saying...the sex, the chemistry...shit, the watch. Anybody woulda got trapped off."

"You're not helping." I was frustrated. Turning my focus to Big Tee, I said, "Maybe I should leave and

230

come back later…Give you a little time to think about it. I know this is some heavy shit for me to lay on your desk like this."

"Impatient ain't gon' get you nowhere, young gunna'. We all on the same team."

"I know, I'm sorry," I apologized to both of them.

A few minutes passed with none of us saying a single word. The silence had a distinct presence, almost as though it was the fourth person in the room. Big Tee was the one who finally broke the silence, "So, lemme ask you this…What did you come here expecting me to say or do about this?" he asked me sternly.

His tone caught Mila off guard. He sounded like he was annoyed with me, like I'd assumed too much in coming to him. She looked at me nervously awaiting my response. I thought for a second, and then said, "Well, what I expected you to say was… *'Don't even trip lil' homie. I'ma handle the muthafucka. Lemme make a few calls…we'll have it right in 48 hours or less.'*"

He leaned back in his chair thoughtfully shaking his head. Seemed like he really dug what I said. He looked me square in the eye and repeated my words, "Don't even trip homie. I'm on the muthafucka. I'ma make a few calls, and we'll have the shit straight in 48 hours or less."

For the first time since everything had gone from sugar to shit on me, I had a feeling I might just come out on top. I looked as Big Tee eased back in his chair with his sly grin on, and I smiled ear to ear. I knew from dealing with him that when he told you it was going to rain, you got an umbrella.

Mila wasn't quite as confident and asked him, "How do you track her down with no trail?"

"Ole' girl 'bout as smart as they come. She got plenty cash and them stones ready to roll…What's gon' slow her down is them pills. No way she gon' risk everything hittin' the road with all them drugs. Right now she lookin' to sell...Just so happens that by tomorrow the word'll be out that I'm lookin' to buy...I ain't gon' find her...she gon' come find me."

It was like watching your big brother figure out a puzzle that had been busting your ass for weeks. Mila and I shook our heads in agreement with the ingenuity and the cleverness of his plan. Provided Chaine hadn't already sold off the pills, selling them would be the only thing keeping her in the city. She couldn't have known there was going to be drugs in my stash. Without a sale already lined up, it would take her at least a day or so to get something together. If big Tee did manage to put a deal together, that represented my last chance at catching her before she vanished forever.

"What you need me to do?"

"All you need to do is decide how you wanna play it once she pop her head up. After I draw her out, it's your show. For now ya'll can just fall back and let me work my hand...Besides, both of ya'll done had enough action and adventure for one day."

His comment almost slid by unnoticed, but after it hung there for a second, Mila and I both realized the implication. We looked at each other for a moment, and then looked at him. He had his head cocked to one side with a raised eyebrow. I didn't know how, but he knew Mila was in on the heist. Maybe I'd slipped or maybe his reach was just that long and he'd heard through the grapevine, then put two and two together.

"How'd you..." Mila started to speak, but I grabbed her arm putting the brakes on her question. She was hip to a lot, but had yet to learn about that "gangsta silence."

"Aiight, Big Homie, I'ma be lay low in' by Mila's crib. Can't rest at my spot while Queen Snake still got my keys. When you know something, hit me over there." I stood to leave tugging Mila's arm to roll with me. She took the hint, and we headed for the door.

When we got to the door, Big Tee said, "Depending on how you decide to play it, we may need some flash money."

"...follow the snake back to the nest," I added, realizing I would probably have to tail Chaine back to her lair. It was a new problem I hadn't thought of. The transaction would probably have to go down if I wanted anything other than just to kill Chaine.

Noticing my hesitation Big Tee added, "I could probably get you some scratch, but the juice gon' be runnin'."

"Nah, he's straight. A player always keep a little something for a rainy day," Mila chimed in, before pulling me the rest of the way through the door.

In the hallway outside Big Tee's office she handed me the knapsack and her keys. I took the keys, but hesitated to take the bag. She said, "Do me a favor Lex, miss me with the male ego stuff. Take the money, give it back to me when you get right."

"I can't, this is your come up..."

"If it wasn't for you, I wouldn't of seen dollar one of that money. We come up together...ride or die."

I reluctantly took the bag from her. I was so moved by her gesture that I didn't even know what to say. All the time her and me had been friends I'd been so caught up with my work that I never recognized just how good a friend she was. She was selflessly willing to risk her fortune to help me recover mine. Little by little as my crazy situation unfolded, what I was starting to see more than anything was that I had some really good friends. For the longest I'd just had trouble seeing them for who and what they were.

"I'll have this back to you as soon as I can," I said, as I slung the bag over my shoulder.

"I know."

I gave her a warm hug with my free arm and whispered "Thank you" in her ear. She went back out front to the bar, and I went and pried Bubby away from his constituents. On the way over to Mila's I brought him up to speed about the plan to lure Chaine out. We'd more than likely have to tail her, so I told him to make sure he didn't ride anything too out of the ordinary when it was show time. He laughed at my stating the obvious, and told me not to worry.

Mila lived just a hop and a skip from Mt. Vernon, in the Baychester section of the North Bronx. The duplex she rented wasn't far from where we went to high school. We pulled in front of her place and I was about to get out, but I noticed it seemed like Bubby had something on his mind. Usually a lot of things went unspoken between him and me, but it was time for a change.

"What's good?" I asked him.

"Just thinkin', is all."

"Lay it on me," I pressed.

"I don't wanna seem like I'm tryna' guide your actions or nothin' like that..."

"Speak your mind."

"Well...It's looking like you got a fair shot at catching up with ole' girl, and I know you probably got your mind made up as far as how you wanna deal with her."

"Yeah...pretty much," I responded.

"I was probably outta line puttin' that bug in your ear when you went to see Helena, but ya'll got history, and I ain't wanna see you do nothin' rash."

"I know you was just lookin' out. I appreciate it."

234

He shook his head and stared blankly out the window at the deserted street. "Lex, I could tell you really loved that girl," he paused, but I didn't respond so he continued, "love ain't no one-way street. The way you described it, I think she loved you too."

"Hell no! That bitch a snake," I grumbled.

"Be that as it may, there had to be something, some type of circumstance, that made her do what she did."

"Whatever her reason, she did it. She shoulda killed me when she had the chance."

"Why didn't she?"

As his question hung there, I realized he had a point. Why hadn't she killed me? Maybe she did have some type of feelings for me and those feelings had made her sloppy, just the same as mine had made me. It was too late for all that though. The only thing the rage inside me would allow me to do was show her that leaving me alive had been a fatal mistake.

"She didn't kill me 'cause she thought I couldn't catch her." I said it, but I knew it wasn't the truth.

"You gon' do what you gon' do regardless what ole' Bubby say, but when the time comes, you should just consider finding out why she did it."

"Yeah, aiight." I patronized him. I had no intentions of discussing anything with her besides my stash and a bullet in her brain.

After thanking Bubby for the advice, I got out of the car. As I closed the door, he shook his head ruefully. He knew that this time around his words had fallen on deaf ears.

I was surprised to find it was well after midnight when I let myself in Mila's dark apartment. I turned on a few lights in the modestly furnished space and hooked myself up a little spot on the sofa to crash. Once I lay down I found I was more hungry than tired. There was some ground turkey in the fridge, so I fixed myself some turkey burgers with mushrooms and Swiss, and checked out Sports Center on ESPN.

When Mila got in from work a couple hours later, she was dead tired and headed straight to bed. I would have liked if she'd stayed up and hung out a while, but after the day she'd had I couldn't blame her. I was left with nothing to do but lie awake recounting the events that led me to where I was. I plotted on what I'd do and say when I caught Chaine, but I knew it wasn't really that type of party. If and when Big Tee managed to draw her out, I'd play the hand as it was dealt. Until then it was a waiting game. While I waited I was haunted by the echoes of love lost.

Eventually I got some light sleep, but even then my dreams were of lost love and lost millions. Mila and I kicked it the following day. She did a good job of trying to keep my mind off things despite that it was an impossible mission. We basically just watched movies and took turns staring at the phone, trying to will it to ring.

The wait was hellish, to say the very least. It would have been even worse if Mila hadn't traded shifts to keep me company. She made us a light dinner that evening and even though we were nowhere near the 48 hour mark, I started to wonder if Chaine hadn't eluded me completely. Big Tee must have sensed that a brother was under extreme stress because at 8pm, not even a full 24 hours from getting on the case, the call came in.

I snatched the receiver off the cradle. "What up?"

"It's a go, homie!"

"When?"

"Queen Snake'll be in the garden in the witching hour. She bit at a ticket. Fall through 'round ten so we can get situated."

236

"One."

"One."

Big Tee came through as promised...Midnight couldn't come fast enough.

Chapter 15

Bubby and I sat reclined in the leather seats of a Dodge Magnum parked halfway up the block from the Third Rail. From behind dark tinted windows I anxiously eyed everything that moved on the quiet block. It was just after midnight and everyone was playing their positions waiting on Chaine to show up.

The consensus among Big Tee, Bubby, and Mila had been that I should snatch her up as soon as she showed herself, take her into the storeroom, and "persuade" her to tell me where the money was. The problem I had with that strategy was that there was no way to be sure she'd talk, and by letting her talk I would be giving her the opportunity to lie. I'd decided to go against their advice and chose to let the deal go down and then follow her. I figured that with a million cash in hand there weren't too many places you went to other than your stash.

I fingered the grip of one of my pistols while I watched and waited. The beginnings of feelings of worry began to creep into my mind as the moments past midnight ticked away. I started to think she was a no show because fashionable lateness was for clubs and parties, not million dollar drug deals. I had just begun to plot what my next move would be if she didn't show up when a black Lincoln Town car eased past us down the block. When the brake lights lit up and they slowed to a stop in front of the spot my heart started pounding so fast I thought it was going to explode. My hand instinctively wrapped the rest of the way around the pistol grip and I had to make a conscious effort not to hop out and do a "Rambo."

The rear door opened and the passenger put one leg out. She paused. From the tight fitting jeans and high heeled boots the only thing I could tell for sure was that it was a woman. Seemed like she was giving her driver some last minute instructions before getting out. As I sat there watching and saturated in anticipation, my breathing began to mimic my irregular heartbeat.

Despite the ambient light from the bar, I couldn't see her clearly when she stepped out onto the sidewalk because she was wearing a knitted Dior sweater with a hood that covered her like a rain poncho. She leaned inside the car retrieving a black bag and her purse from the backseat, and then headed inside. I knew that figure and her unmistakable walk, but I needed to be sure.

I practically had my face pressed against the glass trying to peep her when Bubby cleared his throat reminding me that I had another option. Big Tee had given me his Blackberry so I could watch the video feed from the cameras inside the bar. I snatched the device from the dashboard and turned it on. It glowed to life with an image of the woman standing in the vestibule. The picture came on, and I finally saw for sure that it was Chaine.

She had paused in the entryway to unfasten the clasp of her handbag and reached inside it to adjust something that I knew undoubtedly had to be a weapon. It came as no surprise. Big Tee and I had expected her to be holding. When I'd warned him he had waved it off with a smile.

She entered the bar and I switched to the camera mounted over the door that gave me a view of the entire barroom. The men in the room instinctively took notice and the women shot her jealous stares as she crossed the room. Watching a rear view of her sexy walk my mind wanted to go somewhere else until I saw Mila make an unscripted move toward her from behind the bar. Bubby and I exchanged puzzled glances while Mila walked up on Chaine intercepting her just before she got to the hallway.

"Shit," I mumbled. Mila's cold expression told me what she had on her mind, but she had no idea who she was dealing with. I love a good catfight as much as the next man, but this one would never go the distance. I feared for Mila's safety as they stood toe to toe having a verbal exchange. I would have given anything to have sound with the picture and hear what was being said. I finally found relief when Mila smiled and made a gesture toward Chaine's purse. That's when I realized Mila was just giving in to her feminine curiosity to meet the woman behind my headache. I guess she'd seen Chaine was carrying a brand new Fendi spy bag and used the opportunity to get a close up. I was mad she'd deviated from the script, but there was no harm done once she pointed the way back to Big Tee's office. In a way it helped that Chaine knew she had been seen and identifiable, thereby lessening the chances she would try anything funny on Big Tee.

I skipped the hallway and went straight to the interior of the office. Big Tee had just popped the door and sat back in his chair behind steepled fingers. He looked like a big black judge, and in the center of his desk sat his gavel, his nickel plated .50 caliber Desert Eagle.

When Chaine entered the office he greeted her with a curt nod and gestured for her to have a seat. They spoke briefly and Big Tee said something that made her laugh. She had her normal poise and grace sitting across from him with her long legs crossed. Her pose was deliberately sexy and designed to throw off any fool who

240

didn't think their life could end the moment she reached into her purse. Big Tee was hip to her, but I could tell that she was a lot more attractive than he'd expected.

The transaction took about ten minutes. As I watched her sitting there flirting with the big homie, I wondered if maybe I shouldn't have just run down on her then and there. I had no idea where she was going for sure after the meeting. By choosing to follow her, I was virtually risking the bird in the hand for two in the bush.

My doubts didn't have a chance to solidify. Big Tee pointed to the "Louie" knapsack hanging on the coat tree in the corner behind the door. Chaine picked up her black bag from the floor, unzipped it, and gave Big Tee a peek at the pills inside. He nodded his approval. She set the bag down and made for the door. She said something I was very curious to hear as she grabbed the knapsack, peeking inside on her way out the door. When she was gone Bug Tee looked directly up at the camera and shook his head indicating that he now had a much better understanding of how I got got

When she emerged from the Third Rail I'd already turned off the screen so its faint glow didn't give us away. Her ride pulled up right on cue and whisked her away. Bubby let another car go by before pulling out into traffic behind them. He left enough room so that only a well trained professional would know they were being followed. I sat back and let Bubby do his thing.

Even though I was trying to relax, he noticed me staring at the sedan's brake lights. "Lex, you over there looking like a one eyed cat peepin' in the window of a seafood restaurant," he joked. We shared a brief laugh, but I was only momentarily at ease.

After everything that had happened to me I thought there wasn't much that could catch me by surprise, but when the Town Car got on the highway heading south into Manhattan I realized I was wrong.

We maintained a safe distance behind them. Although it was after midnight there was still moderate traffic, and we remained unnoticed. While Bubby focused on keeping us close enough, I began to silently panic. Why would she be going into Manhattan? Of all the places I'd considered that she might be hiding, Manhattan didn't even make the list. I couldn't fathom that she would have stolen from me and hid out in my own backyard, so when they pulled up in front of the W hotel in midtown I just assumed she was stopping off to handle some business.

A light drizzle had begun to fall over the city. When Chaine stepped from the vehicle the hotel's doorman scurried over with an umbrella and escorted her inside. As she passed through the glass doors her driver sped away into the night. That wasn't as important to me as her having the knapsack in tow. Whatever reason she was at the hotel probably involved that money, and I was not prepared to let her too far out of my sight with it. I made a split second decision to follow her inside. She'd already made off with my fortune, I wasn't about to let her get away with Mila's.

I watched her walk into the hotel lobby and stop at the front desk. While she had a brief exchange with the night desk clerk I turned to Bubby and tried to hand him one of my pistols. "The safety's off," I said.

"Nah, I'm good." He refused.

"Take it just in case," I insisted.

"I'm good."

"I rather you with it than without it."

"Don't worry about me," he said. Before I could respond he added, "Heads up, Lex! She on the move!"

I holstered the pistol as I hopped out of the car and dodged traffic crossing the street. The doorman shot me a puzzled glance trying to figure out what my hurry was. I ignored him and kept watching Chaine crossing the lobby through the plate glass windows. She kept her hood drawn keeping her incognito, but it also kept her oblivious to my presence. She also took no notice of the man seated on one of the couches watching her. As I passed through the large glass doors he was the first thing I noticed in the ornately furnished hotel lobby.

Night staff and hotel guest went about their business, but this one cat stood out to me for three reasons. First, he was wearing a real nice suit. British cut, had to be straight from Saville Row. A black man with a neatly manicured goatee and short dreads didn't usually stick out, but this guy was almost too clean. Next, he's sitting there dapper as a mofo', after midnight, lone reading a paper. Third, I just got this vibe off him. Normally when a man checks out a woman he'll let her know he's watching, but this guy was real careful not to let Chaine see him watching her. I sized him up, and he wasn't strapped. If I'd have had an extra set of eyes they would have stayed on him, but I had Chaine to deal with. She was a handful.

The hotel lobby spread out in two directions. To the far right were banks of elevators that took guests to rooms on the upper floors. On the left were a few shops that were closed for the evening and a restaurant that was still open. I could tell from the faint tinkle of keys that the place must double as a late night piano bar. Chaine had gone to the left. I was relieved that she hadn't headed for the elevators because I would have been forced to make a move on her in the lobby. There was no way I could risk losing her to the hundreds of rooms and suites upstairs. It would have made more sense to take my chances with the dozen or so bystanders milling around.

I stood by a potted palm and pretended to dial my phone as I watched her walk down the corridor and enter the restaurant. After waiting a few moments for her

243

to go inside and get situated, I followed her. My steps down the corridor, although silent, echoed inside my head like thunder in the mountains. To say I was nervous about the impending showdown was understating it. I felt like the butterflies in my stomach had gone into a sudden frenzy. This restaurant wasn't my first choice for the confrontation, but with nowhere for her to escape to, I knew it was about to go down.

To my surprise there were about 20 people, mostly couples, having drinks in the dimly lit restaurant. Near the center of the room a middle aged white guy in a cheap suit played an old Richard Marx ballad on a baby grand piano. He had a few bills in his tip glass, but for the most part the crowd was more worried about late night rendezvous than music.

I looked past him anxiously scanning the place and spotted Chaine at the far end of the room. She was perched on a stool at the bar having a glass of wine. Either she felt very safe or she was already drunk because she had her back to the entire room and the knapsack on the stool next to her like it was all good. That struck me as odd because as a professional hitter and a wanted woman one would expect that she would be extra cautious, checking her six o'clock every few moments.

It was her sloppy technique that put me much more on point as I began to approach her. I crossed the room in my classic glide/stride fashion with one hand ready to draw, but not exactly reaching. As I passed behind the cheesy piano man I had an impulse. I stopped and whispered a few words in his ear and dropped a $20 bill in his glass. Chaine still hadn't turned around by the time I closed the distance between us. It seemed her wine glass had her full attention. Catching her seemed too easy. I stood just a few feet behind her hesitating and wondering if it wasn't some type of trick.

244

The room fell silent as the Marx ballad ended and the piano man got ready to play his next song. The opening of Alicia Keys' song "If I Ain't Got You" sprinkled over the room like the light rain that fell over the city. Watching Chaine closely I detected what looked like a deep sigh from the rise and fall of her shoulder. It kind of surprised me that she had any reaction at all, but it was too late for sentiment. Almost everything that had happened between us had been set to music, so I figured that the last scene should be too. Call it poetic justice.

"Is this seat taken?" The sound of my voice startled her. She must have taken me for a damned fool because she casually began to reach for her purse.

"Anything but hands folded in your lap'll get you two hot ones and a headache," I warned.

She complied grudgingly, and placed her folded hands on top of her dramatically crossed legs. I knew for sure it was her, but I still couldn't believe how easy catching her had been. I snatched the hood off her head. As she turned toward me I was momentarily startled to see she had cut off all her hair, and now had a neat low Caesar. I didn't have the luxury of being taken aback by how good she looked with the short hair-do. Her eyes met min as she turned toward me. She'd been crying. I paid her tears no mind though. Instead I shot her a scorching look from murderously blazing eyes. Her red-rimmed gaze seemed to have a story behind it, but I was in no mood to hear it.

"I didn't think it'd be you," she said.

"You thought a new haircut and a hood would keep you safe?" I asked through clenched teeth.

"No, I just figured some no talent headhunter'd be the one to luck up. Some type of cruel irony, you know?"

"A bar, just like where it all started ain't ironic enough?"

"So, I guess the music was you too, huh?" she asked.

"Hmph."

"Well…you got me, now what?"

"Now you got a choice: Gimme what you stole from me and maybe I'll let you take your chances with the headhunters…"

"Or?"

"Or, I hot you right here, collect a fraction of what I lost, and be done with this whole fiasco," I sneered.

At hearing the second option she gave me a "you-don't-really-expect-me-to-believe-that" grin and began to reach forward. I halfway drew my pistol getting ready to shoot her. She regarded me curiously and said, "Easy, Cowboy. I'm just taking a sip of my drink." I nodded for her to go ahead. While she sipped I took her purse and set it on the floor. Its weight told the whole story.

"You know, it's bad luck to put a woman's purse on the floor."

"It's on you to make your own luck. You got two choices. Where's my money?"

"Or what, you'll shoot me?" she asked arrogantly.

Her confidence disgusted me. The vein in my neck pulsed and swelled dangerously. My face became a dark mask as I said, "I've killed for less. You sure you wanna try me?" The million in that knapsack'll make up for part of my loss. The rest I'd pay to be done with you."

She scrutinized my face looking for clues as to how I knew about the money. I stood there stone faced and didn't satisfy her curiosity. "Lex, if you didn't come to kill me then we have no business," before I could interject she continued, "I went by your place earlier this afternoon and returned your money and your diamonds. Your keys are in my purse, I was trying to give them to you when you walked up."

I appraised her with a long sideways glance. "You expect me to believe that?"

"It's the truth."

"You can't speak the truth, you got a forked tongue," I spat. She sat silent and teary eyed. "And what about the money in the bag? What's that, your reward for returning what you stole?"

"No, that's child support," she said matter-of-factly. Her words blindsided me, but through the shock I was immediately mindful of her deceptive ways. Curious, but skeptical, I said, "Oh, you're expecting? Congratulations!" She rolled her eyes. "When you due?" I asked sarcastically.

"Nine months from one of the many time we had unprotected sex," she simply stated before sipping her red wine.

Her words had gravity. Our countless sexual escapades popped through my mind like paparazzi flash bulbs. There was a definite possibility she could've gotten pregnant, but then I remembered who I was dealing with. I said, "So, you're pregnant and still drinking...You make it real easy to believe you."

She silently slid her glass over to me. I hesitated to drink from her, but she'd been drinking it herself. I took the glass and sipped. Cranberry juice. I quickly snatched her purse off the ground and opened it. She had a phone, some cinnamon Altoids, a hotel key-card, a small semi-automatic pistol, and my keys. I fished out my keys and put the bag back on the floor. The keys weren't enough to convince me, but they had me wondering.

"That's what I came to your place to tell you...Remember? When you fucked me like a whore and were about to throw me out in the street," she explained.

"You must really think I'm some type of sucka," my voice rose with indignation. "I don't believe you. You came to my place with every intention of stealing from me."

"Taking your money was a contingency plan."

"A contingency plan? You didn't even tell me what the deal was. I never stood a chance. Robbing me was your only plan."

"Lex, you said you didn't even wanna be with me, much less with me and a baby. I wasn't trying to trap you."

"Hard to tell from where I'm sitting," I shot back, "I gave you a chance in Jamaica."

"I didn't know I was pregnant then," she argued.

"How is that my fault? You chose the game, remember? In a way I envy you. It must be nice to be that in love with your work."

My harsh words cut her like glass. She had made a series of bad choices, and we both knew it. As a tear welled up in the corner of her right eye I didn't feel sorry for her. I wanted her to feel my anguish. She got it together as best she could and said, "Look, inflation notwithstanding, it costs $850K to raise a kid. Like it or not, I snooped your stash a few weeks ago and you had a million plus. I was just seeing to it that you fulfilled your fiduciary responsibility to this child."

"Unless you got six buns in the oven you kinda went overboard," I replied.

"I didn't expect all the stuff you had in the bag. I was spooked, so I just took the bag and ran."

"And the pills?"

"I'm not even going to try to guess what you're into besides contracts 'Mr.-I'm-not-a-dope-dealer,' I put your money back and then I sold the pills at a fair price."

248

"Even if I believed all this crazy shit you sayin', I should still hot ya' ass off general principle. You sittin' here talking 'bout taking money from me for future child support…"

"What was my option?" she asked, cutting me off. "I'm on the run. You don't need me to explain life on the run. You know it costs. Without that money me and your unborn child don't stand a chance."

Something still wasn't adding up. I said, "You was just ballin' a couple weeks ago, taking shopping sprees and trickin' on big watches." I shook my Versace in her face as a reminder. "Now you tryna tell me you ain't got no stash…You made $750k on Wolf alone."

"I got some paper stashed, but not nearly what I should have. My stash will get me down the road a ways. Then what? Then how am I supposed to live?" She let her barrage of questions linger a moment, then added, "If you have a better option I'm all ears, but if not I need that money."

Her face etched with sorrow told a big part of the story. I had come with every intention of killing Chaine and now I was standing there considering helping her. When I came all the love I felt for her was pushed neatly aside with getting my money back taking center stage. The introduction of the possibility that she might be pregnant had changed things. I was also gravitating towards being sympathetic because as she laid out her situation I saw she had been living a lot like I was before I had hit Imperial. Job to job and spending like it would never run out. Sure, she probably had a million cash saved, but it was just one. In the game one is too close to none. She was right, with people chasing her she'd burn through that in a flash.

"Why all the women in my life gotta be master manipulators?" I grumbled.

"What?"

249

"Never mind…If you telling the truth I'ma help you skate, but it's gon' be on my terms. Them Darkhearts is serious business and I don't think they too far off your ass."

"Why can't you believe me?"

"Because the devil is a liar, and more than likely a woman. If all this is a plot, I promise it'll be the last lie you tell."

"I'm not ly…"

"Let's go." I cut her off. I snatched the knapsack off the stool and slung it on my back. She tried to pick up her purse, but I bent down and quickly scooped it up.

Recognizing my skepticism, she asked, "Where are we going?" in a huff of frustration.

"First, to get a pregnancy test, and then to my place to make sure you really got over your case of sticky fingers."

"We don't have to go anywhere. I have a test upstairs in my room."

I gave her an incredulous grin. I didn't trust her, or me for that matter, in a room with a bed.

"I promise it's not a set up. I bought like five, but I gave up after three positives."

I hesitated.

She pleaded, "Please, I just don't wanna be in the streets. It's after one;, we'll be all over the place trying to find a drugstore."

I stood there thinking about it, and she had a good point. I had no desire to be running around the city with someone with a price on their head if I could help it. We could grab a test from her room and then shoot straight to my place. It was a lot safer than the streets.

Standing aside I gestured for her to lead the way. As we walked out of the restaurant I was obligated to watch her closely. I think she knew that and put just a little something extra in the switch of her hips because I was watching.

When we came out into the corridor I realized how unnatural we looked with her in front of me like a prisoner, and me with her purse and the knapsack she'd been carrying following behind her. I quickly slipped the pistol from her bag and put it in the back of my waistband. I gave her purse to her and she smiled briefly, but it evaporated just that fast as she judged the bag's weight and realized the pistol was gone. I smiled briefly at her dismay and then offered her my arm in consolation so that we could stroll through the lobby under the guise of lovers headed upstairs to do what lovers do. She pasted a plastic smile on her face and played the role.

As we passed through the center of the lobby I wondered how strange it must look to Bubby to see Chaine and I heading upstairs arm in arm. The slick guy in the suit was still on the couch, but he was engrossed in his paper when we went by and didn't appear to notice us. Something about him still didn't sit right with me, and maybe if I hadn't been processing so much information at the time, I would have heeded the warning my senses were giving me.

Standing next to Chaine in front of the elevator's stainless steel doors I stared at our reflections on the shiny surface while we waited. I notice how pretty she was with her new short hair-do. We had made a really good looking couple, and as the elevator doors opened, I was just picturing her at nine months pregnant with me standing by her side. I realized that despite what had happened, I wanted to have a baby with her. I decided that if she really was pregnant, I would do everything in my power to see to it that she stayed safe.

The elevator doors were just sliding closed when I took one last look around the lobby. Chaine was busy pressing the button and didn't see what I saw. The slick cat in the suit folded up his paper and had taken out his cell phone. He headed for the door animatedly talking to someone. In his excitement his voice rose just enough that a tiny fragment of his conversation carried through the spacious lobby. I was sure he'd said the words "red hair" just before leaving. That phrase put everything in perspective, and I realized why the vibe off him had been so strong; he was a spotter and Chaine had just been spotted.

On her way in she'd had her hood drawn, so he hadn't been able to I.D. her for certain. We'd just walked through giving him a clean look at her. Enough of a look that he knew it was her without the fuchsia (red) hair.

I startled Chaine as I lunged for the "door open" button but it was too late. The powerful modern elevator already had us halfway to the sixth floor. I quietly muttered curses and leaned back against the elevator's mahogany paneled interior. Whoever that spotter was working with would be on us in a matter of minutes. I couldn't think of a worse situation than being boxed in and not knowing who was trying to get me or how many of them there were. I hesitated to get out when the doors opened on six. She stepped off the elevator and looked back at me regarding me curiously. I stood there a moment weighing our options. For as second I considered going straight back downstairs and making a break for it, but there existed a strong possibility that we could walk out of the elevator into a hail of bullets.

Sensing something was wrong, Chaine asked, "What's wrong with you? You look like you saw a ghost."

"Worse," I said stepping out into the hallway. "I think we got company in-bound. Where's your room?"

Her lips formed a mute 'Oh,' as my words registered. "Shit! How?...C'mon." She dashed down the hall and around the corner with me on her heels. In front of room 6605 we stopped and she was about to put her keycard in the door but paused.

I knew what she was thinking. If they were on to her, maybe they placed a device in her room while she was out. It crossed my mind too, but I was 99.9% certain they'd only just now ID'd her for certain. Planting a bomb meant you knew for sure you had your mark. Slick had only just now made her in the lobby, so whoever he was calling had to be en route.

I snatched the keycard from her trembling fingertips and pushed her aside. I drew my pistol just in case and opened the door. Nothing. I took a couple steps inside and gave the room the once over. It was clean except that the T.V. and all the lights were on, and I knew she'd left them all on to make it seem like someone was there. I'd have done the same. She walked in behind me and went past me heading straight into the bathroom. I took a look out the hallway before closing the door. It would probably take whoever was coming a few minutes to find which room we were in and that was all we had as far as an advantage.

She was only in the bathroom a few moments, but while she was gone I couldn't help but check the closet and under the bed looking for the Coach bag that held my stash. As it stood she was the one on the contract, not me. I had everything to lose just being near her.

The situation was more than likely going to escalate long before we made it to my place, and I needed something other than just her word to go on before I got in too deep. I was looking around the room for anything that might bolster my confidence in her story. I found what I was looking for in a waste basket next to the nightstand. Just as she came out of the bathroom behind me I scooped the discarded pregnancy test stick out of the trash. My jaw dropped as I looked in the small window and saw a red "+" symbol. Breath caught in my throat forming a lump. Chaine came around beside me. She smiled demurely. "Do we still need these?" she asked, waving two unused pregnancy test kits.

The shock hadn't worn off but I forced it aside. "No!" I responded. "But you gonna need this." I pulled her pistol from the back of my waist and handed it to her. I gave her a conspiratorial grin as she accepted the weapon. That was when she surprised me. Without the least bit of warning she kissed me. Had I seen it coming I might have ducked or turned away, but once her lips touched mine I had no desire to fight it. I wrapped my free arm around her waist and drew her close to me. We kissed fiercely with bodies pressed together, both of us with pistols held at our sides. The room spun, and all the events that brought us there stripped away bit by bit leaving behind just us. For just a moment we floated. Our moment of resurfacing passion was short lived. The tingle of senses warning me of eminent danger snatched me back from paradise.

"We gotta get gone," I said, abruptly ending our tender embrace.

She looked confused for just a second, but quickly came to her senses. Her silent nod seemed to say what I was thinking without quite saying it. There was a lot that needed to be said between us, but we didn't have the time. "We'll talk later," I said.

"Promise?"

I looked deeply into her eyes and said, "I promise." I knew that I was essentially promising her that there actually would be a later for the both of us, and I meant it. If I didn't ever do anything else with my life, I was going to get her out of that hotel safely. The resolute look in my eyes seemed to comfort her.

Without another thought I scrambled into the bathroom. Using the butt of my pistol I shattered the mirror. I took a piece of glass and rushed past a confused Chaine for the door. She got behind me, pistol at the ready, as I checked the peephole and then opened the door just a crack. With the small piece of mirror I checked the hallway and found it all clear. We cautiously padded out into the corridor. She walked backward behind us holding down our six while I keenly led us forward.

We were about to turn the blind corner heading back to the elevators and stairwells when I paused. Playing it safe I used the mirror to peep around the corner. I was just about to rule it all clear and make the final push for the stairway when a booted foot stepped off the elevator.

The booted foot belonged to the first of three men getting off the elevator. They were all black men and one wore long dreads. It wasn't hard to tell they were there for us. I could tell that without having seen that they all wore long coats like the "dusters" in Western flicks.

Not to seem a fan of racial profiling, but even in the middle of the night three black men in long coats should have raised some flags. Where was the government's war on terror when I needed it? They were no doubt strapped with some significant firepower under their coats. I sized them up for a moment while they got their bearings. As soon as they figured out which way the room was and started heading toward us I pulled the mirror back. I looked at Chaine and my quick nod told her it was all bad. We bolted back to the room and quickly holed up inside.

They had us cornered, flanked, outnumbered, and outgunned. Butch and Sundance probably had a better hand on the cliff. Best I could tell from looking at them, they were actual Darkheart crew members and not professional contractors. They must have taken finding Chaine as a top priority if they'd farmed the job out and were still working on it themselves. I was "glad" they weren't seasoned professionals because a thug could be easily tricked, but then again a heavily armed man was a heavily armed man any way you sliced it. They were no more than a few seconds from the door. I tried to formulate a strategy but there was just no time.

The best plan I could come up with was to take cover by the nightstand on the far side of the room. I motioned for Chaine to go and get in the bath tub to keep her safe from the initial gunfire. Hopefully I could draw them into the room enough that Chaine could pop out of the tub and take them out while they were focused on me. It wasn't a great plan, but a bad plan beat no plan seven days a week.

Chaine hesitated to follow my instructions to get in the bathroom. She was a smart chick and it wasn't hard for her to see what I was planning. I showed her the grenade trying to ease her reluctance, but it was like she was refusing to let me risk myself for her.

As our valuable seconds ticked away I pleaded with her with my eyes to just cooperate. At that point bearing most of the risk was all I could think of. For all the contracts I'd filled it was like I had just been killing for more and more money. For once in my life I'd found something that I was willing to die for. Strangely enough I didn't feel scared, I felt liberated.

Apparently Chaine wasn't with my plan at all. Like most hotel rooms there was a door inside the room that opened to another door that led to an adjacent room. Most people kept their doors locked unless you wanted to book a few rooms and open the doors and connect the rooms. I'd seen the door, but wrote it off because the other door behind it was obviously going to be locked. I tried to grab her as she rushed over to it, but I missed her arm by a fraction of an inch. She snatched the first door open and found the second door locked like I thought it'd be. Before I could say or do anything she produces a butterfly knife, from God only knew where, and sticks it between the door and the frame. She rocked it back and forth a couple of times and, Viola! The door swings wide open to the unoccupied adjacent room. I swear, if I hadn't already been in love with her, I'd have fallen in love with her right then.

I crept lightly following her into the next room, and carefully closed the doors behind me. As I was closing the second of the two doors, I heard a knock. We had only narrowly escaped the arrival of our unwanted guests. Chaine and I stood still, enveloped in the quiet darkness of the adjacent room. I wanted to hold her there in the brief calm before the storm, but I knew we didn't have the luxury of time for an embrace. The men in the hallway knew she was in the building somewhere, and they were set on getting her. Them thinking we were still next door gave us a slight advantage, and I intended to use it. We silently navigated the dark room and took up positions by the door leading to the hallway, waiting for our opportunity.

The eerie silence made my skin crawl. Silence was often said to be the last thing you heard before death. When I heard the sound of a boot kick the door off the hinges next door followed by a short burst of automatic gunfire, I welcomed it. I waited. After the gunfire I heard the men rushing into the room, and no doubt finding it empty, I could hear them swearing in heavily accented voices. They tossed the room. These guys surely weren't pro's. They sounded like bulls in a china shop, and I could tell everything they were doing without seeing.

I cracked the door and drew my other pistol getting ready to make my move. They filed out of the room heading back to the elevators. Although there were three of them and one of me with less fire power, I couldn't have had a better vantage point. They never saw what hit them. With my two guns up I sidestepped out into the hallway behind them as they walked away. They were just about to turn the corner when I made it rain. I alternated double taps on both triggers sending shots in rapid succession. The two men closest to me tried to turn around and return fire as my hot slugs caught one guy twice in the back and the other in the shoulder and neck. They both went down hard without getting a single shot off.

The third man, the one with the dreads, had been walking in front of the first two and was actually partially shielded from the onslaught by his partners. I caught him in the shoulder blade, but he was somehow able to stay on his feet and make it around the corner. I briefly turned to Chaine astonished that he'd taken that hit and managed to stay on his feet. As she came along side me she "tsked" and shook her head, teasing me about only getting two out of the three. Before I could react she ran past me to the corner where she dropped to one knee. She let off two quick shots up the hall, and dropped the fleeing injured man.

I'd know Chaine was about her business, but seeing her at work was another thing entirely. I felt a rush of heat to my face from a combination of surprise at her smooth technique and embarrassment at being shown up. I caught up with her as she rounded the corner. she looked at me seductively and said, "A woman's work is never done."

Up the hall, preceded by a trail of blood the dread lay sprawled out with two close holes in his back in addition to my "miss." As we passed his corpse heading for the stairway I was impressed. In another place and time Chaine and I might have made a good team.

We were just ducking into the stairwell as the first two hotel guests started opening their doors and peeking out to see what was going on. They'd been careful to wait until the shooting stopped. Terrified shrieks told us when they saw the bodies. If someone hadn't already called the cops, it wouldn't be long before they did. I bounded down the stairs on instinct trying to put as much space between me and the bodies as possible. A couple of floors down I slowed down for Chaine to catch up, but surprisingly enough despite her heels she was just a few paces behind me.

The lobby drew closer with each step we took. Passing through the lobby presented a number of problems. We were still unsure of how many enemies we were dealing with, and if there were more of them, what they looked like. With the impending arrival of the cops, it wasn't like we could just burst through the lobby with guns out, but rolling through there unarmed wasn't an option either. For the umpteenth time I found myself between a rock and a hard place.

In the end I just left it to common sense. A murder charge beat getting murdered, so as we passed the first floor and descended the final flight of stairs I holstered my pistols. Taking her cue from me, Chaine tucked her burner underneath her sweater. I could tell she wasn't particularly comfortable with that, but we had no choice.

I peeked through the stairwell door and found that the lobby wasn't nearly as chaotic as I'd expected. There was no mass exodus of guests fleeing the gunshots. Actually, there were a couple of people that passed through apparently unaware that anything was going on. The only indication of a problem was the

259

woman at the front desk. In between whispering instructions to various employees, she answered calls on an incessantly ringing phone. Word hadn't quite spread throughout the building yet, but I could tell from her nervous expression that she knew. All the calls she was fielding probably came from guests and she was probably lying her ass off trying to keep them calm.

I scrutinized all the people I saw trying to determine who was friend or foe. Of the half dozen or so people no one looked like a threat. The street out front wasn't visible, but what I could see looked like smooth sailing. I took Chaine by the hand and drew a deep breath as we stepped out into the lobby. For the most part no one paid us any attention, but Chaine laughed and smiled at some joke I never made just for appearance sake. It made us look natural as we leisurely strolled like lovers toward the door. The woman at the desk exchanged fake smiles with Chaine. To her we were just two more guests she wanted to keep comfortable.

As we got closer to the exit I could hear the faint wail of police sirens in the distance. Through the plate glass windows I could see Bubby idling patiently in the Magnum. The rainfall had gotten heavier. I carefully scanned the street out front and nothing looked out of place. The doorman with his umbrella was gone, but I hardly noticed. Maybe the three men upstairs had been the extent of the hit squad. I looked at Chine and she nodded that it looked all clear to her too. It was time to get gone because I surely didn't want to be hanging around when the cops or more Darkhearts showed up.

Approaching the possibility of a flawless escape excited us, and our steps quickened as we neared the large glass doors. There was a tinted out black S-class Mercedes sedan parked directly in front of the entrance. It hadn't bothered me at first glance, but the rear passenger window rolled down just as I started to push the door, and I knew I had made a huge error in judgment. I saw the nozzle of an automatic assault rifle, and I had only a fraction of a second to react. I turned around and shoved Chaine to the ground just as the staccato roar of machine gun fire erupted.

I had spent a significant portion of my adult life intently focused on taking life. I'd never imagined that one day I'd save one. Even more inconceivable was the possibility that I might actually give my life for someone else's, but as I felt the searing pain of hot lead piercing my own flesh the reality of it all materialized. The impact threw me forward and I fell to the ground beside Chaine. All around us shards of broken glass cascaded like crystal raindrops. I writhed there on the floor, my senses flooded with pain that was unimaginable. It hurt so bad that for a moment I couldn't even tell where or how many times I'd been hit. I saw blackness, but wondered if I was dead why I was still feeling pain? The gunfire still pounded.

The pain localized and decreased slightly. It was still excruciating, but I could feel that I was hit high in my right shoulder. The blood felt hot and sticky oozing from my torn flesh. Realizing I wasn't dead I started trying to open my eyes. It was hazy at first, but as I focused I saw Chaine's face. She was right beside me shielding her eyes from the flying glass. The bullets whizzed overhead and all either of us could do was try to stay low. Pieces of glass ate into my flesh as I pressed my body against the ground.

The adrenaline that coursed through my veins had me ready to at least try to survive. The gunfire paused. I heard car doors open and slam shut. They were coming to finish us off and I silently wished the whining police siren were close enough that they actually mattered. The two gunmen stuffed fresh magazines into their Ak-47's as they approached. I recognized one of them as Wolf's lieutenant I'd tossed aside in the club. His menacing gold grill said he had murder on his mind. An incredible pain shot through my body as I made a feeble attempt to draw my pistol with my right hand. Beside me Chaine was reaching but it was too late, they were ten yards away from us on the sidewalk bringing their guns up. Strangely enough, I didn't find myself thinking anything other than that I had failed Chaine and the child I would never have a chance to know.

Chaine and I were sitting ducks. Everyone in the lobby had either taken cover or gotten shot. There was no help. I gave the two gunmen a defiant gaze as they prepared to fire. I had just begun to wonder what the crossroads would be like when three successive thunderous "booms" rang out. It seemed slow for machine gun fire, but I figured my final moments were playing in slow motion. I'd expected the last thing I saw to be the flames leaping from the barrels of their assault rifles. Instead I saw a gaping stomach wound open up on the gunman from the club. The sneer on his face was replaced by a snarl of agony. Bright red blood quickly began to soak his midsection as he collapsed.

Chaine didn't wait for an invitation. She raised her small pistol and sent shots at the other gunman who was standing momentarily dazed and confused looking at his fallen comrade. Her shots went wild, but as they struck the vehicle near him he came to his senses. He fired two short unaimed bursts from his AK as he clambered down the block and dipped between some parked cars.

On the sidewalk the shooter who'd been hit lay twitching violently as he bled out. I whipped my head around looking to find where the shots that had saved us came from. In the stupor brought on by my injury I could barely discern that the shots I'd heard were

262

shotgun blasts, much less which direction they came from. I thought that maybe some gun toting rent-a-cop was playing hero, but there was no one in the lobby on their feet much less shooting.

Chaine scrambled to her feet clutching her pistol. Besides a few minor cuts from the glass she looked okay. She kneeled next to me trying to help me from the floor. My legs felt like Jell-O, and even though my pulse raced I felt like lying down. She helped me to my knees and I got my feet under me one leg at a time. I looked at the crimson puddle that had formed beneath me and felt my wet clothes and I knew I was losing a lot of blood. I got on my feet and when I got a look at the street outside I finally saw where the shooting that saved us had come from. Directly across the street Bubby stood holding a pistol grip pump action shotgun as he peered down the block looking for the second shooter. He was a sight for sore eyes.

The confused expression on Chaine's face said she didn't know what to make of him. In a hoarse whisper I told her, "That's our ride!" The sirens had drawn closer and they couldn't have been more than a couple of blocks away. Bubby apparently had heard them too.

He started waving frantically for us to come on. Even though the other shooter was still out there somewhere he was right, if we didn't make tracks now we were in for a world of trouble. There were four dead bodies and the cops would be hungry for suspects.

Chaine took me by the arm and we headed out of the building. She kind of pulled me along and I could tell I was slowing her down. We stepped over the lifeless corpse on the sidewalk. Bubby stood like a sentinel covering us as we made our way across the street. Chaine looked over her shoulder at me and said, "C'mon baby, just a little bit further."

As the words left her mouth some small movement in the darkness caught Bubby's attention. Sparks spilled from the barrel of the shotgun as he let off two thunderous rounds into the shadows. Chaine and I turned just in time to see the gunman roll out from underneath a van parked a hundred yards down the block.

My first instinct was to shove Chaine out of the way, but with my injury I couldn't manage it. Instead she stepped in front of me. She raised her pistol ad took aim down the dark street. Time slowed down the same way it did when I kissed her. It seemed like I could see every drop of rain as it fell. I stood transfixed as the moment unfolded. She fired. The gunman's silhouette laying on the pavement presented a hard target and her first two shots missed. Using the sparks from her errant bullets striking the pavement she adjusted and zeroed in on the small figure.

With her third shot she hit her mark. The gunman fired a short burst from his AK-47 just a split second before Chaine's bullet silenced him. By some obscenely cruel twist of fate he hit his mark too. The force of the impact spun Chaine around. For a moment I thought she'd turned around to poke fun at saving me, but when I saw her face grotesquely contorted I knew she was hit. The bullet she took may have been meant for her, but it would have hit me if she hadn't stood in front of me. Her arms flailed as she collapsed. I slipped my left arm around her waist breaking her fall. Bubby ran over and supported us before we both fell and lowered us to the ground.

I was on my knees cradling her limp body like a child. Her eyes were open and she looked into my eyes with angelic serenity. She looked so peaceful I didn't believe she was really hit. When I looked down and saw two bullet holes in her sweater an unimaginable grief swept over me like a tsunami. The crimson splotches on her sweater spread as she bled profusely. Two bullets had struck her, one in her abdomen and the other in the right side of her chest. I leaned down holding her tightly, and I could hear the gurgling sound of blood in her lungs as she labored to breathe. She tried to speak but all that left her mouth were a faint rasp and a trickle of blood.

"Don't talk. I'ma get you to the hospital. Save your strength," I pleaded.

She affected a brave smile. Her body began to tremble. She was slipping away and the scared look in her eyes said she knew it. Raindrops fell on her face, but I could still see tears making their way down her face. I felt powerless. I looked around desperately seeking anything that might help matters, but there was just me, her, Bubby, and some dead bodies. I looked on in helpless horror as life slipped away from her. I'd made a small fortune as a dealer of death, but what I was watching was something I had never seen before. It had never been someone I loved. She coughed up some blood and then her body went limp. And just like that she was gone.

Her lifeless eyes were fixed on my face. I shook her and called her name through death's cold stare. I knew she was gone, but I was on autopilot. In my catatonic state I mumbled words to her that to this day I can't recall. Bubby's hand on my shoulder and his calm voice snapped me out of my trance. "Lex, there's nothing you can do for her. She's gone and if we plan on leavin' we gotta go right now."

As reality came into focus I looked around. The wailing police sirens were loud now I looked down the block and I could see the flashing lights on the squad cars as they weaved through traffic barreling toward us. They were just a block down and closing in fast. I looked at Chaine's prone figure for one last second. As

Bubby helped me up I closed her eyelids so she could rest peacefully. I'd once heard it said that you deserved it when you died with your eyes open...there was no way I could imagine that Chaine had deserved that. I hated to leave her there on the side of the street that way, but I had no choice. I clumsily got into the Magnum and Bubby fishtailed into the slick street without letting up off the gas.

Before we bent the corner I looked through the rear window and saw the cops had stopped to move the body of the man who'd shot Chaine out of the middle of the street. That couple of seconds gave Bubby some ground on them that I knew they couldn't make up. He whipped a couple of quick turns, sped down backstreets, and picked up the West Side Highway. We crossed the George Washington Bridge, and in what seemed like just a heartbeat we were in New Jersey. The cops were probably combing the city looking for us, but we were in a whole other state.

I needed my shoulder looked at, but other than that we were out of immediate danger. The knapsack was still on my back and its strap cut into my wound like it had teeth. I barely noticed. The physical discomfort was nothing in comparison with the hole that had opened up inside my heart and was slowly getting wider. Deeper. I hurt in a way that I never thought I could. My work as a contract killer had me thinking I was somehow immune to emotion or that some way I'd never experience feeling loss over anyone's death. That night the invisible box I'd created around myself disappeared and seemed like all the hurt in the world instantly came rushing in on me. I felt like I was drowning in the grief that continued to sweep over me in waves like an unforgiving stormy sea.

The lights on the road were a blur. I tried to recall the good moments Chaine and I had shared, but nothing came to me except a picture of her suffering as her life slipped away. I had yet to even begin mourning the loss of the child that was growing inside of her. We'd both been dealt a bad hand from the start, but somehow I knew Chaine would have made a good mother. The chance for us to ever find out had been stolen.

Some people might argue that Chaine had campaigned for and orchestrated her own downfall by killing Wolf. For me, all the rules that had held my allegiance to the murder for hire game were out the window. The shooter who shot Chaine was more than likely dead, but my need for vengeance didn't feel nearly satisfied. Half of me wanted to leave that whole world behind... the other half wanted to return to it and cut a swathe through the Darkheart Massive like they'd never imagined.

In the end there was only one thing I knew for sure...I wasn't the predator I thought I was. In the street with Chaine dying in my arms I felt very much the prey. Not a victim of a Jamaican crew, and not a victim of my environment. My career and my lifestyle had blinded me. I'd given too much trust to the wrong people and not enough to the right ones. Never once had I given myself a chance to really experience and know love. And right there was where I'd made myself into an inviting target. I may have been about my business in the murder for hire game, but I was easy prey...prey for love.

Epilogue

I woke up this morning to the same sight I've been seeing ever since I moved out here to California. I keep that Versace watch Chaine gave me sitting on my nightstand and everyday it's the first thing I see. I cleaned most of the blood off it, but there were still some tiny traces around the bezel. Even if there weren't I'd probably still see blood on it. Almost everything in my new place is brand new with the exception of that watch. The diamonds cashed out at $3.5 million, almost double what I thought they would. I bought a new bike, car, and this house with the proceeds. I found a nice spot just outside of San Bernadino and it's comfy, but it still doesn't feel like home. I'm only an hour outside of L.A. and from time to time I take a ride to see how the other half lives.

I still haven't started up that private security firm. The timing just hasn't been right. Maxine is constantly hounding me about doing it. She lives in London now, and she's been out here to visit twice when she's free from an acting gig she landed on a British sit-com. We talk on the phone everyday. Her sister is still with Bizzie. He's been on me about coming back to Jamaica, but he still doesn't know I've been wrestling with the idea of going back. I've tried hard to just put everything behind me, but lately I've begun to wonder if maybe settling up with the Darkheart Massive isn't just the thing to get me back on track.

It's been six months since that night, but everything about it is still burned into my memory and I replay it often...in Technicolor and surround sound. I had passed out in the car somewhere in Jersey and that's probably the only part I don't remember. The hit I took in the shoulder was a lot more serious than I realized at the time. Bubby took me somewhere and got me patched up real nice, but when I woke up with my arm in a sling and a bottle of codeine in my pocket he wouldn't tell me how it happened. Couldn't have been a hospital because they would have called "Johnny Law" as soon as they saw a gunshot wound. He didn't want to tell, so I let him have his secret. My shoulder hurt like a sonofabitch, but I was grateful for the physical discomfort to offset what I felt inside.

After we ditched the Magnum for an El Camino we went to Atlantic City and laid low for a couple of days. I called Big Tee, and while he assured me that the cops had no solid leads about what went down at the W, we both agreed it was best for Bubby and me to stay off the radar for a hot minute just in case. Before we got off the phone he was hesitant but he came out and told me Chaine's name had really been Chaine, Chaine Grey, just like she'd told me from the jump. I'm not exactly certain why, but that little tidbit of information had a huge effect on me. The grief had me boxed in, and telling myself that what Chaine and I had shared wasn't real was my last escape. Now my only possible escape route from the pain was gone.

For a week or so I treated Bubby to a well deserved vacation. He tried to get me out of my suite, but I stayed in trying to heal and make some type of sense of everything that had happened. He gave me my space and went off and made the best of it. Mostly he played poker, which he ended up winning $10 grand at, so the little trip ended up paying for itself. Me? I just spent the days holed up listening to Sade and Luther and staring at that white watch with blood still caked on it. I could tell my shoulder would get better in time, but my "internal" injuries were far more extensive.

We rode back to N.Y. in the middle of the night under cover of darkness. Rolling into town felt strange. Somehow I now felt alien in the concrete jungle that raised me. I knew once I tied up my loose ends it was time for me to move on. There was nothing left for me in N.Y. that didn't in some way remind me of what happened.

The first stop we made was at my loft. I asked Bubby to wait in the car even though I didn't know what to expect. When I walked into my place the first thing I saw was the Coach bag sitting on the kitchen counter right in "that" spot. There was a letter on top of the bag from Chaine. My hand trembled as I picked it up: It read:

My Beloved Lex,

I'm sorry for how things turned out between us, but I want you to know that I never meant to hurt you. What we shared was very real, even though you're probably doubting that right now. I tried to explain everything to you but after Jamaica I know you don't trust me and it would have been hard to believe...Anyway, I think it's important you know I'm pregnant! Right now New York is not safe for me and <u>our</u> baby, so I'm leaving.

Lex, I know you're a good man, and I haven't given you much option in all this, but I promise when the smoke clears I'll be in touch. You may not want anything more to do with me, but I'm not going to take away your opportunity to be a father to your child. As far as "us" I want you to know that I loved you from the moment I saw you, and I will always have that same fire burning inside me for you. Right now it's best if I run on my own because we don't exactly make the greatest decisions when we're together. Please try to understand.

Your stash is here minus the "e" pills. I'm selling them to get some money to help get me and your baby far away from here...You said you weren't a dope dealer, so I'm helping you stay true to your word.

Prey For Love

I miss you already. Until we see each other again, I remain truly, madly, and deeply

Yours,
Chaine.

Hearing Chaine's voice from beyond the grave did something to me. Everything she'd done was put in a whole new perspective for me. I instantly began to wonder if I'd just trusted her at the hotel things could have played out better. That was something that would haunt me for a long time to come because in the end I didn't have anyone to blame but myself.

It surprised Bubby, and I even kind of surprised myself when I went by Nana Helen's. She was happy to see me. Even though she didn't deserve my forgiveness, I knew she needed it, so I gave it to her. I told her I was leaving and she cried, but she knew it was best. Before I rolled out she tried to give me the $500k I'd given her from Imperial, but I made her keep it because you never knew when fast money would slow up. I realized that what she'd done was manipulative and conniving, but she had my best interest at heart every step of the way. Plus, if it hadn't been for her I'd never have met Chaine.

I didn't ask him to, but Big Tee had already gotten the pills sold by the time I caught up with him. That helped a lot because it was one less thing I had to deal with. He got me $1.5 million which was more than I'd intended to get. I didn't take it, though; I made him split it between him, Bubby, and Mila. They all tried to refuse, but I won out in the end. I'd learned what it meant to have real friends from them, and even though it was too late, it was an invaluable lesson nonetheless.

The following morning was when I pulled up stakes and headed out here to California, and I've been out here ever since. The change of scenery didn't have the cleansing effect on me that I thought it would. At night losing Chaine follows me into my dreams, and I spend most of my days trying to escape it. Haven't had much luck so far. It's nice outside today. They say it never rains in Southern California. We'll see.

Usually on a day like today I'd take my Suzuki out and ride up Pacific Coast Highway. Instead of joy riding, I decided to call Bizzie and let him know I'll be coming down in a week or so. He could tell there was something in my voice, and he asked me if it was business or pleasure. That was a decision I'd have to make once I got to Jamaica.

Author's Note
As you may well have figured out by now, this was not just a story about contact killers and marks, hustlers and squares, or risking life and limb in pursuit of living lavish. More than anything it was a love story. It may not seem possible, but the same way it's possible for a rose to grow from crack in a concrete sidewalk is the same way love can take hold and blossom in what would otherwise seem a harsh environment. Chaine and Lex were proof of that. Parts of their story may have seemed hard to believe, but we all know that astronomical misfortune is often times unbelievable. In the end what I hope you realize after having read this is that the choices we make in life are like tossing pebbles into a pond, cause and effect that reaches much further than we intended or could have imagined.

If you took some meaning from this book other than what I intended, that's all good with me so long as you're a better person for it. In the meantime it's about to be count time so I got things to do. Live your dreams, stay positive, and remember that time is luck so don't waste it. One Love and God Bless!!!

www.myspace.com/preyforlove

Raw: An Erotic Street Tale

Money make me cum – money, money make me cum .

Chastity Jones is the real thing. She's beautiful, she's classy, and she's got money to spend. Other people's money. As long as there are men around, 19-year-old Chastity will be rolling in their dough.

It wasn't always like that – her father was sent to prison when she was 16, and after being placed in a foster home, she was brutally raped. She runs away, and starts stripping at a men's club, and there she catches the eye of Legend, a mysterious and handsome 6-4 hunk with straight black hair that hangs over his shoulders. His brownstone parties are famous – attended by celebrities, ballers, and hustlers alike. But the real parties are in his basement; sex parties that include girl-on-girl action, and even occasionally bestiality. His parties are so successful he easily clears $25,000 to $40,000 a weekend.

For Chastity it's love at first sight, but try as she might Legend only treats her like a little sister –and under his tutelage Chastity is soon hanging with the big dawgs. They buy her cars, pay the rent on her condo, buy her expensive jewelry and take her on shopping sprees. But the man she wants most shows her no romantic interest; and that's Legend.

And then she meets Hunter – he's a drug kingpin with millions of dollars, and also Legend's cousin – and he falls for Chastity in a big way. Suddenly Chastity is caught up in a whirlwind of money, sex, drugs and danger – and the only way out lies in death.

www.myspace.com/rawnovel

Harlem Godfather: The Rap on My Husband, Ellsworth "Bumpy" Johnson

Forget Nicky Barnes and Frank Lucas, the undisputed king of Harlem's underworld was Ellsworth Bumpy Johnson.

He was called an old-fashioned gentleman. He was called a pimp. A philanthropist and a thief. A scholar and a thug. A man who told children to stay in school, and a man who some say introduced heroin into Harlem.

Bumpy used his fists and his guns to get what he wanted, but he also used his money to help those in need. To this day – forty years after his death – people still sing his praises.

And no one more than his 94-year-old widow, Mayme Hatcher Johnson, author of *Harlem Godfather: The Rap on My Husband, Ellsworth "Bumpy" Johnson* the only biography of the legendary Harlem gangster.

Read the real story of the larger than life Bumpy Johnson, who was portrayed in the blockbuster movies *Cotton Club, Hoodlum*, and *American Gangster.*

Find out Bumpy's *real* relationship with Frank Lucas. And learn the story of a real man -- who never snitched – and loved as hard as he fought.

www.harlemgodfather.com